A CABOT CAIN THRILLER

ASSAULT ON LOVELESS

Also from ALAN CAILLOU

CABOT CAIN Series

Assault on Kolchak
Assault on Ming
Assault on Loveless
Assault on Fellawi
Assault on Agathon
Assault on Aimata

TOBIN'S WAR Series

Dead Sea Submarine
Terror in Rio
Congo War Cry
Afghan Assault
Swamp War
Death Charge
The Garonsky Missile

MIKE BENASQUE Series

The Plotters
Marseilles
Who'll Buy My Evil
Diamonds Wild

IAN QUAYLE Series

A League of Hawks
The Sword of God

DEKKER'S DEMONS Series

Suicide Run
Blood Run

The Charge of the Light Brigade
A Journey to Orassia

Rogue's Gambit
Cairo Cabal
Bichu the Jaguar
The Walls of Jolo
The Hot Sun of Africa
The Cheetahs
Joshua's People
Mindanao Pearl
Khartoum
South from Khartoum
Rampage
The World is 6 Feet Square
The Prophetess
House on Curzon Street

ASSAULT ON LOVELESS
Book Three

CHAPTER 1

The beautiful, peaceful road wound along the sandy coastline with pines on one side and the bright blue-and-white surf on the other; and we were shooting along it at a hundred and fifteen miles an hour in the Jensen, a special bodied four-seater I keep in Europe because every time I settle down to catch up on my studies—I'm very fond of the processes of learning—at home in San Francisco someone sends me a cable that says come back.

It's an FF model, the four-wheel-drive version of the Interceptor, which isn't a bad car either, and the model I would have bought if I hadn't been sold on the value of four driving wheels and the unique Ferguson limited-action differential. Of course, I had to have the top cut off, since they don't make a convertible in this model, and with a roof over my head there's always the problem of getting in and out; I'm six feet seven, and that can be a bit of a nuisance when it comes to fast and comfortable driving. It also has the Chrysler overhead-valve mill which gives you a mere three thousand on the tachometer at seventy-five miles an hour; not that I often loiter at that speed if I can help it.

Beside me, I was conscious that Fenrek was trying hard not to show just how worried he was, and I said, with a sort of shrug: "Well, you did say hurry, didn't you?"

"Yes, yes I did." I knew that the line of his thin, aristocratic lips was tightening. He said: "She's probably there by now anyway."

He sat hunched up in the glove-leather seat, his tight frame, muscular and efficient, wedged into the bucket and his feet properly braced. Colonel Matthias Fenrek, at fifty-five years of age Interpol's top man in Department B7, here from his Paris H.Q., on a sort of working holiday that wasn't going to turn out to be quite as relaxing as he'd hoped. He'd been expecting to sit on the glorious beach at Estoril and do nothing, with maybe Astrid's lithe and lovely movements to watch (keeping a watchful eye all the time on the men who were always trying so desperately to get close to her); or perhaps watching instead the gorgeous mistress he was supposed to have tucked away somewhere.

Astrid was his niece, a handsome young woman he was very fond of, twenty-seven years old and already a dammed good nurse, on leave from her New York clinic to be with her uncle on the beach for a while. Except that now, she was heading for quite the wrong beach...

I said: "The police will stop her before she can get too close."

"You don't know Astrid as well as I do. She can talk her way past anybody. She'll flash her Carte Blanche at them, use my name in a hushed sort of voice, and sweep right by them all. I thought you said this car would do a hundred and fifty?"

I put a little more weight on the pedal and leaned into the wheel as the road swung gently north. We'd come from Lisbon; and Alges, Queiras, Parede, and Estoril itself had flashed past us with hardly more than a temporary slackening of speed. Cascais, the little fishing town, was gone too, in a blur of white-washed houses and tall-masted shrimp boats. The police here don't like this kind of road racing, and who can blame them? But with Interpol beside me I wasn't too worried; and they'd never catch the Jensen anyway, not with those six and a quarter liters under the hood.

Now, the Bocca do Inferno was on our left, the majestic and terrifying waterspout that's a tourist attraction when it's playing gently, as it does sometimes, but is a thing to keep well clear of when the wind's in the southwest, as it is once in a while. It was showing off gently now, sending a great white sweep of spray over the hot tarmac of the road as the driven waves smashed into the confining caves sixty feet below and funneled up violently into the hot blue air. There were notices there to keep the over-inquisitive away, and the danger area was well fenced off; even at its gentlest, the Bocca was a good place not to get too close to.

The road straightened out again, swinging gently back west, and Fenrek said: "Two and a half miles."

I dropped down to a hundred, down to ninety, did a racing change, and heard the whine as the powerful motor took over and braked us down to sixty, then began to play with the foot brake, the Maxaret system that oscillates so that you can't lock your wheels and spin out of control whatever your speed. And when Fenrek pointed and said, "There..." and the track to the beach was only a hundred yards ahead, we were down to fifty, and I swung the wheel hard over, bouncing over the sand towards the sea.

He said suddenly: "There she is."

I'd seen her; her little rented Mini-Moke, like a toy green box on four wheels, was lumbering easily over the broken ground, five hundred yards ahead and below us. I sounded SOS on the horn, and saw the white-blond head turn to look, and then she waved, a bright young girl in a red cotton shirt and a white scarf at her neck. She waved again, and I growled at Fenrek, "You'd think she'd know an SOS when she hears one."

She was looking back at us and waving one hand in a friendly gesture, recognizing Fenrek and perhaps wondering who I was; she was wearing huge round sunglasses with pink lenses, halfway down her nose. And then I banged on the horn again, imperiously, and swung the Jensen over to jump the ditch on my right, pushing hard on the throttle to get her over, landing ten feet off the track and swinging round to get back on it again at a lower level, in second gear now.

She'd seen the maneuver, and now she stopped. She was just barely close enough for the puzzlement to show, knowing that you don't treat a car like mine quite so disrespectfully unless there's a good reason. She swung round in the seat and waited, and Fenrek stood up, grabbing hold of the windshield frame, and waved his arm and yelled: "Back, Astrid, get back, back up the hill, hurry, fast..."

By now we were close beside her, moving at no more than twenty mph, and I swung the Jensen in front of the Mini and braked hard. Fenrek fell out, somehow landing lightly on his feet, and vaulted in beside the girl and shouted. "We've got to get out of here, fast, every second counts!"

She didn't waste any more time. She pushed the tiny toy car straight at the steep sand of the bank, bounced it up till its nose was almost in the air, and found her way back on the track once more. I followed, more sedately now that the immediate danger was over, fifty feet behind them in their fine red dust, and when we reached the tarmac road again and she'd stopped, I switched off the motor, got out and went to join them.

Fenrek made the introductions. "My old friend Cabot Cain, Astrid Tillot. You've both heard about each other."

Her face was grave, a child's face with shiny pink skin and wide blue eyes. Her cheekbones were high, her forehead broad with the silver-white hair piled high on her head. There were tiny lines at the side of the mouth, as though she was always ready to smile. It was not a beautiful face, but a very attractive one, none the less. The red sweater was high at her neck, the breasts tight and pointed.

She held out her hand. "And are you as inexplicably worried as my uncle, Mr. Cain? It's nice to meet you after all these years of eulogy."

I said: "Just as worried. And I wish our first meeting could have been less...hectic."

She looked puzzled. "But it's not in the least contagious— there's no danger at all. So why you should go to so much trouble..."

I interrupted. "No danger if we know what it is. But we don't."

"But we do!" She said, insisting: "We *do* know what it is. I don't want to be technical, but..."

"You can be as technical as you like."

She took a moment to smile briefly: "Yes, of course. Well, most people call it mussel poisoning, because it's often caused by eating poisoned mussels. But more correctly, it's dinoflagellate fever, and you can get it from eating *any* fish that's been contaminated. It's just that mussels carry it more easily, in a much higher concentration, but so do shrimps, and mullet, and sardines, and anything else. A nasty business, but it can be contained fairly easily, and anyone who gets it can be cured if you catch it in time. That's what I'm here for."

"It's not dinoflagellates," Fenrek said quietly.

She stared. "Uncle, it *is!* Take a look out there."

She pointed out to sea, and I followed the sweep of her bare arm. A couple of hundred yards offshore there was a wide red patch in the sea, half a mile wide and perhaps three or four miles long, a deep red dye against the bright blue of the Bay of Biscay.

She turned and looked at me almost scornfully. "You're from the west coast, you must have seen that once or twice. The 'red tide' they call it, over here as well as back home, and it's quite common in California and Florida. There's a reason for it that we know all about, and though it's pretty deadly it's nothing to worry too much about, unless you're a fish."

I took the Leitz Trinovid binoculars from their case under the dash and handed them to Fenrek. "Take a look, tell me what you think," I said.

He shrugged. "I've never seen it myself. Heard all about it, of course. A bad case of it up in the North Sea last spring. Thirty people died from eating contaminated mussels."

He took the Trinovids and stared out to sea, and then those elegant shoulders shrugged again and he said: "Well named, at least. Just what it is, a red tide."

"And the question is, who put it there?"

Still using the glasses, he murmured: "Who, and why." He grunted. "Everybody out looking for it, and there it is, just what they expected to find. Interesting."

I said: "I can make a pretty good guess at *why*, but..."

I looked down at Astrid. She was eyeing me over the top of those ridiculous sunglasses as if she thought we were out of our minds. She said, exasperated: "But, for God's sake, nobody put it there, it just...just *comes*. To get technical again, the dinoflagellates are single-cell organisms in plankton, and when there's an admittedly unknown combination of marine and climatic conditions, they multiply at an explosive rate for a while, and then just as inexplicably die. But while they last, you've got a red tide, and any fisherman who knows what he's doing keeps away from it till it's gone, and doesn't net fish that turn up dead in the general area. Those poor people down there on the beach ought to have known that, but since they didn't they've taken sick and we'll have to do something about it. Now, if you wouldn't mind..."

I said, "It's cochineal."

She was already reaching for the ignition switch on that ridiculous little car. Her hand stopped, and she stared up at me in the most complete disbelief: "*Cochineal?*"

I felt it was my turn to be technical, just to teach this obstreperous young woman a thing or two. I wouldn't have done that with a stranger, normally, but Fenrek was the strong link between us; it was family. I said: "The females of the *Dactylopius coccus*; if you want more precision." She still stared, and I filled in some time for her. "Did you know that the females of the Dactylopius outnumber the males by two hundred to one? But the males are very vigorous, which is just as well, or else we'd never have had any crimsons or scarlets in our history before the invention of the aniline dyes. Have you ever thought about that?"

She said again, incredulous: "*Cochineal?*"

"They brush the insects off the trees in Southern Spain, dry them in the sun to release the carminic acid..."

"Are you *sure?*" It was impossible for her to believe.

I said: "Quite true. I have a doctorate in Entomology, among other things."

She said, impatiently: "No, not that. Are you sure that it's not dinoflagellates?"

"Not a dinoflagellate in sight. That red tide has been tested and analyzed a dozen times. They can't believe it at the Research Center either."

She shook her head, blinking away the astonishment. We heard the dual-note of an ambulance coming along the road from Lisbon, and soon, white-painted, its red light flashing, it slowed down briefly while the cheerful, swarthy driver leaned out and waggled his hand at us, asking a question.

Fenrek pointed to the beach and said: "*Ali, na praia*, there, on the beach."

The ambulance, not stopping, lumbered off the road and wound its way slowly down to the beach, and Fenrek said, speaking mostly for the benefit of his niece: "They've been inoculated against almost everything in the pharmacopoeia, and they're still in danger down there. A new disease that no one knows anything about, so what's the preventative?"

Astrid said promptly: "There's no such thing as a new disease. What you mean is they haven't diagnosed it properly yet."

Fenrek shook his head slowly. He thrust his hands into the pockets of his grey silk suit and wandered off along the edge of the road, his chin sunk on his chest, staring morosely down to the sea. I helped Astrid out of her toy car, and we walked along behind him, watching the ambulance wind its way down there.

In the silence, I felt her looking up at me, and I said, knowing that sooner or later she'd have to know: "When that first case of so-called mussel poisoning was reported last week, they went looking for the red tide, just as a matter of routine. They didn't find it. Then, during the night, that boat down there was washed ashore with three dead fishermen on board, and this time the tide was close inshore, for everyone to see. It came, perhaps, rather suddenly out of nowhere, but that's the way it usually happens, and no one remarked on it very much."

Walking beside me now, she looked tiny and fragile, with that peculiar silver hair piled up high and *bouffant* and too-carefully groomed; I wondered how she kept it like that in an open car. I said, walking with her slowly: "Again, nothing more than routine, but the Department of Fisheries took samples of the water for analysis. They have to know the strength of the infection so that they can estimate roughly how long it will be before the fishermen can give up starving. And they found that it wasn't dinoflagellates at all, just plain *Dactylopius coccus*. Carminic acid derived from cochineal."

She still didn't believe it. She said flatly: "It's impossible."

"Unlikely, perhaps, but proven possible."

"But for heaven's sake, to make a splash in the ocean that size, they'd need...well, they'd need more of the dye than could ever be picked up in the corner drugstore."

"We guess it would take about fifty gallons of the liquid, and you're right; in a drugstore you might find as much as four ounces if you were lucky. Or, alternatively, we figure you'd need eight hundred pounds of the dried insects, and at about seventy thousand to the pound, that's fifty-six million insects. Stimulating thought, isn't it? The Navy boys are out there now, over the horizon somewhere, pouring five gallons of the liquid into the sea to find out just how big a tide that makes. We'll know soon just how much was used."

"But...but by whom, for God's sake? And why?"

"Quite a problem, isn't it?"

She looked at me shrewdly. "You said you knew the answer."

"Not really, not clearly. Perhaps I was boasting a trifle, but...I can think of at least one possible explanation for the *why*. The *who* is a fish of a different smell."

"All right. Then tell me a why, any kind of a why."

"Let me think about it first. If I'm even half right, there's something quite terrible going on."

For a little while, not pushing it, she said nothing. She took hold of my arm when she stumbled on the rough terrain, and didn't leave go when she'd found her balance again. She looked up at me sideways and said: "Uncle didn't tell me you were working for him. Or is it with him?"

"Neither. I'm off on a different tack altogether, looking for a man who can clear up a nasty business for...I suppose you could say a client of mine, General Queluz, do you know him?"

She shook her head. I said: "Your uncle does. A nice old man, retired now. Retired rather forcibly, through no fault of his own. I'm trying to help him."

She swept a long thin arm out towards the ocean. "And this?"

I shrugged. "Fenrek's baby. We happened to be saying hello to each other when word came through that you were hurrying off down to the beach." I smiled down at her. "You're an impetuous young woman, aren't you?"

She nodded, brooding. "Yes. Yes, I suppose I am."

We'd caught up with Fenrek now. He stood on the edge of the cliff looking down at the beach. Halfway down, where the track we'd been chasing each other on swung abruptly round an outcrop of rock and then steeply down to the sand, three policemen were standing, watching the ambulance that was below them. They'd been posted there to keep anyone who might pass by away from the little shrimp boat with its cargo of three lifeless men that was now high on the beach above the receding tide.

At five-thirty in the morning they'd been washed up, a dead

boat with a dead crew, brought in on the surf and left on the sand. At five-forty, a tired and sad old woman had found them there, a wife and a mother down on the beach in the early hours to help her husband and her two sons land the night's catch. At five-fifty-five she'd caught the early bus that took the fisherfolk into Cais do Sodre for the fish market, and all she'd said to the other passengers was: *O mare vermelho*, the red tide, sitting there in black-robed sadness with her tired old weather-beaten face dry-eyed because this was part of her life, as death itself was always a part of the sea which was the only thing she understood; and they too sat there in silence, and at last the bus driver—an educated man from the City—had said to her, reassuring himself: "You tell the police now? Better you tell them."

She had nodded, and there was silence on the bus again, nobody talking because they knew that for a few days, a few weeks, or a few months, there'd be no fish to sell, nor to eat either. In a little while, one of the men on the bus opened the window and threw out the three fat lobsters he'd been carrying, the lobsters that were to be sold in the market for a week's good food for his family. Soon, someone else tipped out a basket of mullet; a box of sardines was the next to go. And finally, the bus driver stopped, not a word being spoken, and watched glumly as basket after basket was emptied onto the roadside to rot there in the sun that would soon be up and hot in the bright blue sky.

Very little had been said; then the passengers all climbed back on the bus and went unhappy and empty-handed to the market to spread the bad news around.

"West of the Bocca do Inferno," they said, "the red tide. Better we cross river and try in Sisimbra, or we all starve."

Now, down by the water, the two white-coated figures from the ambulance were loading the dead fishermen aboard. The three policemen had found rocks to sit on and were watching idly, smoking their cigarettes and enjoying the sunlight.

Astrid said, brooding: "The woman died, the woman who came in on the bus this morning. The doctor said it was mussel poisoning, and now...now there's the red tide which caused it, and you say it's cochineal. It just simply doesn't make any kind of sense at all."

"Not till we know more about it, it doesn't."

"Could a swarm of the insects find its way into the

sea...like...like lemmings, or something? After all, they live in Spain, and that's not so far."

"No. The males are wingless, and the females won't leave the males. They live, breed, and die, all in the same general area."

"Then what you're saying is that someone...someone, for reasons of his own, went out and bought fifty gallons of cochineal—fifty gallons of it, something a housewife uses one drop at a time, once a year, at Christmas!—and poured it all into the sea, just at the time when there's the beginnings of an epidemic of mussel poisoning! Is that what you're trying to suggest?"

Fenrek turned to her, his eyes troubled. "Not quite. You're almost there, but not quite. The woman died, yes. The doctor diagnosed mussel poisoning, yes. And then, when you heard about that, you came driving out here to see, am I right? If there were any young kids around who might not yet know about the red tide and start eating last night's catch?"

"Yes. I was having coffee with one of the interns and he was called back urgently to the hospital. He told me what was going on, and..." She threw up her hands helplessly. "It just doesn't make any kind of sense at all."

Fenrek said: "And I'm afraid your young intern is terribly sick." Seeing the look on her face, he said quickly: "He's one of the lucky ones, he's going to be all right, I hoped I wouldn't have to tell you, but...the doctor who was treating the woman suddenly collapsed on her bed, vomiting all over the place. Before the nurse could do anything, she keeled over and started vomiting too. And ten minutes later, they were both dead, and nobody knows why. The ward's been sealed off, and—" he made a helpless gesture— "that's when we started chasing after you. Thank God the intern told us what you were planning to do." He took a deep breath. "Mussel poisoning is not contagious, and yet the nurse and the doctor, both with the same symptoms, were dead within a few minutes of coming into contact with a patient who'd been in contact with...with what? Am I making sense?"

Astrid shook her lovely head. "No, no sense at all."

I said: "But that's what happened."

She thought it over for a while. "There hasn't been time for a second opinion, has there?" she asked.

"Yes, there has," Fenrek said. "The Army doctors have diagnosed the same thing. Mussel poisoning. From the red tide. No shadow of doubt, they say. Only it's contagious, which the poison isn't, and that tide out there is a fake, a fake that was deliberately put there, for...for God knows *what* reason."

He looked at me accusingly, an expression on his face that made him look like Astrid. They had a great deal in common, these two. He said: "If you've any wild ideas up your sleeve, Cain, now's the time to let them out for an airing."

I shook my head. "Nothing, nothing more than a wild and...elusive thought that doesn't make any more sense at the moment than a red tide that's made of cochineal. I have some thinking to do, and no one can help me do it. When I have a few truths, whichever way they may point...if they begin to make sense..."

Astrid said suddenly, remembering: "You said the Army doctors were giving a second opinion? Why the Army? What have they got to do with this?"

Fenrek told her gently: "As Cain says, my dear...when we have some truths. Meanwhile, resign yourself to doing nothing, because there's nothing you can do, nothing at all."

She did not answer. She was staring at the ambulance as it lumbered over the rough ground unsteadily up the steep track to the road. One of the policemen waved a casual hand at it and went back to picking his teeth. Soon, it hit the tarmac, and it went slowly, in not too straight a line, across the road to the wrong side and lurched to a sudden stop with one wheel in the ditch.

Fenrek said: "What the devil..."

He started to move towards it, and I held out an arm and said urgently: "No, wait."

The driver was getting down from the ambulance, stumbling, being violently sick all over the road. The door at the back flew open, and the two medicos tumbled out, falling on the tarmac and rolling there as though they were in agony. I saw Fenrek moving, and I yelled again: "No!" Astrid ran towards them, and I threw myself at her and brought her to the ground with my momentum. I dragged her back, struggling, pulling her away from there as fast as I could, feeling her fighting me savagely.

She screamed at me: "Cain, for God's sake, I'm a nurse, a registered nurse!" I held her down, and said: "No, there's nothing you can do, nothing."

She went on fighting me until Fenrek, his deeply-tanned face suddenly white, said quietly: "We've got to watch it, haven't we?"

Holding tight onto Astrid, I said: "Yes, we do, and we stay upwind of them as well. Not an inch closer, none of us."

She stopped struggling then, staring at the men on the road with something very close to horror on her face. She suddenly turned away and buried her face in my shoulder, and I could feel her body shaking. And then she pulled away from me and began trying to reach them again, and I held her tighter still. She screamed: "Let me go, damn you!"

I yelled back. "No, it's hopeless, there's nothing, don't you understand? Nothing you can do, nothing any of us can do."

One of the men was yelling a long stream of obscenities; it was the driver. The other two men, the doctors, lay still and I knew that they were dead. And then the driver made a convulsive movement, arching up his body and twisting it round, and then he too was suddenly still and silent and not in that dreadful pain any more.

Fenrek's voice was hollow. He said: "They're dead, all of them, and we watched them...God in Heaven, we stood here and watched them die."

Astrid was staring at the three bodies lying there. The motor of the ambulance was still turning slowly, idling. She said, echoing his words: "We stood here and watched them die..."

There was a little silence. And then Astrid said, her eyes on me with all the anger and hysteria gone from them: "All right, perhaps now you'd better tell me. The Army doctors, you said. What has the Army got to do with all this?"

Fenrek said quietly: "Everything."

CHAPTER 2

The little pieces of the inexplicable always fit together if you take time cut to examine them carefully enough and see where they're supposed to go. Sometimes there's an imponderable or two left over, so you think some more; and soon, they drop neatly into place as well.

I went to see the General.

His house was one of the old mansions built by the Marquis of Pombal in the eighteenth century, after the earthquake that leveled the center of Lisbon. On that terrible day, at half past nine on the morning of November 1st, 1755, nine thousand buildings were demolished in the space of six seconds, and thirty thousand people lost their lives. The violent winds carried the flames through the city, and by eleven o'clock the whole of its center had been obliterated from the face of the earth.

It was a fine old building, the General's house, faced with painted tiles and wrought iron, that stood on the edge of the Alfama, at the top, standing like a highly-decorated fortress with its brick patio looking down over the Alfama's rooftops and its deep, cavernous streets, so narrow in places that the tops of the houses seemed almost to touch, all piled close together up the sides of the hills. They all seemed to lean outward here; in one place, though the street below is eight feet wide, you can stretch your hand out of the upper windows, up on the fourth floor (which is the ground floor on the other side) and touch the walls of the house opposite.

On the steep steps below that were the main streets of this

quaint little quarter, with bright pots of scarlet geraniums and pale blue ageratum everywhere, with honeysuckle trailing carelessly over trellises; kids were chasing each other in bursts of childish energy, racing up the stairs and down again, like ants scurrying in and out of their runs. A plump, well-fed woman was doing the day's laundry at the public fountain in the miniscule courtyard there; and over the rooftops you could see the masts of the ships in the harbor, with the blue sea beyond and the grey hills across the broad river Tagus in the distance. A concrete Christ was up on the hill there, half hidden now in the mist that was rolling in from the bay, and the long, high Salazar Bridge ("the American Bridge", they call it) sent its slender red steelwork like a ribbon across the water; you could fancy, without much effort, that it was swaying slightly, as any ribbon ought to.

The General was a politician, and though I'm not usually very high on politicians, he was a good one—or he wanted to be. General Jaime Dom Pedro Queluz had retired four years ago after a major tragedy in Angola, where he'd been sent to put down the guerrillas and re-impose the strict discipline the Portuguese have always demanded. It was a tragedy that was not his fault at all, except that he wasn't the right man for the job there and had allowed a most unmilitary gentleness to intrude into a very rough situation. A commando of mercenaries had broken into his H.Q. and had blown up the whole installation while the General was attending a so-called "appeasement meeting" with the rebels.

In Angola, in those days, you weren't supposed to talk with the enemy at all—especially while they were planning to kill off all your staff officers at that precise moment—and Dom Pedro had been brought home to face a court-martial which had resulted in his retirement.

I'd been home in San Francisco then, and a report of his speech to the Tribunal had appeared in one of the Spanish papers that I take regularly. He had said, at the close of his defense (which he conducted himself):

We will never realize the full potential of our culture, and nor, indeed, will any of the civilized Powers, until the world's great armies can learn to build as efficiently as they can now destroy.

When we use our understanding as expertly as we use our weapons, then we will at last be able to hope for peace on earth, and armies, perhaps, will become redundant...

I was deeply impressed by this little piece of philosophizing, coming as it did at a time when half of Africa was badly in need of understanding and wasn't getting very much; though it didn't do him much good in front of a Military Tribunal.

Now he was making a comeback, or trying to. He needed a coup, a dramatic triumph to put himself once again in official favor. And that's why I was there.

A short, stubby sort of man, with gentle eyes and thinning white hair, a kindly man with an air of vague distraction as though his mind was forever playing with ideas that had nothing to do with the matter under discussion; a man who had the peculiar ability to stay absolutely still while he talked, frozen in the same posture for minutes on end, without the twitch of a muscle or the blinking of an eye. He would be moving around, and would suddenly stop still, and not move again, so that you felt you were talking to a statue; and then, he would suddenly come to life again and make broad, incisive gestures with his thick, muscular hands.

He had a good reputation in the Army. They said that in spite of his gentleness he was a terror to his officers, that he demanded from them a state of vigorous competence to match his own—something that was, very hard to come by in Colonial Africa, where lassitude and laissez faire are much more easily accepted characteristics.

I was late, two hours late for our appointment, but he waved aside my apologies. "I heard...I heard about Colonel Fenrek's niece nearly getting herself killed." He broke off and grunted. "A strange thing. We've had that damned red tide before, but it's never before been contagious. Seven deaths, all within a few hours, and two more likely to die if we don't find out what's truly wrong with them. The SME's very worried about it. And how are Fenrek and his niece?"

I said: "So far, no trouble. We were all of us very close to three of the victims, but there was a good strong wind blowing away from us."

Standing there, immobile, he asked: "Inoculations?"

I shrugged. "Against what? We don't know what it is that killed them. Fenrek insisted on being vaccinated, every vaccine the hospital could suggest. But his niece and I, we've both got more sense."

He frowned. "The army doctors are inoculating everyone with a mild compound of...piperidylester, I think they call it."

I said: "To be precise, ethyltripiperidyl cyclopentylphonylglycolate. But it isn't everybody who can take that, even a very mild dose."

The muscles galvanized themselves and he changed position and froze again, his eyebrows raised. "I didn't know you were a medical man, Senhor Cain?"

"I'm not. But, as you may know, I read a great deal, I have a memory that can only be called freakish, and microbiology has always fascinated me." I shrugged. "Put all that together, and...that's why Astrid and I refused all those inoculations."

"Astrid? The *minena*, the young lady? I've never met her, I'm told she's extremely attractive, in a Nordic sort of way."

"Very attractive. Perhaps I can introduce you to her."

"That would be delightful."

We wandered across the patio to where a plump and smiling woman was cutting some roses. She turned and waited expectantly, and the General said: "Senhor Cabot Cain...my wife, Dona Clara."

She took my hand and smiled. "Our house is the better for your presence, Senhor Cain." Her voice was all up and down the musical scale, a softly-lilting voice with the accent of the mountains of the northwest where the Spanish influence is strong. The roses were the very rare Sharastenaks, a variety of the old Provence Rose, the *rosa centifolio* that Pliny wrote about more than sixteen hundred years ago; I was surprised and delighted to see them here, in their neat little bed heavily mulched with walnut shells. We moved over to the edge of the steep drop down to Alfama's cavernous little streets and leaned on the railing there while she went back to her work.

The General said: "But that's Fenrek's problem, isn't it? Let's get down to our own. The problem of Major Arthur Loveless."

I said: "I read the file you gave me, and I think I should know more about the man who told you Loveless was here."

"My old servant, a man I trust implicitly." Queluz jumped away from the railing as if a wasp had stung him and then froze again. "Let me go back a few years. On that memorable occasion that was to give me so much heartbreak, out in Angola, I received a note from the rebels saying they were prepared to discuss peace terms with me personally. Their leader then was an African called Ojugo, a good man, really, and a fine soldier too. One day he'll probably rule the whole of Angola, and he'll be a very good ruler too. He wanted me to meet him in the bush, alone, and in secret. The kind of secrecy he demanded usually means, out there, a trap of some sort, and I debated long and carefully with myself before accepting the invitation. I kept the news of it even from my staff officers, and when I went to the meeting place I took with me only one man, my servant, whose name is Nacimento, Corporal Nacimento. Now, Nacimento was born in Angola, the son of immigrant settlers who had a coffee plantation there, and he knew the bush like the back of his hand. So he followed me to the meeting place and kept well out of sight, his rifle ready just in case of the treachery which I half-expected but which, as you know, took a rather different and much more violent form.

"While I was talking with Ojugo, and giving way much too much, incidentally, Nacimento saw, from his hiding place, a small commando of four mercenaries moving back along the way we'd come. He thought at the time that they were merely being posted along the track to make sure that one of our own commandos was not following me and preparing to take Ojugo himself. But, of course, subsequent events showed that they were on their way to blow up my H.Q., an act of violence which resulted in the deaths of eight senior officers, and subsequently in my own...dismissal."

I said: "Let me interrupt you. Was Ojugo alone?"

"He was."

"And presumably he knew about the attack. Presumably, he even planned it."

"No." The General was very emphatic now. He said: "Later, Ojugo told me personally that the attack was carried out without his knowledge, and I believe him."

"That's a very hard thing to be so sure about, isn't it?"

"No." He shook his head. "I am absolutely sure. I'd stake my life on it. I'm a good judge of character, Senhor Cain, and if Ojuge says black is white I'd believe him, because that's the way it would be."

I accepted that.

He went on, slowly, frowning: "But perhaps I should have warned my staff officers after all. In my absence..." He sighed. "It was always hard to keep them on their toes, and the moment I turned my back, ever, they all tended to sleep too soundly. And after the attack, as you know, this man Major Loveless, a guerrilla working for Ojugo, openly boasted that his commandos were responsible for it."

"And all we know about Loveless," I said, "is that he's a Scotsman, a deserter from the British Army of the Rhine, and a little more competent than most of the mercenaries working in Africa."

"And many of them," the General said, "are extremely competent, make no mistake about that. They work for the highest bidder, and they are not as responsible as soldiers in a regular army, but they're highly trained professionals, most of them with long experience, and they're very dangerous men."

He sat down and put his stubby hands on his knees, staring at his wife as she took her roses into the house.

"But that one coup not only disgraced me," Queluz continued, "it also put Loveless at the top of his profession, and he became...should I say, famous? Or notorious? And ever since, I must confess, the problem of this man has obsessed me. I believe to this day that Ojugo, who still commands the rebels out there, was acting in good faith. I believe to this day that had Loveless not carried out that attack there'd be peace in Angola now, through my efforts and Ojugo's. We're both intelligent men, may I say...humane men? And, to tell the truth, he didn't really demand very much that I didn't think he was entitled to. It all boiled down to...to recognition of the Africans' right, and I'm the last man to deny them that. But he had engaged mercenaries to fight for what he felt was a good cause, and...if you give a professional killer a gun, he's liable to use it wrongly, and Ojugo could never control his mercenaries—most of them had nothing but contempt for him."

I said politely: "So much, General, I know."

He laughed shortly. "Yes, of course you do. But at that

meeting Corporal Nacimento got a very good long look at Loveless. In fact, he trailed him for a short distance until he was half a mile or so from the meeting place, and then he decided he'd better go back just in case I got into trouble. And as you also know, we left the meeting shortly, with a concrete plan for peace that came to nothing because of the commando attack which wiped out my staff. Clear?"

"Very clear."

"Good. After my dismissal, Nacimento stayed on in the army, and he's a sergeant now, in the Honor Guard at Castelo de São Jorge. He got a bullet in the foot, so he's been...put out to graze, a good man now in a peaceful, comfortable job. Now, ten days ago, Nacimento came to me and told me he'd seen Loveless with two other Europeans, down in the Baixa. And he was absolutely sure that it was Loveless. Absolutely and completely sure, with no shadow of doubt at all. That's when, on Fenrek's recommendation, I called you over here. Because, if you can find Loveless for me..." He sighed. "How wonderful it would be to tell them, to prove to them, that my negotiations with Ojugo would have paid off after all but for that one irresponsible act."

"Which, you are sure, Ojugo himself did not order. It all hinges on that, doesn't it?"

"Yes, it does. And a confession from Loveless that he was acting on his own would never reinstate me. But it would at least inform a public that's tired of the constant guerrilla warfare out there that I was not as wrong as they said. That's all I need." He looked at me a trifle wistfully, and said: "The country needs people like me—can I say that without arrogance? We've been a stable and well-run Dictatorship for more than thirty years now, and at last...at last that stability might end." There was a little twinkle in his eye now. "I won't pretend that we have a Democracy, provided you won't pretend that Democracy can solve all the world's problems, agreed?"

"Agreed. Could I have a drink?"

I thought for a moment he hadn't heard me. Suddenly, he came alive again and his face fell. He threw up his hands. "There's so much on my mind these days, can you ever forgive me?" He went to the door, tile-decorated, that led into the house, and tuned back and said: "I could offer you our local Antigua, but I seem to remember Fenrek said you were a cognac man?"

"Cognac would be fine, thank you."

"*Muinto bem, tambem para mim*, I'll have one too."

He disappeared inside, and I strolled over to the iron balustrade and leaned on it and watched the woman washing her clothes down there. Close by, a young girl brought a small brazier out from her front door, set it down in the middle of the narrow street, and began fanning the red coals; the blue smoke drifted up and scented the hot air, cooling off a trifle now that the sun was getting lower; and soon, I watched her throw on a couple of small fish, and the scent changed.

Then Queluz came back, followed by a white-jacketed, white-gloved young man who looked at me stolidly, and bowed slightly, and looked again with a very sharp, appraising glance that somehow startled me. It was a glance that denied any of the self-effacement I would have expected, a quick, almost impudent look, but it was gone almost at once. He put down a tray on which there was a bottle of cognac with two delicate glasses, lovingly handmade, I imagined, in the old glass factory on Rua do Alacrim.

We stood for a while by the balustrade and watched the sun slowly sinking, casting its glorious gold light over the red roofs and the white stucco and the green vines all around us. Two small Naval Patrol boats were moving slowly into the harbor, coming up the broad river, so wide that now, in the evening mist, you couldn't see the opposite bank, and I jerked my head at them and told him:

"They've been dying the sea red with cochineal."

He stared at me, just as Astrid had done. "Cochineal? But why?"

I said: "That red tide that's got Fenrek so worried turned out to be just that and nothing else."

"What an extraordinary thing: There must be a reason, I suppose?"

I said: "There's a reason that comes to mind a little too easily, perhaps."

"Oh?"

"There is a virulent poison down there somewhere that looks like mussel poisoning but turns out to be something else. It occurred to me that if Portugal had a department for bacteriological warfare, someone just might have made a mistake, maybe allowed a slight leakage. And if so, that someone might just try to cover up that mistake by simulating a red tide—to brainwash the civil population."

He was quite offended, which I'd rather expected. But I had to know. He said tartly: "You are presupposing an extraordinary degree of irresponsibility in the army, Senhor Cain. And we don't have a bacteriological arsenal, in any case."

"Not even for Angola?"

"Emphatically not," he said smoothly—and there was no gentleness apparent now. "It's only the major powers who are building up arsenals of these terrible weapons. We've neither the ability, nor the wish to do so."

"I just wondered. And it's Fenrek's problem anyway, not mine."

He wasn't so easily fooled. He said slowly, watching me very carefully: "Though why Interpol should be interested in what is surely a medical question, I can't imagine. Can you?"

The way to acquire knowledge, sometimes, is to exchange what you know for something you don't know.

I said: "There was a similar case in the Farne Islands, off the coast of Scotland three months ago. Mussel poisoning that turned out to be something else, and they never found out exactly what the something else was. Eight or nine sudden deaths, and one of them not so sudden. One man, a truck driver, lived long enough to make one cryptic comment that brought the police, and then Interpol, into it. He said: 'It's all my own fault, if I'd left the stuff where it was...,' and, then, he lay down and died. Same symptoms. But everyone wanted to know, *what stuff?* They found out that the driver was the kind of man you hired if you wanted stolen goods moved from one place to another, with no questions asked. It seemed to indicate enough evidence of some illegality or other to justify criminal investigation. So, when much the same sort of thing happened here, Colonel Fenrek came to take a look. Just a watching brief, really, while he took a much-deserved holiday. There's already an Interpol man here who's looking into it—banker, I believe. Fenrek knew I'd just arrived to work for you, and came to say hello. Then we learned that Astrid, who's a trained nurse, had scurried down to the beach to see what she could do."

"An impetuous young woman."

"Yes, indeed. But we stopped her in time. What's the African population in Lisbon?"

He shrugged. "Who knows. We don't keep records of that sort. If they're not from Angola, or Mozambique, they're Portuguese citizens like anyone else. What's on your mind?"

"It might be easier to find newcomers from Angola than a European hardly anyone has seen. Unless there are any photographs of Captain Loveless around, and I don't suppose there are likely to be many."

"None. Just Nacimento's description, which you already have."

"And which could apply to almost anyone."

The General said, worrying: "If we only knew how long he'd been here, that would be a help of some sort."

I told him: "Less than four months, that much we know."

"Oh?"

"There was a report in *Jeune Afrique* four months ago. According to them, Loveless is a bit of a hero. They said he'd left Angola some time back, was then fighting for the Biafrans in Nigeria, and about to leave West Africa on a 'special mission.'"

The General said instantly: "Biafra. A good cause to fight for."

"Perhaps. It seems he led a raid on a bank in Lagos, to get funds for the Biafran army."

We were sipping our drinks together, and suddenly the General remembered his manners again. He said, leaping up: "And I didn't even offer you a cigar. I don't smoke, myself, and I sometimes forget."

I said: "And neither do I. A foolish habit, I've always felt."

"Ah, good then." He sat down again and asked: "Did the report say whether or not the Biafrans had actually benefited by the raid?"

"It did indeed. Roughly a hundred thousand dolars' worth of local currency was stolen, and the Biafrans got half of it. The rest, according to *Jeune Afrique*, was being 'held back,' whatever that means, for a 'special project.' Whatever that means too."

He said thoughtfully: "Nigeria. So Angola's been made too hot for him. Is that a small triumph?"

"Not really. The only triumph will be when we get him. If we can persuade him to talk enough to clear you. And that's a moot point, isn't it?"

"And Biafra's liable to be too hot for him soon, too. Not many places left for the mercenaries to work, are there?"

Well, he was quits wrong there.

I said: "Out of all the new countries in Africa that have emerged in the last ten years, there's fighting going on in ninety-nine percent of them. That means plenty of scope for the professional fighter, on one side or the other. And if Africa ever settles down, there's always Central America, with South America about to go the same route, too. And by the time that's all finished, they'll have started over again in Africa. If, indeed, they ever stop. If you know how to use a gun, and you're short on scruples and long on toughness, there's always someone to hire you. Loveless presumably speaks good Portuguese?"

"Yes, apparently he does."

"Well enough to fool a Portuguese?"

"Well enough to fool an Angolan. There's the question of accent, of course, it's quite distinct."

"We can assume that he's traveling either without a passport or with a forged one."

He shrugged. "A landing somewhere along the coast, a small boat from Tangiers, it wouldn't be difficult."

Now I wanted the *quid* for the *quo*.

I said: "Now tell me, General, why the Army doctors are interested in Fenrek's red tide."

"Oh, that..."

It didn't seem very important to him, and, to tell the truth, it wasn't very important to me either. But I'm a curious kind of man, and anything that seems even a trifle out of kilter, I want to know about. It's strange how far apart cause and effect can apparently be and still be part of the same pattern, I recalled that Goethe had made that point once. On the surface, Fenrek's little problem had nothing at all to do with mine, but...Well, you can't just let the oddities slip by without inquiring about them, or you'll go through life in an intellectual vacuum.

He looked at me sharply all of a sudden, and asked: "You think there's a connection?"

"A connection? How should there be?"

He shook his head. "It occurred to me that you're concerned with a soldier, a professional fighting man, and Fenrek is dealing with the Army, you're both here in Lisbon at the same time...Is there a connection?"

"No stronger a connection than you've implied. But I still want to know. Why is the Army interested at all? We can accept Fenrek's involvement in what ought to be a purely medical matter, because of those criminal overtones in Scotland. But the Army? Why, General?"

He sighed. "You are a persistent man, Senhor Cain! And I wasn't trying to evade the question. It's simply that the Army was supposed to be carrying out a small-scale exercise during the night along the beach where those fishermen died. It was called off at the last moment because one of the three landing craft involved broke down. They're rather...ancient. But it occurred to someone that a small detachment had just escaped being wiped out. They wanted to make sure that it was merely coincidental."

"And was it?"

He didn't take his eyes off me. "Of course. Obviously."

A little pause, and then: "Wouldn't you say so?"

I couldn't think why he should want to fence with me so carefully. The natural discretion of the good politician? I said, not wanting to hide anything from him:

"If the nebulous thoughts at the back of my mind ever begin to make sense, then there'd be a very plausible reason for a minor attack on a small military contingent."

He had the intelligence—or the grace—not to look surprised. He just stood there, his fists at momentary rest on his hips and looked at me, and he said at last, very quietly:

"A test of some sort?"

"Exactly."

He said: "If you're thinking what I think you are thinking...You might be on to a very dangerous business, Senhor Cain." Almost without stopping, he shook his head suddenly and said: "No. No! Whichever way you look at it; it just doesn't make sense!"

I said: "But it just *could*. It just might be a very logical progression. Can I call on Nacimento if and when the problem of identification crops up?"

"Of course. He's up at the castelo, any time you want him."

"And I can trust him implicitly?"

"Implicitly. He's a very good man. Our Army's not very democratic, I suppose, but we occasionally do have promotion from the ranks, and I once almost gave Nacimento a Commission. He'd have made a very good officer."

"But you didn't?"

He sighed. "No, though in retrospect, I wish I had. I think perhaps I was being a little unfair to him. I just didn't want to lose him. And when I realize how I've been held back from a career that would have been very close to my heart, then I feel that on a smaller scale I really inflicted the same kind of obstruction on Nacimento. But he is very happy now, a sergeant in the Honor Guard."

Passing through the house on my way out, I shook hands again with Dona Clara, and admired her roses, set off now in a beautiful silver urn on the hall table. The servant was there, holding the front door open and eyeing me slyly when he thought I wasn't looking. I had to bend my head to get through the door.

The General said, shaking hands; "Come back and dine with us tonight, can you do that?"

I said: "I would like that very much. May I bring Fenrek's niece with me? Astrid Tillot?"

He beamed. "Of course, my dear fellow, we'd be delighted." His mood changed suddenly. He said, sounding worried: "Do you think you'll be able to find this fellow Loveless for me?"

"Yes. It might take a little time."

"It would mean so much. My country is coming into a very difficult period now, and if I can get the Ministry I want... There's so *very* much I can do. I like to think that were basically a very *good* people, we Portuguese, and I'd like to help our country along to much closer *rapport* with the rest of the world, good neighbors to everybody. Is that too much to hope for?"

"I'm sure it's not."

"If we can persuade Loveless to speak out, to let them know that I was on the right track." He threw up his arms helplessly: "All I can do, is try. And if you'll help me, Cain..."

I said: "I'll help you, General Queluz. *Ate logo.*"

"And thank you."

The servant was watching me go, making sure I didn't say an unkind word to the old man, guarding him like an affectionate, but wary, watchdog.

CHAPTER 3

Fenrek was in the hospital, fuming,

His face was red and swollen, his eyes puffed up, and he looked like hell. He said, glaring: "Those damned injections, why didn't you talk me out of them, Cain?"

Astrid was sitting there with him, looking pert and cheerful in a bright green shirt and white slacks, her silver hair flowing loosely now. She said: "He told you, Uncle, and I told you, too. You've only yourself to blame."

I said: "And you've never looked better anyway. How are you, Astrid?"

"Fine."

"Good." I said to Fenrek: "It's your lousy metabolism. You don't drink enough. What's the latest on the red tide?"

He scowled. "The Navy report. The five gallons of cochineal they poured into the ocean colored roughly a tenth of a square kilometer. So whoever made that artificial tide for us must have used about forty gallons or so."

"Did they drag up any dried insects?

"No, none. They must have used the liquid."

"And I suppose you've got people out checking on sales of cochineal in liquid form?"

"Of course. Every pharma in town has at least a small amount in stock except in one area. In the Alfama, there's not a drop to be had."

"Ah."

"A bottle here, a bottle there—someone bought up every ounce they could find, but only in Alfama."

I said sharply: "Someone?"

He scowled again. "Correction. Three people, three different descriptions, they went from store to store looking for cochineal till there wasn't a drop to be had anywhere. And you'll be interested to know that they all spoke with the same sort of accent, I don't know if it means anything, but..."

I interrupted him. "If it's an Angolan accent you're thinking of, it means a hell of a lot. It answers the big question."

He stared, then pulled a handkerchief from under his pillow and wiped at the sweat on his neck. He eased himself back into the pillows and said at last: "All right, Cain, let's have it. What's Angola got to do with it?"

"Wasn't it Anatole France who said that chance, in the last resort, is God? I think God's come to our rescue. He may be a bit late, but..."

"Angola, Cain."

"All right, I'll tell you. At least, I'll tell you the half of it. I came here to find a man called Loveless, a mercenary Captain from Angola, the man that got General Queluz dismissed, you remember?

"Go on."

"You came here because this mysterious red tide turned up and might, just might, have been connected with a similar occurrence in Scotland that turned out to have criminal overtones, even though no one, not even Interpol, knows what they were. Two separate and disparate facts. Problem: find the connecting link, if any. And the connecting link is Angola. Angolans buying cochineal to throw you off the scent, and an Angolan mercenary is the man I'm looking for."

"Lisbon's full of Angolans. They're Portuguese citizens, remember?"

"So it's pure coincidence? Balls."

"It might be," Fenrek said.

I said: "I've got a file on this man Loveless, a good one. There's always someone keeping a watchful eye on the appearances and disappearances of these mercenaries, there has to be, because whenever they appear on the horizon you can expect trouble. In this case, General Queluz has given me the Angolan Military File on Loveless, everything they know about him, which is considerable though still not enough. First of all, he's a Scotsman from the Farne Islands. Does that ring any bells?"

He sat up suddenly, and winced with the pain of it.

"Yes, I thought that might interest you. A short while ago, *Jeune Afrique* published a somewhat laudatory paragraph about him. They said he was an orphan, born on one of the Scottish islands. As soon as his name cropped up with Queluz, I did a little checking. Orphan my ass. His father is still living, but his mother died when he was a child."

I waited, and Fenrek said gloomily: "I know all about your unlikely likelihoods, and if you tell me she died of mussel poisoning..."

"She did. Precisely that."

"And that also turned out to be something else? Interesting, I'll admit that."

"No. What's interesting is that it really was mussel poisoning. Dinoflagellates. Part of a quite frequent pattern up there. Five or six islanders killed off, and she was one of them. Don't you think it's possible that we have a seed planted there?"

Astrid said: "The germ of an idea. It's possible, I suppose, but you're presupposing some medical knowledge in this man, you realize that?"

Fenrek said crossly: "He's not. I know exactly what he's going to say next."

He probably did, but I said it anyway. "And then, thirty years or so later, here's an epidemic in the Farne Islands of what is apparently the same thing, only it isn't. And that's a connection with Loveless too, because it's his own home ground and he'd be bound to hear about it, wherever he is."

"And where was he?"

"In Katanga, fighting for Tshombe against the United Nations, as a matter of fact. At least, that's where he was supposed to be. But it doesn't matter a damn *where* he was—the mystery of the inexplicable disease was loudly trumpeted all over the world. He'd have heard of it, and there's our connection."

"A very tenuous one." But I could see that Fenrek was impressed. He screwed up his face and said: "This bloody fever's going to kill me."

"I doubt it." I said: "Look at the progression. As a child, Loveless' mother is killed by mussel poisoning caused by a red tide. Next there's an epidemic of a similar disease *without* a red tide..."

Fenrek said glumly: "Thirty years later."

"That doesn't matter. Think of a man with boyhood memories. Next. The same man turns up where there's another deadly epidemic, and this time there *is* a red tide, just as there should be if we're not going to have another—and this time, far more serious—investigation on our hands. Only the red tide's a fake. And who bought the cochineal to make that fake? Loveless and a couple of friends."

"That's a preposterous assumption, and you know it," Fenrek said.

"By itself, it would be. But not as part of the progression. Who's your best man in Scotland?"

He frowned. "Say again?

"The best Interpol man in Scotland."

"Oh. Superintendent McGivern, in Edinburgh. Why?"

"Can I use the hospital phone, do you think?" I reached out and took the phone and said to the operator: "*Minena*, will you get me a Superintendent McGivern in Edinburgh, Scotland? At Police Headquarters. You can charge it to Senhor Fenrek's account." I put the phone back and told him: "They only asked you to come here because of that driver, didn't they?"

His mind wasn't functioning as well as it did normally. He thought for a while and said: "Ah yes, the driver who stole something or other that killed him. I remember. A professional thief."

"You remember his name?"

He said tartly: "Since I came here to see if there might be a connection between Scotland's trouble and Portugal's, yes, I remember his name. Does that surprise you?" He was in a bad temper today, and Astrid reached out and touched his hand soothingly: "Now be a good boy and maybe we'll find you a rattle to play with." He glared at her and said: "His name was Stewart, Alexander Stewart, a nice uncommon name in Scotland."

I said calmly: "Common or not, it's all I want to know at the moment. Do you know about the island of Gruinard?"

His temper was abating, but he glowered and said: "Yes, I do, and you're not supposed to know anything about it."

I shrugged. "Only what I read in the papers. I hear it's been closed off, put off limits to everybody."

"So have many others of the remote islands, come to that."

"But not for the same reason. Ah…" The phone was ringing, and I took it and heard the operator say: "You call to Scotland coming through, Excellency."

"Thank you." I gave the phone to Fenrek and said: "Just introduce us, will you? I'm now going to solve your problem for you."

He sighed and took the phone, muttering under his breath. A nurse came in with a bowl of barley soup, and he took one look at it, sniffed it suspiciously, and snarled at her. She put it down on the table none the less, and he said into the phone: "McGivern? Fenrek. How are you?" He waited a moment then said: "As a matter of fact, I'm probably dying, and it's nothing to do with the beautiful Portuguese women either. I want you to talk to an associate of mine, tell him what he wants to know…What? No, you can tell him anything. Here he is. Cabot Cain."

He handed me the phone, took up the bowl of soup, sniffed it again, and put it back on the table. He snuggled closer under the bedclothes as Astrid tried to feed him.

I said: "Cabot Cain, Superintendent, how do you do? You remember that epidemic in the Farne Islands that killed off eight or nine of the islanders?"

His burr was strong, his voice ripe: "Aye, I do that, Mr. Cain."

"The truck driver who died, a man named Alexander Stewart. Do you know anything about him?"

"Aye. What was it you wanted to know?"

"Was he a local man?"

"Aye, he was that. From St. Agnes."

"And just before he died, say a few days before, did you ever find out if he'd been away? If he'd made a trip anywhere?"

"Aye. As a matter of routine, we investigated thoroughly, but we never found out where he'd been. He'd been away from St. Agnes for five or six days. But the Farne Islands, ye ken, are no Scottish, they're British, and we don't get the cooperation from them we might like to have. They're Sassenachs there." He sounded as though that explained everything, and when he said "British" there were half a dozen *R*s in the middle of it.

I said: "In six days, he could have gone to Gruinard and spent a day or two there, couldn't he?"

The heavily-accented voice was suddenly very cautious, "Aye, he could that, I suppose."

"And what is it precisely that they were manufacturing on Gruinard, Superintendent?"

There was a long pause. I saw that Fenrek was watching me, suddenly very interested. The Superintendent said at last, very ponderously: "The Island of Gruinard, Mr. Cain, is a closely-guarded military installation, and what they're up to there is an equally closely-guarded secret."

I said politely: "But not, no doubt, from Interpol."

"Aye, from us too."

"And from you personally?"

Another long pause. He said at last: "I don't know if I've the right..." He sighed. I waited, and he said: "It's a Bacteriological Warfare Research Center, Mr. Cain."

I said patiently: "As a matter of fact, I knew that already. What I want to know is...what *exactly* are they manufacturing there?"

That pause again. He said at last: "Could I speak with the Colonel again, if you don't mind?"

I handed Fenrek the phone and said: "Tell him, Fenrek. This is what we've all got to know. And now."

Fenrek said into the phone: "If you know, Superintendent—even if you're not supposed to—tell him."

He gave me back the instrument, and I heard the rich ripe voice say slowly: "They're manufacturing a thing called botulinum toxin, Mr. Cain, though I'll not be able to tell you much about it because I'm happy to say that I don't know very much. All I know is..."

I interrupted him. I said quietly: "Don't bother, Superintendent, I know a lot about it. Do you know a man named

Loveless?"

"Aye. Michael Loveless is our Minister of Education."

"Wrong Loveless. This one's Arthur, born in the Farne Islands, in St. Agnes, but now lives in Africa."

"St. Agnes, Mr. Cain?" I could hear the wheels turning.

I said: "Aye, but don't let it bother you too much. Except that there's a likelihood he knew your Alexander Stewart. What's the population of St. Agnes?

"About eighty souls, give or take a couple."

"Then he did know him. They must have been kids together. And that's all I wanted to know. Thank you, Superintendent. You want to say hello to Fenrek again?"

"Aye, but tell me...what's the matter with him?"

I said: "Nothing, now. He'll be on his feet again in five minutes."

I passed the phone over to Fenrek and listened to them exchanging small talk for a moment. I tasted his barley soup; it was excellent. And when he'd rung off, I said: "You'd better pass the word around. What you're fighting is botulinum toxin. Under ideal conditions, that's a toxin of which one ounce is the fatal dose for sixty million people."

He stared at me.

I said: "More precisely, one sixty-millionth of an ounce is a fatal dose for one person. Somehow, some of it has found its way to Portugal, and the question of finding Loveless is now a good deal more worrisome, isn't it?"

He said: "But why, Cain? For God's sakes, *why?*"

I said: "And there's a very simple reason there, too."

He thought for a while, turning the possibilities over in his mind. He said at last: "If Loveless was behind that theft the driver spoke of...what in hell is he doing in Portugal? Is he...for God's sake, is he planning to wipe us all out here? A residue of his Angola enmity?"

"I doubt it. I think he's got a better plan, one that makes a lot more sense."

"But that's something he *could* do, if he were so inclined..."

"Yes indeed. And all he did was make a casual attempt to wipe out a small military contingent that was due to land on the beach by the

Bocca. Just a small-scale business all round."

He didn't know about the Army exercises, and when I told him he sank back into the pillows and said wearily: "I still think it's a lot of nonsense, but I'm not fit enough to argue with you. For God's sake, take Astrid to dinner and leave me to enjoy my suffering in peace, will you do that for me? And, for your information, if they're really playing around with botulinum on Gruinard, nobody's going to steal any of it. *Nobody.*"

I said: "And you might as well get out of bed, your fever's breaking. I'd like you to do a little job for me tomorrow."

Suspiciously, he squinted up at me out of the pillows. "Tomorrow? What sort of job, Cain?"

I said: "I want to know if a sour cream factory has changed hands recently. Quicker for you to find that out than for me, wouldn't you say?"

"A sour cream...Oh, for God's sake!"

"No. For the sake of the Devil."

I took Astrid's arm and we went out together. On the stairs, I told her: "There's a nice old man waiting to meet you. Were going to see General Queluz, a friend of your uncle's. They say he's got the best cook in Lisbon."

But we had no dinner that night. The drama became suddenly personalized.

We drove over in the Jensen to the fine old house above the Alfama, and parked in Praca Santa Lucia by the railings that are high above the narrow streets of the lower quarter, looking out across the rooftops at the river for a moment, listening to the noisy night sounds, coming up from below there; a lottery-ticket seller was shouting his wares, calling out in a melodic, high-pitched voice that broke off sharply and left the last syllables hanging. We could hear the mournful notes of a *fado,* the sad-sweet love song of the Portuguese; somewhere down there a woman was mourning a lost love.

We went over to the house and knocked on the door, and the white-gloved servant was there, with an expression of abject contrition on his sly face. He said, and he sounded very worried: "The General is not yet back, Senhor. All I can do is ask you to wait. And I know he would expect me to offer his apologies."

"Oh? Back from where?"

"He went out, Senhor, to one of the *lagosterias* beyond Cascais, to find Sergeant Nacimento. A *lagosteria* near the Bocca do Inferno."

"Bocca do Inferno? What would Nacimento be doing there at this time of night?"

He shrugged his narrow shoulders. There was a trace of worry on his face. "I do not know, Senhor, I only know that someone called and said Nacimento was there, with something to show the General, urgently."

"Someone?"

"I do not know who he was."

"And you're worried?"

He could not easily hide the concern that was there. He said slowly: "Perhaps it is nothing, Senhor, but there is a parade of the Honor Guard tonight at Castele São Jorge, and Nacimento would not miss this. I do not think he would go out to the Bocca when he is expected to take his place in the parade."

"And does the General know about the parade too?"

"Perhaps. Perhaps not."

It didn't sound right at all. I said harshly: "What time was this?"

"At half past five, Senhor."

"Get me the castle on the phone, can you do that?"

"*Sim Senhor, de uma vez...*"

He hurried away, and we followed him into the high-ceilinged, paneled library. I poured a glass of cognac for Astrid and one for myself, and told her: "This just might be all the dinner you're going to get tonight."

In a moment, the call came through, and I took the phone and said urgently to the operator at the castle: "I don't want to interrupt the parade, Senhora, but do you know Sergente Nacimento?"

The connection was bad, the line crackling. She said: "Yes, Excellency, I do."

"Then tell me if he's on parade, can you do that?"

She did not hesitate. "Of course, Excellency, he's leading the Honor Guard."

"And what time did the parade start?"

"At four-thirty, Excellency."

"And the sergeant has been there all the time?"

"*Sim, Excelencia, certamente.*"

"*Obbrigado, Senhora.*"

I slammed the phone down, grabbed Astrid's arm, and lugged her with me to the outside. As we ran to the car, she said: "But for heaven's sake..." and I told her: "You'd better stay with me, I don't like the way things are shaping up. I don't like it at all."

Would it have been safer to have left her there? I just don't know. All I knew was that something was happening—had perhaps happened already—that I should have expected and been prepared for.

I pushed the starter button, reared round in a tight U-turn, and headed straight down the hill. I kept my finger on the horn and went fast down Rua da Regueira into the impossibly tight alley of San Miguel, the walls of the houses no more than an inch from the sides of the car, swung into Beco do Meixas, and bit the square at the bottom at sixty miles an hour. I braked hard and skidded over the cobbles where the water was running down the steps, past the vegetable stalls there where a man leaped back in the nick of time and shouted an obscenity at me, and pushed her hard out into the wide street of the Trigo.

We'd gone no more than a few yards, but we'd dropped a few hundred feet as well, and Astrid took a deep breath and asked plaintively: "Couldn't we just get out and walk?"

The streets were heavy with traffic now, and we had to fight donkey carts and push barrows till we got to the broad and beautiful Praca do Commercio, the stateliest square in Europe, with its huge quadrangle of pale-green painted buildings and the fine white marble statues of Vasco da Gama, Alvares and Viriatus and the Marquis of Pombal on top of the Arch of Triumph, lit now by the bright beams of the floodlights. I speeded up and shot past an angry traffic cop, and hit the Avenue of the Fourth of July at seventy-five; and once we passed the beautiful Tower of Belem, where the traffic was thinning out, I put my foot down and pushed her really hard.

The powerful motor hummed, but the Michelin radial-ply tires, steel bound, hung tight to the road as we left the town and hit the highway along the coast. I heard a siren behind me, and saw two motorcycle police coming up fast in the wing mirror, so I pushed a bit harder and lost them when we topped a hundred and ten. I switched on the long-range driving lights, the Lucas Flame Throwers that light up the road ahead as bright as day for a mile or more.

We by-passed Estoril by taking the second-class road, then slowed to eighty to go through the back of the little fishing town of Cascais, taking the inland road through the pines to by-pass the traffic, and braked savagely to a skid round the bend to hit the coast again; and two minutes later we saw the lights of the *lagosteria*.

I took a short cut by jumping the ditch at the side of the road and pulled up under the brilliant overhead flare that was meant to keep away intruders and let the watchman see anyone who might come sneaking round the tiny growing lobsters in their dark deep caverns; lobsters are expensive now, even in Portugal, and the guard always carried a shotgun.

Only he wasn't there. And I had a premonition of disaster.

I said to Astrid, whispering: "Stay here in the car. Keep the engine running, and at the first sign of anything you don't like the look of, head for home, fast. You know how to drive with a stick shift?"

She nodded. "But can't I...can't I come with you? I'm scared."

I hesitated. The danger was nebulous, inexplicably worrying; there'd been no evidence that anything was really wrong, and yet...I had a nasty feeling that someone, *somebody*, knew of my interest in whatever it was I was supposed to be interested in here. I couldn't explain it, even to myself; but I always play my hunches, it's wiser. I wished I'd brought the General's tough little servant with me to look after Astrid.

I said, a little dubiously: "All right. Stay close to me, all the time."

She said fervently: "I will, don't worry about that."

I reached into the glove compartment and took out the flashlight, and we went quickly down the steep slope of the sandy bank towards the broken rocks of the beach.

The Bocca do Inferno, the Mouth of Hell, is well named. When the wind is in the southwest, as it was not now, thank heaven, the driven sea beats into a monstrous complex of caves that lead from a tight funnel at sea level down under the hundred-foot cliff. There's a gorge that cuts through the middle of it all, well-wired off at the top to keep the curious tourists away, and the sides of the gorge are pitted with smaller caves and tunnels, some of them boring deep down into unexplored recesses deep under the cliff.

A party of spelunkers had been there last year to explore the deepest of these. They reached a depth of four hundred and eighty feet before the ground gave way beneath their feet and buried all six of them, five young students from the geology class at the University and their teacher. Now, this tunnel too has been wired off.

We gave it all a very wide berth and moved along the beach to where the *lagosteria* is. It is part of the same complex of caves, but far enough away from the Bocca itself to be quite harmless, unless you're fool enough to lose your footing. Here, there's a deep slice into the cliff that is man-made, a squared off passage that was cut by hand, no one knows how long ago or why, that opens up into a huge chamber, some eighty feet square and fifteen feet high, with a smooth floor of ancient cement. When the cavern was first discovered, they found that the cement used was made with egg whites, which presupposes the work was done by the Romans; but some say that the Phoenicians carved it out while they were on their way to build Gadir, the "wall fortification" in Spain, that later became known as Cadiz; that was eleven hundred years before Christ.

Be that as it may, some of the minor caverns, the safe ones, have now been put to a more prosaic use; lobsters are bred there. The owners of the various *lagosterias* have cut great square holes in the concrete floor, below which—and a few feet down—the water of the sea is gentle and subdued, in surprising contrast to the fury of the turmoil just round the corner, where the waters of the Bocca are driven up sky-high through the deep cleft in the rock.

In this huge backwash, several hundred square yards in area, the young lobsters come by the hundreds, and they are trapped here by a series of heavy wire grills and left to feed on the thousands of dying fish which are trapped by the rise and fall of the tide. It is as though a false floor of concrete had been built across the uneven floor of the ocean, some two or three feet above it—a great deal more above it in parts, where the bottom drops away into natural reservoirs—so that there is easy access from a sensibly stable platform into the dark and murky depths below. The cut holes, in turn, are covered with massive slabs of concrete which are moved aside, when collection time comes, with a simple rope and winch, and as many lobsters as are required can then be hauled up by hand. It is a profitable business, and the heavy slabs are there to make sure no inquisitive explorer goes home with his rucksack full of lobsters at twenty *escudos* a head.

These are not true lobsters, of course, not the *Homaridae* whose major legs terminate in crushing claws; these are the *Palinuridae*, the spiny lobster or crawfish that taste so well when they're cooked in a mixture of court bouillon and cognac, or grilled over an open hearth and brushed with black butter. But they crowd their confined homes here by the hundreds, scarcely moving in the darkness except when the rising tide deposits their food for them and then falls back to leave it there.

I shielded my eyes against the glare of the big lamp at the top of the cliff and waited for someone to yell out and ask what I was doing there; there was only the boisterous sound of the sea, and I wondered where the watchman was; down there himself?

I went quickly down the sand-blown concrete steps that have been cut into the side of the cliff, with Astrid nervously following, and the spray coming up and soaking us both, and landed in the relative quiet at the bottom to find the wooden door that leads to the cavern ajar; the padlock was open with the key still in it. I turned the bright beam of the flashlight over the cavern and studied it.

High in the roof, the water was dripping slowly; we could hear the sound of the wash below our feet, and the flashlight showed me why—one of the huge concrete slabs had been pulled away on its winch to open up a trap. We skirted it carefully, peering down into the murky depths of the water below, and swung the light down each of the many tunnels that led God knows where, one after the other. There was a sign on the rock wall, painted in red letters on white near the entrance to one of the many subsidiary tunnels that lead down into the black silence there; it said: *Caution, the roof is unstable, do not make noise.* I called out none the less: "*Guarda!* Watchman!" Some rubble trickled down from the roof, and my voice echoed back a dozen times, the sound dying away slowly, reluctantly. I called again, louder; only the echoes came back; and more rubble.

I swung the beam of the light slowly over the walls. An electrical cord ran along the ceiling, with bare bulbs hanging from it at intervals, and I followed its line and found the switch and flicked it on. The bulbs lit up and cast their eerie shadows over the red and yellow rocks.

And there, swinging from an iron support in the ceiling, swaying still at the end of a rope, was the body of General Queluz.

CHAPTER 4

Astrid's scream reverberated through the chamber, a scream that went on and on and on as she clutched at me and buried her face in my chest.

I said: "For God's sake!" I tried to stifle the sound, and before I could say another word, another small shower of stones and rubble fell from the ceiling. She gasped.

I said gently: "There's nothing we can do, and screaming won't help. You'll just bring the roof down on us." She turned back to stare at the swaying body, staring as though hypnotized, and I said roughly, trying to throw some sense into her: "You've seen dead men before, in your business."

Her voice was a whisper: "Yes, but not...not like that."

I broke away from her and went to the body and touched it; it was cold. And then, in the terrible silence, I became aware of something that shouldn't be there. I moved swiftly to the light switch and flicked it off, and in the darkness I heard Astrid gasp; she whispered urgently: "No, no, not the darkness."

I felt for her and took her arm and guided her carefully back the way we had come. She began to say something, and I put a finger on her lips and held it there, feeling her freeze. I put my mouth very close to her ear and whispered: "No sound at all."

Very carefully, very slowly, we moved together, step by slow step, towards the iron gate; I tried hard to visualize just where that gaping hole was in the floor, and reached out an arm to search for the rope of the winch in the darkness. I found it, and we skirted the entrance to the trap and moved on.

The scent that had alarmed me was stronger now; the ripe, sweet scent of tobacco.

I don't smoke, myself, and I can smell a cigarette a long way away. The General was a nonsmoker too, and if it was the watchman, why hadn't he answered my call?

There was no alien sound, just the murmur of the water, a faint lap-lap in slow cadence. The darkness, after the bright flare of the lights, was impenetrable, and Astrid's lithe body was stiff as she walked beside me, trying hard not to make a noise, walking on the tips of her toes and the leather scuffling the concrete floor. And then, suddenly, the lights went on again.

We'd come to within a few feet of the wooden door, and there they were, two of them, with their weapons pointed straight at us.

One of them was a tall, gangling man, with cadaverous cheeks and an unhealthy pallor to his skin, a man with lank hair falling over his forehead and dark, resentful eyes. He wore an off-white sweatshirt and khaki trousers, with a broad leather belt and a loosely-cut jacket of worn-out Bedford cord, and he carried a sawed-off shotgun very easily and nonchalantly in one hand, with the butt tucked under a bony elbow and the barrel pointed straight at my stomach.

The second man was quite different, a slight, stolid looking man with fair hair and a very bronzed complexion wearing a blue Naval coat and a pair of dirty white trousers, with dark blue sneakers on his feet. To my astonishment, he carried a bow and arrow.

It was not an ordinary bow, but a small, brightly shining bow of what looked like brushed steel, not much more than thirty-six inches long, small enough to slip down a trouser leg if need be to hide it from watchful, curious eyes. The string was drawn back, but only a trifle, and his thumb was hooked over it in the old Mongolian draw—almost the first time I'd seen this. The arrow was about twenty inches long, and quite heavy, an unusually thick arrow made from steel rod with a hunting head on it, what looked like the Howard Hill broadhead, and instead of feathers it was fitted with a fur fletch. There was a quiver across his back, high up at his neck, with another twelve or fifteen shafts in it. It startled me to see so unusual a weapon, and I wondered what sort of man he was.

I turned round to see who was at the light switch, and there he was, a thick-set, burly man with close-cropped hair and pale blue eyes, well over six feet tall and looking very tough indeed, with huge, well-developed forearms under the tightly rolled up sleeves of his khaki shirt. He, too, carried a sawed-off shotgun, and there was an indescribable air of affinity among the three of them; they looked like a wolf pack together, as though each were part of the others. The close-cropped hair gave him the look of a soldier, and the tan was straight out of Africa.

There was a look of controlled impatience on his face, like the face of a schoolmaster who's found one of the boys in the pantry in the middle of the night. He looked quickly at Astrid and back to me, his expression not changing, and he said, quite quietly and with no sort of expression in his voice:

"Well, who are you, and what are you doing here?" There was no anger in his voice at all; it was as though the question were purely academic, as though, almost, he didn't really expect an answer.

I said mildly: "My name's Cabot Cain, and I came looking for General Queluz. Simple enough."

He didn't waste any time on more formality. He held his shotgun loosely in his hand and moved to one side a little, a move that seemed on the surface to have no meaning at all till I looked back again at the two men by the door. They had moved out, each to one side, and the third man had merely moved instantly and casually out of their line of possible fire. I looked back at him, and he jerked his gun towards the hanging body and said:

"How did you know he was here?"

I shrugged. "We had a dinner appointment. His servant said he'd come down here, so we came looking for him."

"Just the two of you?"

I didn't expect to deceive him, but I thought that at least I might try. I said: "Just the two of us and my driver. He's outside somewhere."

The man with the bow laughed, a sudden, inexplicably queer sort of laugh. He held the bow and the arrow in one hand, the index finger of the left hand curled round the shaft to hold it still in position, and made quick, elusive gestures with his right. So we'd been watched as we arrived. The third man nodded, accepting the signal. He jerked his head towards the open hole in the floor that was the lobster trap and said briefly:

"Get down there, both of you."

I said: "No."

A flicker of impatience crossed his face. Still no anger, just a touch of irritation. He said roughly: "In there, or I'll blow both your heads off."

I looked up at the sign on the wall. "And bring the whole lot down on us?"

Staring at him, Astrid whispered: "Did you...kill him?"

Now there was a curious look in his eye, and I knew why. We'd been talking Portuguese—his accent was Angolan—and Astrid spoke it badly. He looked at her sharply and switched to English, with a strong Scottish accent:

"Och, so you're Americans then. Aye, and it's a natural characteristic, is it not, minding everybody's business but your own? Now, get down there, the both of you."

I said again: "No."

There was a little silence. He took a deep breath, a sigh almost, and said carefully, a schoolmaster explaining to a not-too-bright schoolboy: "Look, the world I live in we don't worry too much about risks, we just take them. You'd probably call me a very careless fellow, but in my language that just means that if a chance has got to be taken, then by God I'll take it. If I bring the roof down on us we're close enough to the door to make it. Now, get down there, I won't tell you again."

It was all a question of likelihoods, and likelihood is stronger than truth. There was a look on his face, not a temporary expression but a strange set to the line of the mouth, a composure in the eyes that told me he was not exaggerating. I suppose an old-fashioned term for it would be a kind of guts written all over his face, a look of casual determination that said this man would take the most extraordinary chances and think nothing of them at all. You meet that kind of man sometimes; and it's mostly in wartime; they make the best soldiers.

I looked at the other two, and I suppose I was unconsciously calculating their capacity. The thin man with the shotgun did not stir; he was chewing a piece of tobacco nonchalantly. But the other man, the one with the bow, suddenly made a move. He pulled back the string and let fly with a shaft, and then, so fast that I literally did not see the movement, another arrow left the bow and a third was there, drawn back, in its place. I heard the thump as the arrows struck home; they'd both passed between Astrid and me, and we were standing close together, so close that our bodies were almost touching. And he hadn't even aimed—just the instinctive aim that a boy uses with a slingshot. I looked back over my shoulder and found that both the shafts had found a mark in a heavy wooden spar that supported the winch to the lobster trap.

And then he laughed again. With his wild eyes and his tousled fair hair, he looked like Harpo Marx; but only temporarily. In a moment, the madness in his eyes was a violent fanaticism. He stood there now with his feet apart, his body loose and controlled, and remained immobile and placid and...expectant. I looked at the two arrows again; they were buried deep in the oak, two inches deep or more.

I shrugged. I moved over to the edge of the pit and jumped down in. I'm six feet seven, and the water came up to my waist, and the massive concrete closure was a foot above my head. The smell of lobster was ripe in the air now, and I was standing on them, feeling them wriggle as some of them crushed under the weight of my two hundred and ten pounds; they must have been packed tight down there, five or six deep. I held out my arms for Astrid as she stood looking down at me, the harsh light showing up the terrible fear on her face.

I said gently: "It's not as bad as it seems."

The cadaverous man moved in swiftly behind her and put out a straight arm and shoved, and she fell into my arms with a strangled sort of a sob, and I held her there and watched them reaching up for the rope on the winch, staring up into the light and waiting. In a moment, the concrete slab swung into place with an oddly metallic ring, and there was only absolute darkness,

I heard Astrid sob. She said, her voice low: "Oh, God..." I held her tight for a moment or two, clear off the bottom, listening; but there was only silence to hear. Her body was wet and cold and frail, and I thought: it's going to be a lot worse.

I said to her, very quietly: "I'm going to put you down. The water will come up to your shoulders and you'll be standing on a mass of lobsters, but they won't hurt you."

There was silence again. And then, inexplicably—and something which pleased me enormously—she said with almost a grunt: "Then I'd better pull myself together, hadn't I?"

I said: "Yes, you had indeed." I put her down at once, and she squealed and hung on to me, and said, not quite so fearfully as before: "Lobsters with claws?"

"Crawfish." I said callously: "If we die, they'll eat us, but we're not going to do that. We've got an hour or so to get out of here."

"An hour?"

"High tide."

There was a long pause. She said at last, whispering: "The water may reach the roof before high tide."

"No. The floor above was dry, and down here it wouldn't dry off in twelve hours if any spilled up onto the concrete. And there still might be an inch or two of air even when the tide's at its highest, so there's plenty of hope."

It wasn't very true; one of the tunnels had sloped upward and there were concrete manholes up there too, which meant we were in one of the lower ones. And the floor had been *thoroughly* wet, only I hoped she might not have noticed or might have forgotten. Anyway, she seemed to take my word for it, which argued a nice sensibility.

The water was freezing, and those dammed crustaceans were squiggling and writhing under our feet, paying us back for eating their brothers and sisters.

I said: "We'll give those men five minutes to get clear."

"And then?"

"Then I'm going to shift that cover."

"You'll never move it."

"I can, and I will."

"It took two men on a winch to move it, and even if you could...they might still be there, waiting."

I said: "No. With a dead body hanging up there, they'll get clear as soon as they can. At a guess, if we'd arrived five minutes later, we'd have missed them. And I wouldn't have liked that at all."

"What? For God's sake!"

I said: "That was Major Loveless, the man I came here to find. Well, now I've found him, haven't I?"

I knew that her silence was a rebuke. I said: "Well, at least I know what he looks like now. Don't worry too much, we're not going to stay here forever."

She thought for a while. I heard her squeal when the mass under her feet heaved, and she clutched at me tightly. She said: "That cover must weigh a ton."

"It was roughly five feet by three, and about eight inches thick. Say, eleven cubic feet. If it's reinforced Portland, which it probably is, then a cubic foot weighs a hundred and forty pounds. So we have a matter of fifteen hundred and forty pounds to worry about. Not easy. Not impossible either."

There was still time to wait out. I said: "Or look at it like this—the rope was on a standard sheave pulley, which has a mechanical advantage of a trifle under one to six. If an average man can comfortably move two hundred pounds, then the pulley system presupposes about twelve hundred pounds total weight. You noticed that the two men were hauling on it with no effort at all, so that makes our reckoning probably about right, wouldn't you say?"

She shrugged. "No man alive can lift that much."

I said: "We don't have to lift it. I need a six-inch rock and maybe a stick if we can find one."

My casual tone was having the right effect. She began to laugh suddenly, then stopped and squealed again, the squeal turning into a shriek. I felt her trying to climb all over me, and she said, aghast: "They're biting me."

"It's your imagination. There's too much good food down there for them. They're not going to bother with your feet. Now, hold still and wait for me."

"Wait for you?"

I took a deep breath and ducked under the water. My hands clutched at lobsters, dozens of them, feeling the powerful flap of their tails as they shot out of my way, forcing their way through the crowd, thrashing about madly in their fear. I groped around for a big enough stone, and couldn't find exactly what I wanted, so I had to make do with something a trifle smaller than I would have liked. But I turned up a stone at last about the size of my fist, came up for air and handed it to her.

"Hold this. Step one," I said.

Then I went back under and groped around for a stick, a piece of old lumber, anything that might serve the purpose I had in mind; there was nothing. I came up again at last and said:

"Well, we'll manage without."

I put my feet wide apart, kicking aside lobsters to get a firm footing, and reached up with both hands flat and widespread dead center on the underside of the cover; and I pushed.

The slab was absolutely immobile. I pushed until my arms were aching from the effort, and then shifted my position and tried again. I put my palms at the extreme edge of the slab, knowing that here there'd be the question of leverage to help me; one edge of twelve hundred pounds weighs less than its whole. It would not budge, even though all I had to do was tip it a trifle.

I relaxed and took a breather, the sweat running down my body and mixing with the salt water, and then I went under again and groped around with both hands among those damned shellfish till I found a large boulder that was loose and seemed to be about the right size. It was flattish, and about two feet thick, and not impossible to lever into position under the water. I got my shoulder under it and shoved, and felt it move. And then, slowly, laboriously, I rolled it over on its side, feeling Astrid's long slim legs in the way (her feet hopping now and then among the lobsters). I came up and said:

"Move over a bit, well to the left, I'm rolling a rock around down there."

When she'd moved away, squealing again, I went down once more and rolled the rock heavily over onto its side. It settled into place with a rumble, and I came up, gasping for air, and stood on it. And now, I was eighteen inches or so higher, and the slab above was close enough to make me bend my shoulders. Just what I wanted; with my shoulders I can move the earth itself.

I bent my legs, put my hands on my knees, put my right shoulder under the edge of the slab, and slowly straightened my legs. I felt the slab move, just a trifle. I let it fall into place again, eased my position, and said to Astrid, quite happily now:

"Now it's up to you. Climb up round my waist, put your arms round my neck, wrap your legs tight around me, and hang onto that rock I gave you. When I tell you, shove the stone into the opening—it'll wedge the slab open just enough."

She reached up and clambered up me, holding her- self tight in the position I had given her. I felt long legs locking themselves at my waist. I said: "Keep your head out of my way, twist over to the side a little"

She did as I told her, and I put my shoulder back under the edge of the slab and once more began to straighten up. The edge tilted slightly and hung there; I pushed some more, laboring against it. And then the damned rock down there heeled over and slipped, and we both fell, foundering, into the water. Above our heads, the slab thundered home again with a roar to wake the dead.

She waited, Astrid, while I submerged again and set the boulder once more into position; the smell of crushed lobster was overpowering now, and I fancied I could hear them tearing at the dead flesh of their fellows down there; well, at least it would keep them away from Astrid's toes.

We got back into position, and I started again. The edge went up slowly, more and more, till it cleared the lip and a rush of cold air came suddenly through it. I pushed harder, raising my hands and adding the effort of my biceps. Astrid was already fumbling with the stone, trying to get it into the gap. She said excitedly: "A little more, an inch or two..."

I straightened up fully, and now there was a four inch space between the edge of the cover and the lip of the opening. I said: "Now! Make sure it's steady." She held the stone in position while I gently bent my legs and lowered the slab once more. It stayed firmly wedged on the stone she had put there, leaving a gap wide enough for a thin arm to reach through. I took hold of her by the backs of her thighs and hoisted her up higher, and said: "Now, reach through there and feel around for the rope, it's there somewhere."

She reached out and groped about, and said disconsolately: "It's probably on the other side, if it's there at all."

I said: "No, it's not on the other side, why do you think I opened up this edge and not the opposite one? The winch is well off-center, on that side, and that rope's got to be within easy reach. That's what I wanted a stick for, but we don't have one, so quit cribbing about it and reach for it." I could feel her straining, catching her breath, and I said: "My arm's longer but it won't go through that gap very far, so if you can't find it I'll have to find a bigger stone and we'll start over."

She said suddenly: "I've got it!" She reached out far, half her slim shoulder disappearing through the opening. She said impatiently: "Dammit, missed."

I was wondering if there was still someone out there, watching with a kind of interested amusement, ready to kick the stone out of the way and crush her arm with the heavy slab; I wished I'd been able to find a bigger wedge that would have allowed me to do the groping myself. But it was dark up there; the lights had been switched off, and that meant they'd probably gone.

She said triumphantly: "Got it!" and in a moment she dragged the free end of the winch rope down through the opening.

I said: "All right, climb down again and leave me some room."

She slipped lithely down me, clutching at my waist as she landed among the lobsters, and said: "I'll never eat another one as long as I live."

Grabbing the end of the swinging rope, I said: "Personally, I'd like to take a few of them home for us, what do you say?"

I felt her shudder. I heaved on the rope and heard the wheels of the pulley creaking as they turned. The huge slab swung ponderously out of the way. And in less than thirty seconds we were up on the concrete floor again, standing there dripping wet and cold in the darkness, listening to the silence and feeling the sea breeze on our soaking bodies.

I left the cover where it was, and in silence we crept to the door and found it locked. There was a padlock, I remembered, on the outside. So I put my shoulder to it and smashed it open, making a mental note to come back one day and pay the owner for the damage. We went up the concrete steps together into the cold, moonlit air of the night.

For a moment we huddled together in the darkness, sheltered

under an overhang of rock. Silhouetted against the bright glare of the lamp I could see the Jensen, sitting there forlornly as though waiting for me. I whispered: "There's just a chance someone may be watching. We'd better leave it there." She nodded. I said: "A run along the beach to dry off, it'll do us both good."

We clambered down the steep track to the beach, and I took her hand and we ran together in the sand close under the cliff, running at an easy, loping pace, Astrid taking off her shoes and running barefoot. The murmur of the sea was friendly, a peaceful sound, and the white surf caught the steel glint of the moon. And, fifteen minutes later, dry and refreshed but wrinkled and dirty, we were on the outskirts of Cascais.

There's a telephone at the base of the fishermen's wharf there, put there for the exclusive use of the lobstermen who call the trucks as soon as they bring their boats in, and it's far enough from the town itself to be deserted during the night; or mostly so. We disturbed a young couple making love in the sand, and apologized for nearly tripping over them, and I went to the telephone and asked the operator to give me the Santa Maria hospital, I got through to Fenrek in no time at all.

I said: "I need a car, Fenrek, at the fishing wharf in Cascais, unobtrusively."

His voice was plaintive at the other end. "I was just in the middle of a beautiful sleep, Cain. What the hell are you doing in Cascais at this time of the night?"

I said: "Trying hard not to be seen. Unobtrusive, all right?"

"Unobtrusive it shall be."

"And somewhere to clean up and hide cut for a couple of hours. Don't you have a house tucked away here somewhere?"

"Yes, I do, and you're not supposed to know that."

"Up on the road towards Sintra, I believe. Can I borrow it?"

I heard him sigh. "All right, I'll get hold of Pereira—I suppose you know about him too?"

"Your banker friend? Well, of course I do. Not only that, I've met him, though he probably doesn't remember?"

"Not remember *you?*"

I told him precisely where to send the car, what the driver had to do, and rang off. We sat down on the lonely sands together, and waited. It was cool and pleasant there in the moonlight, and Astrid leaned in close to me and put an arm round my waist. I held her tight for a while, feeling the softness of her body and saying nothing.

The car came along in twenty minutes, an old and disreputable looking Citröen. It stopped at the head of the wharf, and the driver got out, opened the back door, pulled out a heavy wicker basket of fish scraps, lugged it to the end of the wharf, and tipped it into the sea—a fisherman emptying the refuse into the water like any other fisherman. He'd left the rear door of the car open, and he stood there for a moment lighting a cigarette, then flicked the burning match in a high arc into the water.

I said to Astrid: "That's us, come on."

Bent low, we ran up to the car and climbed quickly into the back and lay down on the blankets that someone had thoughtfully laid out on the floor; no back seat here, an old sedan converted, with all the trimmings taken out, a fisherman's car with room made to haul away his catch.

We waited. In a few moments the driver came back, slammed the rear door nonchalantly, climbed in the front, and drove off. When we were clear of the street lighting, he slowed down, pulled into the curb, turned round, and grinned down at us; it was Fenrek's man Pereira, the banker. Only now he was dressed as a fisherman, with a high-necked blue sweater and a cap on the back of his head.

He said: "We've met, Mr. Cain, but I don't suppose you remember? At the Contessa Salina's party...Pereira."

"Of course, and it's nice to see you again. I hope you don't mind all this...masquerade?"

He spread his hands wide, delighted. "But I love it! I sometimes wish the Colonel would make more use of me. A little excitement once in a while. And my wife gets a tremendous kick out of my nocturnal exploits."

"Well, how very convenient. This is the Colonel's niece, Miss Astrid Tillot. Senhor Jose Pereira."

He inclined his head gravely, then reached into his pocket and pulled out a flask. "May I? Would you care for some Antigua?"

I took it gratefully and handed it to Astrid. She took a long swig, and as I helped myself liberally, Pereira handed us a wrapped bundle and said: "And I thought, this time of night, you'd be hungry. My wife made up some sandwiches for you, rather hurriedly, I'm afraid."

"Ah, splendid, I'm starving."

I broke open the packet and handed one of the sandwiches to Astrid. The bread was still warm from the oven, the butter thickly-spread and salted. And the lobster filling was plentifully doused with mayonnaise and garlic. I said: "Can you manage to eat someone when you've already met his family?"

She began to eat hungrily, wolfing it down. She said: "Delicious."

CHAPTER 5

There was no question of going back to my hotel, and Astrid couldn't go to hers. I usually do what I think is right for the moment, and it seemed to me then that it would be right to disappear for a while, if only for a few hours. There is a kind of psychosis we all suffer from, even the best of us, which suggests that when someone has just tried to murder you, you should lie low and well out of sight until you've got your breath back.

A hunted animal does the same thing; it gets under cover at the sound of the first shot, whether or not the hunts liable to continue. And so, we ran to ground, unseen, unheard, and unsuspected.

We lay uncomfortably on the floor of the car, just for the sake of that security, my legs cramped up in the confined space and my arms always getting in the way of Astrid's slim body. I said to her: "For what it's worth, we'll keep out of sight till I can see a little further than I can see at the moment. I want a few answers to a few questions before I show myself on the streets. Let them think were dead, and they'll make no more attempts on us, will they?"

She said: "Who are they, Cabot? I mean...why, for God's sake?"

I said: "One of them, the one who spoke, is called Loveless. A Major Loveless."

"Oh? What army?"

"His own. He is a mercenary from Africa, and out there he's got an army of fifty, sixty, maybe a hundred guerrillas. English,

French, German, American, Cuban, Spanish—a bunch of riff-raff from all over the world with only one thing in common. They are a dying breed, the professional warriors with only one kind of competence, a dangerous one."

"And he killed the General? But why?"

"Yes, that's a nasty business. I'll take a guess at why. The General's ex-servant from Angola saw Loveless down in the Baixa somewhere and recognized him. It's a fair assumption that Loveless saw at once that he'd been spotted, realized that his presence here would be reported to the General, and decided there and then that the General was a potential enemy. Anybody who knows just who and what Loveless is can be put into that category, because, if the reason I've got for his presence here is the right one, and I'm damn sure it is, then *anybody* who knows him is liable to put a spoke in his wheel. And to a man like Loveless, like any of them, that means only one thing; it means wipe out the lability at once, fast. It means kill him off before he can put two and two together and come up with the round dozen that it all adds up to."

"What kind of man...?"

I said: "*His* kind of man. In his world, everyone's against him, it's important to remember that, and human life is the cheapest thing there is. It just doesn't matter a damn to him. The only thing that worries me, because it doesn't make sense, is why he waited so long. He was seen on the street, Loveless, more than a week ago, and yet it wasn't till tonight that he made his move, a quick, easy, and callous move to remove someone who could just possibly stop him from doing what he came here to do by merely knowing that he was here. Why did he wait so long? It's a worrisome question because it doesn't make sense at the moment, it's not logical. It's not even likely. But there'll be a reason for that too, somewhere, and it'll turn up sooner or later."

The car was turning steeply up the bill towards Sintra, the road twisting and turning as it wound slowly up towards the little town that Lord Byron called "a glorious Eden," winding in sharp hairpin bends with a splendid panorama of the shimmering sea at every curve as it climbed up the edge of the Sierra. There was the sound of muted music coming to us as we passed a low and rambling building that hung on the edge of a steep escarpment, with grapevines hanging over the trelliswork of its patio. In the headlights we caught a glimpse of white-jacketed waiters serving drinks there, at little tables under the trees, and there was a sign in ornamental tiles, in the *azulejos* the Portuguese love so dearly: RESTAURANTE ALENTEJANO. I turned and stared at it as we drove slowly past, a charming, secluded nightclub tucked into a fragrant corner of the hills.

We climbed higher and higher. A poet's refuge, this. Robert Southey described it as "the most blessed corner of all the habitable globe," and maybe he was right at that. The red volcanic rock was covered along the roadside with hanging moss, and the moon was shining on the sea far below us. The little white villas were bright in the car's headlights as I got to my knees to see where we were going, with bright bougainvillea and honeysuckle trailing over them.

Hearing me move, Pereira turned round and smiled. He said: "Just a short way now, Senhor Cain, a house where you will be safe. I am sorry it should be so uncomfortable for you in the back there, but it is better no one sees you, no? I would have brought my good car, it is more comfortable, but better we play the masquerade, is it not? And in the house...in the house, you will like it much more."

We turned off almost immediately, and passed through a pair of wrought-iron gates set in high stone walls. Someone swung them to behind us, a shadow moving among the trees and vines with scarcely more than the glow of his pipe in the darkness to show that he was there. We drove for a hundred yards through high laurel bushes; and found a small white house with a tiled portico and a faint light burning beside it.

And Fenrek was there. He was even thinner than usual, and pale and drawn, and as I got down from the car and shook hands, I said: "What the hell are you doing out of the hospital, Fenrek?"

He said: "Chasing you. I had to find out what it is that you're up to." He showed no surprise at all when Astrid stepped out of the car, but kissed her briefly and let her feel his forehead in a proprietary sort of way. She clicked her tongue at him and he paid no attention at all. We stood for a moment looking out across the dark hills to the still sea. Down there; far away, the waves were washing on the *Baia do Guincho*; the Shriek Bay so called because of the howl of the southwest wind that blows such havoc at the Bocca, or perhaps because of the Shriek Bird that's supposed to come there once in a while, though no one's ever seen it.

He said at last, impatiently: "Well, let's go inside, shall we? And then you can tell me, Cain, just what the hell's going on."

I said: "A nice house, who owns it?"

He turned away with an exaggerated kind of vagueness. "I'd introduce you to the owner, but she's not here for the moment." The secret mistress he was supposed to have tucked away here somewhere? I wondered; I just thought it would be nice to meet her one day.

The door closed behind us, and Fenrek turned to Pereira. He said, looking at his watch: "You'd better get home now, and thank you."

"If you need me again, Colonel."

"Of course. Again, thank you."

Pereira made a little bow to Astrid, took her hand and: kissed it, accepted my thanks, smiled a cheerful goodbye, and was gone.

We went on into the small living room. A fire was burning in the grate, a wood fire of eucalyptus logs; it was cold up here in the mountains, and Fenrek went to a tall chest of beautifully carved chestnut that might have been made in Belgium at the turn of the fifteenth century, opened it, produced a bottle of cognac and three snifters, set them out on the small oak coffee table that I thought might be from the period at the end of Louis XII's reign, just before the French craftsmen switched from oak to walnut for their prized pieces. He sat back in a red velvet armchair, indicated the glasses, and said:

"All right, do us the honors. For the moment at least, this house is yours."

I said: "I like it." It was a very feminine sort of place, with a minimum of furniture, all of it fine. A splendid carpet on the floor, a Tournai from Belgium, was surrounded by a border of highly-polished oak parquet, and one wall was entirely covered with a sixteenth century tapestry from Mortlake, woven in wool and silk. Opposite, the wide window was covered with velour drapes in an unusual and striking shade of dusty rose. A small bookcase in a corner, carved oak from Spain, was full of books; to my surprise they were about classic cars, mostly in French; I made a mental note to look at them more closely when I got a moment.

I said, wandering around: "If this is my house, can I take that Mortlake back to San Francisco with me?"

"No."

"I thought not. Have you read this book on the Bugatti? It's been out of print for nearly fifty years now."

He said impatiently: "Will you sit down, Cain? And I want to know all about sour cream factories—what they've got to do with an imitation red tide."

"Ah, good. That means you've found what I hoped you'd find. A long shot, maybe, but this is a long shot sort of operation, isn't it? And we're pulling it off all the way along the line. A nasty, dirty business." I couldn't get out of my mind the image of the old General 'So much I can do for my country,' he had said.

I poured three drinks and handed them round, then sat close to Astrid on the velvet sofa, stretched out my legs, and took a long slow sip of the cognac. There's nothing like a good cognac to make the world seem sane when we all know it's mad. Astrid curled up with her legs underneath her and watched me. There was a puzzled, hesitant look in her eyes.

I said: "First of all, I'm afraid General Queluz is dead."

He stared. "What...?"

"Left hanging in the *lagosteria* near the Bocca do Inferno. At nine o'clock, I'd say he'd been dead about two hours. I'm afraid I had to leave him there, for reasons which will be obvious to you."

Fenrek went to the telephone and picked it up, I said sharply: "No! Let him be found in the course of time, it's the only way to play it. A good man murdered, and we've got to leave him there till someone else finds him. I don't want it known that we weren't murdered too, not yet."

I saw him throw a quick and worried glance at Astrid.

She said gently: "I was in good hands, Uncle."

He put down the phone and stood there, looking at me and waiting. I said:

"Off the top. We went to dinner with the General tonight, and found he'd been called out to the *lagosteria* by a man named Nacimento, the man who first reported to him that Major Loveless, the man I'm looking for, was here. A report that resulted, as you know, in my being called here by the General to find him. We wanted to clear the General's name so that he could make a comeback."

Fenrek said glumly: "He'd have made a damn fine Minister too."

I said: "Only, Nacimento was on duty at the Castelo São Jorge and didn't make that call or cause it to be made. Obviously, there was trouble about to happen, and I hoped we'd be in time. We weren't. I'm afraid I took Astrid along because it occurred to me that if an attempt on his life were in fact being made, and if it failed, another might be made at his house. The house could have been dynamited, for example, and I wanted to make sure that Astrid was safe. I thought she'd be safer if she stayed with me. Perhaps I was wrong, but there it is."

Fenrek said nothing. He sipped his cognac and waited.

I said: "We found him hanging there, and also found Major Loveless, with two of his men. They forced us into the lobster traps— you know them?—"

"I know them."

"—and left us there to die. High tide would have seen to that in a matter of less than an hour, and we'd never have been found, for obvious and rather disgusting reasons. We got away, called you, and here we are."

Fenrek took a deep breath and sat down again. He said: "All right, a couple of questions. How do you know it was Loveless?"

"There's a good description in the file the General gave me."

"Two other men? Who are they?"

"I don't know. Yet. But both...shall I say, the mercenary type. Tough and efficient and reckless, all of them. Straight out of the African bush."

"How do you know this man Nacimento didn't set it up?"

"It's hardly material, but he was on duty at the Castelo São Jorge when the call to the General was made."

"The General took the call himself?"

"I see what you're driving at, but the caller did not say he was Nacimento—he merely said Nacimento was there."

"All right." Fenrek thought for a moment or two, and then said: "Now, the crucial question. What about the sour cream factory?"

"So one has been sold recently. Good. Tell me about it."

Fenrek made a gesture of impatience. He said: "Doing precisely as you asked so casually, I inquired if any factories had changed hands recently. The *Lateria Agosta*, a small outfit in the Alfama, was sold ten days ago. Nothing particularly strange about that, except that it was sold for cash—a rare thing in Lisbon—and to a man no one has ever heard of, a complete stranger no one knows anything about. Except that he spoke with a strong Angolan accent. And that was enough to make me realize that you know more about all this than I gave you credit for."

I said mildly: "That shouldn't surprise you."

He took a deep breath. "All right, what about sour cream, for God's sake?"

Astrid slipped a hand under my arm and sat there quietly, very close, listening carefully.

I said: "Sour cream makes all the difference in the world. Till now, I was only half sure, though perhaps I had enough to make me certain. But now...now all those elusive thoughts jell together, and I know exactly what's going on. And it's terrifying."

Fenrek said: "And I'm still waiting."

"All right then. Listen carefully. There's scarcely a country in Africa where there's any kind of constant peace. In Nigeria, until recently the most stable of all the emerging countries, the Ibos are slaughtering the Haussas, and the Haussas are slaughtering the Ibos. In the Congo, even though we don't hear much about it anymore, there's still a major guerrilla war being fought. In Angola, Mozambique, Ghana, Guinea, Mali, Mauretania, Senegal, Rwanda, Zambia, Malawi, Gabon and the Sudan—God dammit, in almost every single one of the new countries and half of the old ones—Africa is at war with itself. Wherever you turn, there's a rebel force of some sort fighting against the government, or one tribe trying to seize power so that it can wipe out all the other tribes. And with the exception of the Sudan, where the Egyptians are methodically exterminating the Northern Sudanese, the only really efficient fighting force on either side, however small, is the force made up of white mercenaries. Almost every single country is employing them, for the sad reason that the whites have a long history of more efficient wars than the blacks. You can argue that the Africans are more savage, if you like, and I'll deny it. But you can't argue that the European professional soldiers are not a hell of a lot better than the people who are employing them out there. Wherever the mercenaries turn up, the tide turns in their favor. It's axiomatic that whichever side has the best mercenaries is the side that wins—because they're much more efficient than the Africans can ever hope to be. They fight for money, they fight for the love of it, or they fight because they're simply born killers; but wherever they've been fighting, they've been winning. Until recently. Can I pour myself another cognac?"

"Your house, Cain."

I helped myself, and said again, the crucial point: "Until recently. But now, the major powers are pumping modern weapons into Africa so fast that what used to be tribes of primitive Africans with obsolete weapons they didn't really know much how to use, now turns out to be heavily-equipped, European-trained armies. Only five years ago, there was hardly a tank in Nigeria. Now, Britain is pumping modern equipment in there for the Federal Army so fast that the Biafrans have been almost, but not quite, wiped out. The white mercenaries are still holding out with a few Africans under their command, but they're losing the battle, fast. They're licked, and they know it. You want me to tell you which of the major powers are supplying arms to Mali? Or to Ghana? Or to Zambia?"

Fenrek said wearily: "No, it's not important, I get the point."

"Do you? Make sure you get it well. The picture's the same all over Africa. Some of those mercenaries are smart men, born leaders, savage and absolutely ruthless. Under other circumstances, they'd turn into Stalins or Hitlers, and in their own fields they've got just about as much power. But they're losing, wherever they go. Some of them have become well known, like Rolf Steiner in Nigeria, or Bousson in Malawi, or Black Jean Schramm in the Congo. There are dozens of them. And all it wants is for one of them to come to the obvious and inevitable conclusion and to do something about it. And that's what we've got on our hands now. Loveless has realized that for survival and now for more than mere survival—the mercenaries need a new weapon."

Fenrek sat up straight in his chair and stared at me.

I said: "Nuclear bombs? Of course not, they haven't the capability of making or using them. But what about chemical warfare,

Fenrek? America, Russia, England, France, Germany...we all know that they've stockpiled chemical and bacteriological weapons, it's common knowledge. We know that our own people are using mild forms of them in Southeast Asia and the Egyptians have been using them in Yemen...So what about Africa? Conditions are ideal there. Six men with one small vial each of *Bacillus anthracis* could infect the whole of Nigeria with fatal septicemia in a matter of three or four days. Properly inoculated, they could move around through the bush contaminating water supplies or fields, and move out with complete impunity to await the results a few days later. What about *Brucella melitensis?* Spray this from a light plane and a pound of it will incapacitate every man, woman and child within an area of anything up to a couple of thousand square miles. One ounce of that is enough to infect two *billion* people, though not usually fatal. But Loveless has got hold of *botulinum* toxin, hasn't he? And shall I tell you about that?"

Astrid's face, beside me, was white. A tight line was setting around Fenrek's mouth. I said:

"Just under a year ago, in a Naval exercise, a Swedish destroyer sailed upwind along the coast of Sweden, releasing, from a single aerosol canister, a yellow cloud of smoke made from *olioethyldiacine*, a substance which is quite harmless but happens to have the same persistence factor as botulinum in the specified concentration. The idea was that for as long as the yellow cloud was visible to the naked eye, just so long would the botulinum it was simulating be fatal to anyone coming in contact with it. Of course, they had the sensors out measuring it too, but...Do you know that it remained faintly visible for four days, and in that time covered seventeen thousand square miles? But the sensors were still picking up a simulated lethal concentration four weeks later, as far away as the east coast of Finland, a matter of five hundred miles downwind. That means that in those four weeks, the entire population of Sweden would have been wiped out—eight million men, women and children—if that yellow cloud had been the real thing. That was a single aerosol canister, Fenrek, containing less than a pound of simulated toxin. And I'd have you know that this stuff is being manufactured, and stored in quantity, by the Americans, the British, the French, and the Russians as well. Under the tightest possible security, of course, but...How tight can that be to a really determined man? And can we entirely discount human carelessness?"

In a hushed voice, Astrid said: "There was a case in the States, in Utah, some sheep were killed."

I said: "Sixty-four hundred sheep killed overnight by an accident for which no one ever admitted responsibility...A place called Skull Valley, twenty-five miles from one of the Military Research Centers. That was probably one of the anti-cholinesterase nerve gasses, most likely a derivative of the old German Sarin. It is relatively harmless when you compare it with botulinum. And that's the stuff that Loveless has got hold of. And I wonder how much of it he's got?"

In a strained voice, Fenrek said: "Any of these things look like mussel poisoning, Cain?"

I told him: "There's an island off the Scottish coast called Guinard. It's been off limits ever since World War Two, and that's more than twenty years now. For why? The British ran a limited disease-warfare experiment there in 1944, small-scale stuff, they merely dropped a bit of spore on the beach. But the last survey showed that the whole of Guinard will probably be infected for the next hundred years. The next hundred years, Fenrek!"

"Spores? What kind of spores, Cain?"

I said: "Botulinum. Very similar symptoms to those caused by your red tide."

"And the sour cream?"

"A question of techniques in production. If you're already making yeast, or yogurt, or sour cream, you're already halfway to manufacturing botulinum toxin. There's one consolation. If he's planning to manufacture it, it's obvious he hasn't got hold of very much, and therefore..." I stopped to think about that for a moment. Reading my thoughts, as ever, Fenrek said:

"He doesn't *need* very much, does he?"

"As much as you could put on the head of a pin would be enough to wipe out a small army. Provided he knows how to cut it and distribute it reasonably well."

"Does he have any technical training?"

I said: "No, he's a self-educated man, he probably doesn't realize just how potent his new weapon is. He can't possibly have insufficient for his needs, it's just not feasible. But if he doesn't *know* that, and feels he's got to make some more...that gives us time to catch him, doesn't it?"

Fenrek said tightly: "I can have a hundred men round the *Lateria Agosta* within fifteen minutes. Five hundred, if necessary."

I said: "We might find there's nobody there at all except a few cows."

"And we might find the Angolan detachments of Loveless' army of mercenaries, armed to the teeth with..."

"Botulinum toxin. And if one man gets away with a vial the size of a ballpoint pen, he'll still have enough for the biggest slaughter in history."

"No one will get away, I promise you that."

"And there's an all-important point to remember. A psychological difference between them and us. They don't mind taking risks. Not only are they unaware, probably, of just how deadly dangerous this stuff is to handle, but they also don't give a damn. Not about anything. About you, or me, or the rest of the world. Not even themselves; it's the creed they live by. Loveless is at war with God, Fenrek, and sooner or later God's going to get him. And I don't suppose he gives a damn when that's going to be. Let's go."

CHAPTER 6

That night, the street lights in the Alfama failed, which I thought was very fortuitous; until Fenrek told me he'd arranged to have them go off at just the right time.

The darkness was not quite absolute, and when the obscuring clouds drifted away from the bright moon, we could see the outline of the arcaded lodge that formed a bridge above our heads and traversed the incredibly narrow alley toward the door to the *Lateria* where they used to make sour cream and now, perhaps, were embarking on other schemes. *Beco da Mosca*, they used to call it, the Alley of the Fly, since only a fly, they said, could scale the steep slope of the tiny street, no more than a few yards long. It's now called St. John's Alley, and though its name is now more prosaic, the ancient charm is still there.

To our left, the winding staircase of Chafariz climbed up into the skies where the Generals house was, on top of the hill, and to the right the ground fell sharply away again down to Trigos Terrace, so steeply as to give the feeling that we were perched here on a narrow ledge, a ledge on which someone had had the audacity to build a row of tiny houses, walled with diamond-pointed bricks back in the sixteenth century when this was a ghetto.

In the darkness, it was easy to imagine all the twisting, turning, winding staircases and narrow alleyways that covered the slopes of the old quarter and made it one of the most picturesque corners of Europe.

We waited, the two of us, standing in deep shadow under the overhang of a three-storied house that on the other side was only one story high, with a balcony that projected so far out onto the street, a balcony only three feet wide, that it almost touched the building opposite, leaving just a narrow gap through which we could see the clouds and the deep night sky.

There was the sound of a train coming in to the station of Santa Apolinia which lay a few hundred yards to the east of us, at the end of the Street of the Tobacco Garden, and there were voices calling out in the darkness, calling for candles which soon lit up in dark windows everywhere. A phonograph was playing somewhere; a child was crying for its mother.

We beard the slight sound of rubber-soled footsteps, and a shadow moved in beside us, a shadow in police uniform. It spoke very low: "A man coming, *Senhor Colonello*, up from the terrace."

Fenrek nodded, and the shadow glided away. We waited.

Soon, we heard the sound of the hesitant feet, saw the flash of a light shining on the house numbers, and then the footsteps stopped. The beam of the light swung round, and we withdrew deeper into the shadows, the recess of the lintel hiding us from anything out there on the road. The light moved past our doorway, traced a pattern on the opposite wall, and then we heard the footsteps again and a man walked past us, not hesitating but moving on as though he had found what he was looking for. He was wearing white shoes, and was carrying a small bag.

The spot of the light held on the tiny gate and moved up to the sign over it: *Lateria Agosta*. And then the man moved forward and knocked twice with the wrought-iron knocker, a gentle, not-too-overt sort of sound. We heard the creak of the hinges as the door swung open, and we heard a whispered murmur, too far away to be more than a susurration in the silence.

I said to Fenrek, very quietly: "He saw us."

"Yes, I think so. But he can't know we're watching the place."

"Can't he? With no one else on the street?"

"All right."

He moved out quickly, stepping briskly forward and whistling once, quite shrilly. From somewhere to our left, high above the steps, a police whistle sounded, drawn out and piercing, and the whole quarter was suddenly bright with a score of pinpoint lights, like cats' eyes in the darkness, flashing here and there over the walls, the recessed doorways, the trailing vines and the flowerpots. There was the sound of hurrying feet, and Fenrek and I ran up to the man who had knocked on the door, and suddenly he was inside and the door was slammed shut in our faces.

I said to Fenrek: "Just give me room..."

I put my foot up against the lock, felt for its point of most resistance, drew back my leg and shoved hard forward, putting all of my weight into the blow. The door crashed off its heavy iron hinges and hung askew there for a moment, then twisted over and toppled to the ground. Three policemen brushed past us, filling the tiny courtyard with their lights; one of them was the shadow who had approached us out there in the archway, a soft-spoken young Lieutenant named Loureiro. I was up by the inner door already; a small wooden door that led into what we knew to be the main curing room of the little *Lateria*. I heard the heavy bolts being slammed home behind it, top and bottom, and Fenrek nodded to the Lieutenant, who knocked loudly and called out: "It's the police, open up there!"

The walls around us were heavy with the tread of policemen's boots as they clambered down into the courtyard, down the steep steps, down the high walls, down the drainpipes, down the grape vines even...On the other side of the building, we could hear the shouts as a sergeant checked the positions of his men. The place was surrounded, and on Fenrek's orders they were making enough noise to make this obvious. There was the sound of a shot inside, a single shotgun blast, reverberating in the confined area and sounding like a mighty roar of thunder at such close quarters.

The young Lieutenant said quietly: *"Com licencia, Senhor Colonelle..."* and blew a short, sharp signal on his whistle. Immediately, three more police poured into the courtyard, armed with rifles. They began to batter hopelessly with their rifle butts on the door, and I said: "For God's sake, let me do that." I got ready to batter it down with my foot, but the Lieutenant said courteously: "Better not, *Senhor,* someone has a gun in there."

I said to Fenrek: "For God's sake, we're wasting time..." But the young Lieutenant was politely insistent. He said smoothly: "Better a little time, *Senhor*, than a little carelessness."

I shrugged and stood aside, and in a few moments the door was forced open. The Lieutenant stepped quickly inside, and in a moment the room was flooded with light. I saw him standing there with one hand sensibly still on the switch, ready to plunge the place again into darkness, his automatic ready in his other hand while he surveyed the room carefully. He flicked his eyes at us soon, and called out: "All clear, *Senhores*, I think."

I murmured to Fenrek: "Nice to be looked after so carefully," and we went inside.

It was the curing room of the factory. Eight big copper urns of milk, each holding maybe two hundred and fifty gallons or so, stood along the far wall, huge round-bottomed pots that looked like witches' cauldrons in the yellow light that streamed from the bare bulbs. There's something fascinating about a good copper cauldron. Maybe it's the evocation of a time long past, when such things were more common, or maybe it's the association with witches and sabbaths and tales of childhood ogres. These were huge, and immensely valuable, hand beaten into shape perhaps more than two hundred years ago, now shaded with the splendid green patina of time except where someone had made half-hearted efforts to polish them up a bit.

A long packaging machine, ready loaded with glass jars, took up most of the adjacent wall, and the other two walls were covered with shelves on which there were boxes and jars and rolled up sheets of paper, and packages of yeast and bottles of rennet, and some old cardboard containers and a few tools. In the center of the room was a long bare table of heavy wood, a butcher's block kind of table, with a big copper tray on it.

And lying across the tray on his back, a dead man was lying with most of his head blown off; a shotgun lay on the floor under his dead hand, just as though he'd dropped it there. I looked at his white shoes, and said to Fenrek: "The man who passed us out there."

Fenrek said tightly: "And he shot himself before he could be asked any awkward questions."

I snorted: "Didn't take him long to find a shotgun, did it?"

Fenrek stared and said nothing.

There was a single door leading out of the room, and the closed windows, two small ones, were heavily barred and dusty with ancient grime. The Lieutenant went to the door and opened it, and signaled to two of the others. He said briefly:

"Search, thoroughly."

The two men, both sergeants, went hurrying through and mounted the stairs, narrow and tight and dark, that apparently led to another floor.

Fenrek was at the cupboards, opening them one by one and carefully inspecting everything he found inside. He pulled a cork-stopped test tube out from under a pile of loose papers, pulled the cork, and sniffed it suspiciously.

I said mildly: "If that should turn out to be the toxin were looking for, don't come too near me, will you? There's a good fellow."

He said calmly: "Dust on it. It's been there for a long, long time."

"Oh. My apologies." I took it from him and sniffed it, and said: "The *Orla-Jensen thermobacterium* yogurt, it's quite harmless. One of the bacteria used for making yogurt."

He snorted. "I had a feeling all along we'd not find very much here, Cain."

I jerked a head at the dead man. "You had a feeling about that too?"

"No. What makes you so sure he didn't shoot himself?"

"No reason, except that he couldn't have known what the danger was he was up against."

"Oh? How's that?"

I shrugged. "The night train from Madrid got in ten minutes before he turned up, and we're ten minutes' walk from the station, so it's a likelihood he was on it. He was carrying a small case too, didn't you see?"

"Oh."

"Which seems to have gone. And he was talking to someone, so where's that someone now?"

Fenrek made a silent signal to the Lieutenant, and the young officer went to the door that led upstairs and stood there for a moment, listening. He went to the door they had broken down, and called in a squad of men and said to them:

"Upstairs, there's probably a murderer hiding up there

somewhere. Two sergeants looking for him, but if he knows he can't get through our cordon he'll turn and fight, so watch out."

The squad stomped noisily up the stairs and left us there, the three of us, looking around the room and wondering. Fenrek went back to searching the cupboards, pulling everything out and examining it carefully before putting it back precisely in its place again.

I went to the big copper pots and admired them, huge gleaming' cauldrons of thick milk, turning sour with the bacteria and curing overnight at room temperature. Two of them had mechanical stirrers gently rocking back and forth; one of them had a half-inch copper pipe hooked over its rim, the other end disappearing down into the pungent, creamy-white yogurt like a vent for excess gas; three of them were covered with cheesecloth to keep out the flies, the yogurt that was ready for bottling tomorrow when the day's work should begin.

Fenrek said: "I suppose we might as well take a sample from each of these vats?"

I shrugged. "You'll find no botulinum there. This stuff's getting ready for local delivery, not what we're looking for at all."

The Lieutenant was busily going through the dead man's pockets; a handkerchief, a bunch of keys, a small box of tablets, a pocket comb, a perfectly blank notebook with a ballpoint pen in its spine, a torn railway ticket (Madrid-Lisbon one way), a pack of Spanish cigarettes and a book of matches, a fountain pen with no ink in it, a stub of pencil, a handful of silver and copper coins. He laid them all out on the table, and I said:

"Where's his wallet?"

The Lieutenant shrugged. "*Ninguem, Senhor,* he doesn't have one."

Fenrek interrupted his searching and came to the table and looked down at the mutilated body. He said at last: "Well, that makes it certain, doesn't it? No one travels without identity papers. Someone doesn't want us to know who he was." He looked towards the stairway. "Just two small rooms up there, they'd have found him already." He said, exploding: "But he can't get through that cordon, it's impossible!" He didn't sound very convinced.

At that precise moment, the two sergeants came back from the stairway. One of them said: "Nothing, *Senhor Colonello*, nobody there. The men are continuing to search for...for whatever they may find."

I said: "And there is no one hiding there? Are you sure?"

"*Certo, Senhor,* absolutely sure. Two small rooms only, a bed in one and some office furniture in the other. A lavatory with a small window, but heavily barred like all the others."

Fenrek stamped his foot on the floor two or three times, listening to the ring of it. He said: "Concrete underfoot. If there's a cellar anywhere, an entrance in the floor, it's up there somewhere on the other level." You can never tell with houses built on slopes as steep as these. On one side of a house there can be three, four, or even five stories, while on the other there's nothing but a single floor, with a perfectly level roof running from one side to the other.

Fenrek turned to the Lieutenant: "Street level on that side, *Tenente?*"

Loureiro said: "About two meters above us here, *Senhor Colonello*." He said dubiously: "There may be a trapdoor in the lower part of the wall up there leading into the sewer that runs along the building, but I don't think so. I would know about it, unless it had been opened up recently. This is my quarter, I've lived in Alfama all my life. There is a sewer, but it's more than ten meters away, with no way into it from this building. If a passage had been drilled, even in secret...I think I would have known about it, *Senhor Colonello*."

Fenrek said, exasperated: "God dammit, there must be one, that's the only possible way out, and it means he's gone!" He looked at me and said: "Well, let's go and find that damned passage, shall we?"

I said pleasantly: "You go. I'd like to look around here a bit more." He nodded, and went off with the two sergeants to join the others searching upstairs.

The Lieutenant stayed behind, meticulously noting down on his pad the contents of the dead man's pockets. I watched him for a while as he counted out the coins carefully, one by one, thirty-eight Spanish *pesetas* and fifteen Portuguese *escudos*. I went and stood over by the copper vats, admiring them some more, leaning against one of them while I watched him, the one with the half-inch copper pipe in it. I said to him:

"All your life in the Alfama, Tenente?"

He smiled. "*Sim, Senhor.*"

"In most parts of the world they don't allow a policeman to work his own territory. You're lucky."

"*Sim, Senhor,* I am indeed. My house is quite close to here, just off the Largo Sac Miguel. When we have finished here, if you would care for a cup of coffee...I should be honored."

"You are very kind." I put up my left hand and took the bent end of the copper tubing between my first two fingers, slipping my thumb over the end of it and closing the vent. I said: "Perhaps I'll be able to do that, it's a cool night, and a cup of good strong Portuguese coffee is always very welcome. I drink ten or twenty cups of coffee every day, almost my only weakness. But a comforting weakness, isn't it?"

He smiled and looked briefly at my left hand, wondering idly what I was doing, then turned away to go on with his work. And then, suddenly, he realized what it was all about. He made a startled sort of exclamation and swung round, quickly pulling out the pistol he'd slipped back into its holster. He stared in astonishment at the vat, the pistol held level with its top, and I said:

"I don't suppose you'll need that, *Tenente*, but it's good to be careful, isn't it? Let's see how long he can hold out down there without air. Another thirty seconds? Forty, perhaps?"

There was a sudden convulsive stirring of the yogurt in the vat. The surface of it erupted like a miniature volcano of rich white cream, a sudden frothing and bubbling and splashing that turned out to be the dripping figure of a man, his hair, his face, his shoulders draped in thick and clinging wet yogurt, the tall, cadaverous man from the Bocca do Inferno, still spluttering and gasping for breath, but his hands reaching out for my throat none the less. I heard the shot as Loureiro fired, and was glad to see that it was a warning shot, no more, fired into the ceiling. And then, the wet ghost was on me.

I let him grab my throat just as he wanted, and felt his fingers sink in tight, professionally, like a steel vise. With my left hand I stopped him from reaching the ground by grabbing hold of his greasy, slippery belt, and with my right I swung a haymaker up from down by my knees somewhere and hit him so hard in the solar plexus that his feet went up in the air and almost reached the ceiling.

His grip on my throat broke, and he fell headfirst towards the ground; but, before he landed, I hit him again, one for the General, a blow to the side of the descending head that sent him slithering along the concrete floor in his own lubricant, to crash into the wall on the other side and then, thereafter, lie quite still.

Fenrek came rushing down the stairs, followed by a crowd of worried policemen, and I told him calmly:

"Down on the bottom of the river, with a reed between his lips. He's one of the men who killed the General."

Fenrek stared at him. "My God, what a mess, where the devil was he hiding...? Oh, I see, the copper tube, I noticed it and thought nothing of it."

He said plaintively, excusing himself: "I'm not a dairy farmer, how should I know that vats of yogurt don't have copper tubes sticking out of them under normal circumstances?"

I said: "What, just one of them?" He grunted.

The Lieutenant was already slipping handcuffs onto the cadaverous man's wrists.

I said to Fenrek: "Why don't we leave them to clean up in here? Presumably they know what they have to do?"

"Indeed they do, Cain."

"And when our friend of the floor comes round he just might give us a lot of information."

"And he just might not."

I said easily: "I don't suppose he'll want to very much. So we'll have to persuade him, won't we?" I said to Lieutenant Loureiro: "Can I take you up on that coffee offer later?"

"Of course, *Senhor,* anytime."

"Don't forget to fish that train case out of the vat."

"No, I won't forget."

"Have you had your inoculation?"

"*Sim, Senhor.*"

"Well, anything looks suspicious to you, leave it alone. Just call in the Army doctors, they're waiting at the station. But I've a feeling they're not going to be needed. Not yet."

Fenrek, at the door, said impatiently; "We'll stake out this place, of course, but..."

"After the horse has bolted? If he was ever here at all?"

"He still might come blundering in here, not knowing what's happened."

I said: "You've never lived in the African bush, Fenrek. That's the first thing you learn there; you don't blunder into anything, it just might kill you. I'm afraid well have to look for Major Loveless somewhere else. But now, we've got a guide, haven't we?"

Fenrek looked back at the slimy, dripping white form on the floor. He said moodily: "And everything he tells us will be a lie."

I said: "That's what you think."

CHAPTER 7

I was eight o'clock in the morning, and the small backroom in the Alfama police station was crowded with observers; an observer from the Army, another from the Medical Service, another from the State Security Force, and no less than three from the Department of Public Health.

The tall, cadaverous man had been cleaned up now, and was sitting stolidly, his face expressionless, on a wooden chair close by the desk that Fenrek had taken over. He was wearing the grey and yellow Portuguese prison garb already, and someone had given him a cigarette. A police stenographer was taking notes on a stenotype machine. There was an armed soldier at the door, another at the window, and two more in the corridor outside. But I noticed, none the less, that the prisoner's eyes constantly wandered over the room, calm and appraising, as though he wanted to know exactly where everything and everybody was. It was the young Lieutenant who conducted the interrogation, and it was polite and formal and quite routine; at first.

"Name?"

"Gerald Histermann."

"Age?"

"Thirty-four."

"Marital status?"

"Single." (That was a lie; there'd been a brief pause.)

"Nationality?"

"Australian."

He spoke quite good Portuguese, with a strong Angolan flavor to it. The Lieutenant surprised me by switching to English.

"And you came to this country...when?"

"Three weeks ago."

"For what purpose?"

Histermann said laconically: "Just looking for work."

"And you bought the *Lateria Agosta* for the sum of thirty-five thousand *escudos*, paid in cash. For what purpose?"

"I didn't buy it. I'm an employee there."

"You have a work permit for Portugal?"

"No."

"And your employer is...?"

He shrugged. "I seem to have forgotten."

"The name of the man you shot is...?"

The prisoner snorted. "I didn't shoot nobody. I let him in when he knocked, there was a commotion outside, he slammed the door, grabbed the shotgun I was carrying, and killed himself."

"And why were you carrying a shotgun?"

"Because I'm a night watchman. My employer gave it to me."

"The man whose name you have forgotten?"

"Right, digger."

The Lieutenant said: "You must know that sawed-off shotguns are illegal here."

"I'm just a simple employee, digger, I'm not about to argue with the man who gives me a job."

"And then you decided to hide it in...in a..." He didn't know the word, and I said:

"A vat full of yogurt."

Histermann looked across at me speculatively. He was wondering just who I might be, or how come I hadn't been eaten by those lobsters. He said smoothly:

"Well, it's like this. As soon as that fellow shot himself, someone started breaking the door in, so I thought I'd better hide. I grabbed a piece of copper tubing, and got down under that stinking cream. It was very uncomfortable. Then someone blocked my air supply and I came up and attacked him, in self-defense." He shrugged.

"I wasn't to know it was a copper, he wasn't wearing any uniform." He looked at me narrowly, and said: "If he is a copper, of course."

The Lieutenant ignored the remark. He said: "You didn't see me at the table, a few feet away? In full uniform?"

Another shrug: "I was too busy to see you, digger."

"Why did you come to Portugal?"

"I told you, looking for work."

"Did you enter the country illegally?"

He said promptly: "Legally. Flew in from Tangiers, used my passport, which I have now regretfully mislaid. And I don't remember the exact date either, though it was sometime in the last year or so." He was getting cocky, and that was a good sign.

Loureiro went on: "And where are you staying, Mr. Histermann?"

Again, there was the slightest pause. Then: "Been sleeping on the streets, mostly. A couple of nights in a couple of hotels, but I don't remember the names of them."

"Where did you learn to speak Portuguese?"

He shrugged and grimaced, and wasted a few seconds while he thought. "I picked it up on a ship I worked once."

"Or perhaps in Angola?"

"Angola? Isn't that in Africa somewhere? Never been there."

I said, with a touch of irritability: "If I don't get a cup of coffee soon I'm going to fall asleep on my feet. Been up all night, damn it."

The Lieutenant smiled. "Of course, Senhor, forgive me." He said to one of the policemen: "Bring some coffee, a big jug full, will you? And some cups."

He went back to his questioning: "The last two years, where have you been working?"

Histermann shrugged. "Tangiers, mostly."

"We can check on that, of course."

"As a matter of fact, digger, you can't. I'll make a full confession, I usually move around without bothering much about papers, and in Tangiers...I didn't have a work permit there either."

"And before that?"

"Oh, just bumming around the world in general."

"Tell me the name of your employer."

"I told you, I've forgotten." It was easier for him now, and he was getting just the right degree of overconfidence. He said: "A Portuguese name, but I've forgotten it." He was getting very pleased with himself.

Fenrek sat there watching, a very faint smile on his face.

I said: "What about General Queluz, Histermann?"

"General...Queluz? Who's he?"

"You know damn well who he is."

The policeman came back with the coffee and passed it around. He said to the Lieutenant: "The prisoner too, *Tenente?*"

The Lieutenant said coldly: "No," and I said: "Let him have a cup if he wants one." I pushed a cup across to him and said: "Another cigarette?"

"Yes, I don't mind if I do." It was all so much a part of the pattern; get friendly with the prisoner and he'll talk; I could see the thought forming itself in Histermann's mind. He began to grin, and I wanted to hit him, but I didn't. He sipped his coffee and said: "They took my cigarettes away from me, so if you could fix me up with a pack..." He was hugely amused. I tossed him the cigarettes on the desk, the Lieutenant's, and said:

"Two of us saw you in the Bocca with the dead body of General Queluz hanging there. And you tried to murder both of us."

He said promptly: "Not me, digger. A case of mistaken identity."

"Uh-huh." He was beginning to think that we weren't very good at this sort of thing, and I thought we'd better call a halt before he got suspicious. I said to the Lieutenant:

"Take a look at his forearm. His left, probably."

The prisoner glanced at me quickly, wondering what was going on, and the Lieutenant got up and rolled back the sleeve over the skinny, malarial-wasted arm. I bent forward to take a look, and found the tiny mark of the hypodermic. Histermann laughed uneasily:

"It's not drugs, if that's what you're worried about. Just an inoculation, that's all."

"Oh? For what?"

Again, there was the briefest hesitation: "For typhoid."

"Who gave it to you?"

"I dunno, some doctor or other, I don't remember."

"Uh-huh."

He looked at me suspiciously. His cockiness had gone, and there was a trace of worry there now.

I said: "Is not very important to anyone except you, Histermann, but a typhoid inoculation is a scratch, not an injection, so give me leave not to believe you."

He shrugged, the overconfidence coming back. He said: "Okay, so it was for mumps, what do I care?"

I said: "You ought to care a great deal. We suspect that you might have taken an injection of BR47, and if that stuff isn't straight out of the freezer, it's no damn good to anyone."

He was suddenly very pale, but he kept up his front. He said stubbornly: "I don't know what the hell it was they gave me. Just one of them injections everybody gets once in a while." He waited for me to say something, and I waited for him, and at last he said, fidgeting: "BR47? What's it for?"

I said carefully: "It doesn't matter to you what it's for unless you happen to know a man named Loveless. And about what's happened to him."

All the expression had gone from his eyes now. He said stolidly: "Loveless? Never heard of him. Who's he?"

I said: "Major Loveless. They picked him up on the street three hours ago, retching his lungs out in the gutter with botulin poisoning. He'd had an injection of BR47 too, though that's not the name he knew it by. But since it wasn't as fresh as it should have been, it didn't do him a bit of good. They're pumping more and more of the stuff into him, of course, but it's my belief it's too late. Once you start retching, that's the beginning of the end. He's probably got a couple of hours to live."

He had taken a tremendous hold on himself. He looked down on the floor, watching a spider crawl across it, then put out a leisurely foot and crushed it. Not looking at me, he said: "You ain't a copper, are you? A doctor, maybe?"

It was time for the big lie. I said: "I'm a microbiologist. My specialty is botulin. It's a filthy thing to have, ever seen it?"

"No. And I don't know any Major Loveless either."

I said pleasantly: "Good, so there's nothing to worry about."

I went to the door and opened it, and turned back and said to him: "I just wanted to make sure that you didn't know him. We can't save Loveless, he's too far gone, but anyone who's been in contact with him...If we catch them before the fever starts, there's still hope." I said, musing: "It's strange...the paralysis attacks the extremities first, then moves up the body, very quickly. It hits the thorax, and then...that's it. With thoracic paralysis, you just can't breathe anymore."

I saw the man posted at the end of the corridor reaching for the intercom telephone on the wall, as he'd been told to do the moment I opened the door, and in a second or two the phone at Fenrek's elbow rang. He picked it up.

I said briefly: "You've got other things to worry about, Histermann," and began to move out. The door was almost shut when Fenrek called out:

"Cain! Just a moment!" I looked back in. Fenrek said gravely: "That was the hospital. Major Loveless just died."

I nodded and went on out. As I passed the man at the phone, I thanked him. "Nice timing, just right." I went into the street, crossed over to the little cafe, ordered a coffee and a glass of cognac, and waited.

A municipal streetcleaner was pushing her shiny aluminum barrow up the steep hill, a plump peasant woman in khaki slacks and bush jacket, with a pillbox cap of the same material. A donkey with two big wicker-covered demijohns slung over its back was standing there patiently while his owner poured out a liter of olive oil to a waiting housewife; the smell of baking bread was coming from the open door, opening directly onto the cobbled street, so narrow there was no room for a sidewalk. Two shirt-sleeved men were sitting on a doorstep close by playing cards, a pile of *escudo* notes beside them.

In a little while, Fenrek came out from the police station and joined me. As he pulled up a chair and signaled the waiter, he said: "I hope this is going to work, Cain."

I said: "It'll work. You know what psilocybin is?"

He frowned. "Isn't that the hallucinogenic agent in marijuana? It's a long time since I took the departmental course in drugs."

"No, that's cannabinol. Psilocybin is much more. I slipped a large dose into Histermann's cup of coffee, and in about an hour's time he'll get dizzy and disoriented, his heart will start pounding, and he'll have a scare to beat the devil. It's unlikely he knows very much about the symptoms of botulin, though he's probably been indoctrinated about it just enough to have a superficial knowledge. And the moment the psilocybin hits him, he's going to be scared out of his bloody wits. And soon after he starts yelling for help, that's when we move in."

Fenrek frowned. "It's all very unethical."

"Yes, isn't it?"

"And where the devil did you get that antidote to botulin poisoning? What did you call it? BR47?"

"Yes. Nice sounding name, isn't it? I just invented it. I didn't see any point in telling him that there's no cure at all for botulinum. Where is he now?"

"Still there. They're questioning him about General Queluz. He's flatly denying that he was even in the *lagosteria.*"

"He's got a nerve."

"No, he's not too worried about that, and I can't think why."

"I'll tell you why. There's no capital punishment in Portugal, so even if he's found guilty, all he gets is a jail sentence..."

"Twenty years to-life."

"...which doesn't mean much to a man of his caliber. He knows it would take him, what, a couple of months to break out of a Portuguese prison? So why should he worry? No, he won't start worrying till the psilocybin starts taking effect."

"And just how dangerous is that?"

I shrugged. "No more so than a dose of LSD. Don't worry about it. But, to ease your conscience...that's why I didn't want you to know what I was doing. Not you, nor any of the police. I just wanted you to plant that piece about Loveless and nothing more. You see how I worry about your ethics?"

He sighed. "One of these days, you'll go too far, and I'll be there, and I'll have the painful duty of arresting you."

I said: "Not a hope in hell. I don't take that sort of risk."

"And Loveless?"

"In a few hours...I've an idea that in a few hours we'll know exactly where to find him.”

It was less than a few hours.

Before we’d taken our second glass of cognac, Lieutenant Loureiro came hurrying across the street. He looked worried. He saluted smartly and spoke directly to Fenrek:

“I’m sorry to disturb you, *Senhor Colonello*, but the prisoner...I think there’s something very wrong. He’s very, very sick.”

I looked at my watch. “Already? That may mean there’s still a touch of typhoid left in him. Interesting.”

Loureiro looked at me blankly and said nothing. They’re not an inquisitive people, the Portuguese, and they’re smart enough to know when not to ask questions.

I said: “Put him in a cell by himself, cell number eight, a guard on the door, and let him stew there for a little while. We’ll be over there shortly.”

“Sim Senhor.”

“And see if you can rustle up a doctor’s bag for me, will you? One of the Army doctors might be kind enough.”

“A doctor’s bag? If you would be more specific?”

“Anything that looks like what it is, I won’t have to use it.”

He was fighting his curiosity, but he saluted and hurried back to the station.

I said to Fenrek: “One more cup of coffee, and then we’ll go.”

I wondered if we were being too cruel. To anyone, even to a man like Histermann, the thought of an imminent, certain, and extremely painful death is a terrible torture. And then I thought of the kindly General Queluz hanging there in the darkness, thought of the terror on Astrid’s face as we went down into that lobster trap to a casual, but certain death...I thought of this man sticking out a straight arm and brutally shoving her down there. And then, it didn’t seem to matter anymore.

Soon we went back into the police station. I collected the little black bag Loureiro had found for me, watched Fenrek switch on the tape recorder that was wired in to cell number eight, and went down to talk to the prisoner.

I was shocked by his appearance. He lay on the wooden bunk, clutching at his stomach, doubled up in pain and grey faced; a man with a naturally yellow complexion doesn't look his best when all the blood has drained away from it, and he looked like hell. His skin was dry and flecked with a pink rash that couldn't really get to be the proper color, so that his hollow cheeks looked like a piece of moldy cheese; I expected the sweet stench of Gorgonzola to rise from him, but it didn't.

I said cheerfully: "Well, what seems to be the trouble? A little fever?"

He said: "For Gods sake, Doctor, I'm...I'm..."

I said: "I'm not a doctor, but that doesn't matter, does it?" I felt his pulse, which was beating at an alarming rate, and opened up the little black bag slowly, and said: "Probably malaria, you've had it before, haven't you?"

He said, gasping: "Not malaria. Botulin poisoning. I need some...some of that...that stuff you spoke about...that BR stuff. Hurry...hurry, for God's sake, I've been sick already, and my feet...my feet are going dead."

I sat on the edge of the bunk and looked at him. "Botulin? What makes you think that? Are you qualified to diagnose your own sickness? I think not, surely. Or have you recently been in contact with a botulin carrier?"

He rolled over again and clutched at his stomach. There was no thought in him now of anything but himself. He tried hard to speak; the panic was taking firm hold. He said at last, spluttering: "You mentioned...you mentioned...Loveless." He couldn't stop the sibilant, and it came out: *Lovelesssss.*

"Ah, then you did know him."

"For God's sake yes, give me some of that stuff, quickly."

I took my time. I stuck a thermometer in his mouth and lifted an eyelid to peer at his pupils. I said:

"Try and stand up with your eyes closed."

He huddled deeper up into himself, a fetus shivering there and squeezing itself into nothingness.

I said: "Stand up, there's a good fellow."

He could barely speak. "An injection, quickly..."

I said severely: "Please don't try to advise me, Mr. Histermann. Now, stand up and close your eyes."

He struggled to his feet, swayed, and clutched at the wall.

"Close your eyes."

He did so, and immediately fell forward. I let him fall to the ground, and he rolled over on his back and stared up at me in horror. A doctor letting a patient fall like that? And now he knew that there was something terrible going on and he couldn't understand what it was. Couldn't understand because of the drug, because for him lights were flashing, fear was sweeping over him, and unimaginable things were happening inside his brain, twisting it this way and that, showing him a clarity that wasn't there at all and then brutally replacing it with a fantasy that was even worse.

In short, he was on a trip.

I said carefully, keeping up the lie: "I can save your life if I inject you within the next half hour or so. After that, I'm afraid it's going to be too late."

"Then...then...hurry, for God's sake. Hurry, man."

He rolled over onto his face and clutched at the bunk, dragging himself up onto it. Halfway there, he twisted his head and glared at me; he knew already.

He said thickly: "Not a doctor at all...you're another...you're a copper, aren't you?"

I said: "It's now nine-thirty. By ten o'clock you'll be over the mark, past the time you can be saved. So, you've got half an hour to make up your mind and answer half an hour's worth of questions, beginning right now. And if you don't tell me what I want to know, I'm just going to walk out and leave you. So help me, I'll leave you here to die."

He had the strength, or the courage, to try and disbelieve me. He said, gasping: "Not only a cop, a crooked one..."

I said: "Loveless is dead, and we don't know where he was hiding. That's the first question."

For a long, long time I did not think he was going to answer. He screwed up his eyes with an effort and stared at me. At last he said: "A deal? How can I know...know you'll keep your end of it?"

I said: "Time's short, isn't it? It might really be less than half an hour, it's hard to tell in these cases."

He said: "You...you bastard! All right, the injection first."

"The injection after."

"A promise?"

He swayed out of control, and suddenly screamed; he clutched at his head and then began banging it against the wall furiously, trying to shatter it in obedience to some unseen and unexpected compulsion. I dragged him away and held him down on the bed, and waited till a moment of coherence came. He didn't know which end was up, now, and all he could do was answer my questions, obey the disembodied voice that was sitting astride his chest.

The coherence was there again, though it was only momentary. He said, with a touch of grim humor: "So this is what it's like...how long have I got?"

I said: "You won't die, not yet, not if you keep talking."

I wondered how strong his loyalty might be, wondered if it could control the uncertainty, or worse still, the incoherence.

He took a deep and painful breath. His eyes slowly crossed and uncrossed again, an extraordinary sight. He said:

"You're all...all green and yellow."

I could only imagine the startling colors that were affecting his vision. He reached out for something in the air and clutched at it, and there was nothing there at all.

I said again: "Where was Loveless hiding?"

He'd made up his mind, or the drug had made it up for him. He said, laboring: "Up by...by the castle."

"São Jorge?"

"Yes, Rua...rua Vicente, number...eleven."

"He sleeps there every night?"

"Yes...For God's sake...Give me a shot..."

"Soon." He was slipping away again, his body going limp. I shook him and said: "How much of the toxin does he have?"

"Four...four...four..." He was silent.

I shook him again, furiously: "How much?"

"Four...ounces."

My God, at thirty thousand milligrams to the ounce, why in God's name would he ever want to manufacture more of it?

I said: "Who was the man who was killed?"

"A chemist...a chemist from Madrid. His name...his name's Serafino, Martinez...Serafino."

Check. That was the name in the wallet they'd dragged up, soaked through with fermenting yogurt. Martinez Serafino, one of Spain's leading psychopharmacologists, a brilliant man with a twisted mind and a chip on his shoulder, a man at war with half the world. I wondered how Loveless had come to find such a ready and valuable protagonist.

I said: "All right, four ounces of botulin. What's it stored in?"

"I don't...I don't under...understand."

I said impatiently: "In glass phials? Or what?"

"Four...four glass tubes in a steel box."

"And where does he hide it?"

"I dunno...I dunno, so help me. He's got it tucked away somewhere."

Another tack. I said: "How did you both get here?"

"Boat...from North Africa. We flew to...to Algeria, landed on...on the beach there...took a boat across. Took all day to get the boat...the boat in...That Great Barrier is murder, the Serpent's Tail..." The incoherence was coming back again, and he was home in Australia, fooling around on the Barrier Reef.

I wondered how long the effect of the drug would last; I know a lot about these things, but I've had very little practical experience of them, I'm happy to say.

I said: "All right, you landed from North Africa, when?"

"Two...two months ago."

"And then?"

"Loveless went off to...to Scotland somewhere. I went to Spain to find...to find Serafino, offer him a job, just like Loveless told me. And Van...Van stayed with the boat. Even there, it's a bit risky, leaving it...leaving it all that time..."

I said: "Where, Histermann, where's the boat now?"

But the drug had taken over again. He said, muttering: "That Serpent's Tail can kill a man, did you know that? When we was kids, out on the Barrier Reef, me and my father used to sail right up to it, we used to watch it, and he used to sail right up to it, we used to watch it, and he used to tell me..."

I said, shaking him back to coherence: "Where do you plan to use that toxin? The botulin?"

"Nigeria, first. Then...anyone who wants us..."

He began to cough horribly, and I got off his chest and let him roll on the floor. His eyes were glassy.

I said: "Why did you have to kill Serafino?" I knew the answer, but I wanted it on the tape.

Histermann shuddered and shook his head, shaking some clarity into it. He whispered:

"God, this is awful..."

I said: "Why, Histermann? Why did you kill Serafino?"

"He knew he was going to make...to make botulin toxin up, in the sour cream...sour cream factory. It was him that told us to buy one."

"And where did you get the money from? Thirty-five thousand *escudos*, that's quite a pile."

He wiped the tears away from his eyes, staggered up onto the bed, leaned back against the wall and sat there, a piece of wet rag. His eyes were clear now; he was coming round, but not there yet; he had a lot more hallucinations coming on. He said, and he even managed a short sort of laugh, half grunt and half cough:

"The money? We've got plenty of money. You'd be surprised...how many people want to support us. In America...in England...in Russia...in China...The left and the right, both sides of the fence, as long as we're holding out they're still ready to send us money. Some for this reason, some for that...It's all very easy, really. You fight for one side, it's the left wing folks sending you cash. You fight for the other, it's the right-wingers. We do both, so...so there's always plenty of money. Easy, ain't it?"

He was in a state of exhaustion, beyond any care now. He said slowly: "Not sick to my stomach anymore...does that mean...does that mean I'm already dead?"

I said: "How many men with Loveless?"

"Just me and Van, the three of us."

"Van?"

"The man you saw in the cave, the archer. Van Reck, he's a

South African. Watch out for that bow, he's murder with it."

"And how did you propose to use that toxin?"

"We got...three aircraft, small ones. We were going to mix it with flour and...and seed it. From the air."

I could feel the blood draining out of my face. Four ounces of it? Enough to kill twenty-four million people?

I said harshly: "You know how many people that would kill?"

He shrugged: "Non-people, all of them." He was too far gone to see my anger. He said: "That's just...just the kind of weapon we need, ain't it, digger? Put us back up there where we was before...in the good times...the good times when we was winning..."

I knew it would be hard to control my fury. I signaled the guard and went to the door. As he unlocked it, Histermann, in a sudden fright, threw himself on me and shouted, begging:

"The shot, you've got to give me that injection!"

I pushed him away with my foot and left him slavering there on the cell floor. I said: "You're not going to die, Histermann. Not yet."

I went out, white with anger, and heard the door being locked behind me. When I looked back through the grill, he was crawling all over the floor, babbling incoherently.

I couldn't help thinking: there are some people who take that sort of stuff for the fun of it.

CHAPTER 8

Fenrek wasn't wasting any time.

By the time I was upstairs again he was there waiting for me. He had a police map spread out over the desk and was touching a delicate finger to it:

"There, Rua Vicente, I wonder why he chose that particular place?"

"Must there be a reason for everything?"

"Yes, of course." He sort of squinted at me and said: "Your argument always is that there's always a reason for everything."

I said: "Well, that will come out in the wash in the course of time, no doubt. High up on the hill? An animal instinct perhaps? That just might be the way a man from the African bush would behave."

"Even in a big city?"

I shrugged. "Habit dies hard. Is there any reason why he shouldn't have chosen a place like that?"

"No. But I was wondering if he's got contacts here. If so, this might be the place they live."

I said: "Or there might be a more plausible reason. We'll soon find out."

He nodded, letting it slide by because he knew I wasn't sure enough to tell him what I was thinking.

I said: "The chances are that Loveless would not carry the stuff with him, he wouldn't risk keeping it on his person. But he just *might*. If we go for Rua Vicente and he's not there..."

"A stakeout then."

"Yes. Someone with a good description of Loveless to watch the place carefully. Maybe from the castle, there are good points of vantage there."

He said grimly: "I'll have a dozen men with binoculars, watching every side of that house, every door, every window."

"Good. And will you do me a favor?"

"Of course."

"There's a sergeant in the Honor Guard at the castle. His name's Nacimento, he used to be the General's servant in Angola, remember? When all that scandal broke out? It might be a nice gesture to let him be one of them. Help to avenge the death of his old master."

He scowled. "A nice gesture? I'd rather use men I know to be fully trained for this sort of thing. This is hardly the time for gestures, the stakes are too high."

I said smoothly: "He knows Loveless by sight."

"Oh. Well, all right. We'd better have a word with him first. We don't want him exposing himself like an amateur with glasses glued to his eyes for everyone to see."

"I'll talk to him. And if Loveless is sighted going in?"

"We'll hit. Hard. As many men as necessary."

"Good. Just in case of accidents, make sure every one of them gets an inoculation and keeps his mouth shut about it."

Fenrek said: "Inoculations? You mean you haven't noticed? There's a hospital truck on every corner in the city, free inoculations for anyone who wants them. They're saying it's for typhoid, and recommending that everybody take one."

There's no inoculation that's any good for botulinum; they just pump you full of Type A and Type B anti-toxin to slow down the destruction of nerve tissue; does no good at all.

"Ah yes, of course. Can I get into the grounds of the castle without being seen? I'd have to pass by Rua Vicente, and there's always a chance I'd be stopped up there. If I were, he just might cut and run immediately. We don't want to lose him at this stage of the game."

"We're not going to lose him," Fenrek said. That's the trouble with the Interpol people. They're so damned good that they get overconfident; it's their only weakness. He said now, puzzling about it: "What was all that about a serpent's tail?"

"Histermann? I'm afraid that drug was taking him further on his trip than I'd thought it would. You can never tell with these things, that's why they're dangerous. He was back in his youth, as a kid, on Australia's Great Barrier Reef. There's a waterspout there called the Serpents Tail, quite a tourist attraction. I hope he's being well guarded. That's the kind of man a jail can hold for just about a long weekend and no more."

"Two men in the cell with him, that should keep him there."

"Don't underestimate him. I was very impressed with the way he conducted himself under the influence of that psilocybin."

Fenrek raised an elegant eyebrow. "You were? It sounded to me as though he was talking his head off."

"His conscious was fighting hard with his subconscious, and they were taking turns at overcoming each other. Impressive is the only word for it. When I asked him where the boat was hidden, he really ought to have answered at once, right off the top of his head. But he didn't. He went off into regression instead, off to the Great Barrier Reef and his childhood. Very impressive. Something I want to think about a bit more."

Fenrek grunted.

I said: "Are you interested in the power of auto-suggestion?"

"Huh?"

"Rather interesting. Histermann said his feet were going dead, merely because I'd pointed out to him that botulin attacks the extremities with paralysis first. Psilocybin doesn't have that effect at all. Pure self-delusion. You just plant an idea in someone's mind, and they do the rest. Thought it might intrigue you."

I went up to the castle in the back of the truck that delivers the daily rations in the late afternoon. I found Nacimento waiting for me in an obscure corner of the beautiful, shady grounds. He had been warned of my coming, and was turned out in his most spotless uniform. He stood at ease, rigid as though he were on parade, under the archway in the northern wall where he'd been told to wait, in the tiny courtyard by the Martim Munez Gate. Here, in 1147, an obscure cavalryman in the army of the great Alfonso Henriques, Portugal's first king, fought off a hundred Moors who were trying to close the gate against the liberating troops; he held it alone, Horatio at the Bridge, and lost his life in the process. All that's left of the history now is a tiny bust of Munez, high in the wall over the gate, cut from soft limestone and eroded by time down to almost nothing.

But there's a silence and an aura of post-war peace in this tiny shaded courtyard, as though all we need is the ghost of a brave man to tell us that peace is the product of virtuous strength.

And, come to think of it, that's a commodity that's pretty hard to find these days.

A small man, Nacimento, nearly sixty years old by the looks of him, with a sharp and somewhat bitter look to his face, and a scarcely noticeable limp. His white hair was cropped short, his brown face scraped shiny-clean except for a startling black moustache. There was an air of alert efficiency about him, the air of a man who, under better circumstances, would have gone a long way in the world; but he was an old horse put out to pasture, a horse that could still show its mettle if it were given half a chance. I thought: forty years in the army, and still a sergeant, with nothing but a once-a-month parade for a breath of the glory that might have been his. It's important to the Portuguese, the glory bit, and to the soldier more than any of them.

I put him at ease, not without difficulty; there was a feudal barrier between us, which was going to be hard to break down. I wandered about among the acacia trees, making him walk with unaccustomed leisure beside me; I felt he wanted to salute every time he opened his mouth.

I said: "He was a good man, the General. And he spoke very highly of you."

He said simply: "When they find the man who killed him, Senhor, it will be hard not to break all the rules and shoot him, myself."

"I know. That's how I feel too."

"May I ask a question, Senhor?"

"Of course."

"Was it Major Loveless?"

"Yes, it was."

He frowned. "I cannot think why the Major would want to come to Portugal at all. But I suppose..." He looked up at me sideways. He was having trouble with his feet, trying to march and to keep in step with me at the same time. "I suppose there must have been a good reason for him to leave Africa."

"Yes, there was. He was looking for a new kind of weapon, a weapon that would give his mercenaries the edge over the opposition. The opposition was getting too strong, too sophisticated, and he needed a giant step forward if he was going to stay in business."

"Oh? You mean...tanks? Heavy artillery? He would not easily get these in Portugal, Senhor."

"No. Something more easily portable, and much more deadly. He is going in for bacteriological warfare."

He stared at me, and I explained:

"The major armies of the world are all manufacturing bacteriological weapons, and not one of them will use them until and unless the other side does. As a matter of fact, there's been a treaty in force ever since 1925 banning the use of bacteriological weapons in war. Only some of the major and minor powers never ratified it. The United States, Japan, Uruguay, Brazil, a few others...But everyone's stockpiling them just in case, in heavily guarded arsenals in the more secluded parts of the world. But Loveless was in Scotland recently, and there he stole enough of a deadly bacteria to wipe out half of Africa in a matter of hours. Not a very nice thought, is it?"

He did not answer. He was staring moodily at the swans that were sitting placidly on the small tree-shaded pond.

I said again: "A nasty business, wouldn't you say?"

He nodded. "If there is anything I can do, Senhor...I would be glad of the chance to help."

"Good," I said, smiling, "that's what I really wanted to know."

He looked up at me quickly: "How could you doubt, Senhor? The man who murdered my General...?"

"All right then, listen carefully. Loveless has a hideout, just across the street from here, in Rua Vicente, number eleven. In case you don't know it, it's the very narrow house next door to the Peseda Cafe, three narrow stories high with a blue and yellow tile facing, you know the one I mean?"

He nodded gravely, watching me. "I know it, Senhor. I pass it frequently, on my way to take a glass of wine in the evenings."

"Oh? In the Peseda?"

He smiled deprecatingly: "No, Senhor, the Peseda is a little too expensive for the likes of me. I go to the Modana, at the lower level. Wine in the Modana is only *vint tstoes* a glass."

I suppose you could translate *vint tstoes* as two bits, but it's really only about three cents; not very much for a glass of good wine.

"I see. Well, we're setting up a watch on number eleven. We want to see when Loveless goes in there so that when we raid it were sure of finding him at home. We'll have a dozen men watching the house, unobtrusively. I thought you might like to be one of them."

"I would like that very much, Senhor. And...may I say? That is a very kind thought. I think that not many people would be so understanding."

"But there's one very important point. It is absolutely essential that nobody sees what you are doing. The other men are all trained for this, and one of them will show you what to do, so as not to be seen by anyone. One little carelessness now..."

"I understand, Senhor. If there is carelessness, it will not be mine, you have my word."

"Good. So that's settled then." I said: "Someone will be along very soon to instruct you. Just remember—absolute security."

"I will, Senhor."

A couple of young people, arm in arm, passed by us and stood by the edge of the water, feeding the swans. We watched them for a while, the image of all that was peaceful, and I sighed and said:

"He brought a man in from Spain, a chemist, to make more of that bacteria he's stolen, can you imagine that? As if he didn't have enough of it already."

Nacimento clicked his tongue, "Terrible, Senhor."

I said: "But it's fortunate for us that he did."

The sergeant looked up at me with a look of worried puzzlement on his face. "Oh? It does not sound very good, Senhor."

"But it is. Because every day he stays here now, to make up his damned bacteria, is another day for us to apply to catching him. He's not the kind of man to know much about microbiology, fortunately, so he doesn't realize that he's got more of that botulin already than he could ever possibly use. He plans to cut it with flour and seed it from an aircraft, the most wasteful way he could possibly do it. If he used aerosols instead, he'd have enough to cover half the Continent."

He was not too sure what an aerosol was. I said: "Any kind of canister, sergeant, with the bacteria suspended under air pressure inside it. Deadly, absolutely deadly."

"I see." He smiled sadly and looked at the ground and said, with a sort of deprecating laugh: "No, Senhor, I do not see. I am not a very educated man. But I will take your word that what you say is correct."

I sighed. "If he knew about aerosols, knew just how potent that stuff is, Loveless could be on his way home tomorrow. And then...then, our chances of finding him just might be nil. But let's hope we get him in the Rua Vicente house. And for that, Nacimento, we're counting on you to help us."

We shook hands, and he saluted me twice for good measure, and I left him and went over to the edge of the fine old battlements that looked out over the town, the red roofs bright in the hot sun, the seven hills of the city crowded with stucco and tile-faced houses piled one on top of the other in splendid disarray.

Strange how it's always seven hills, not nine or six, when the tourists pamphlets describe a beautiful city: Rome, Hong Kong, Rio. There are supposed to be seven in Lisbon too, and I started to count them once and gave up when I reached ninety-two.

The great wide square of the Rossio was busy with traffic down there, far below the walls, with the Elevador da Santa Justa beyond it, a tall, slender elevator of grey-painted ironwork, built by France's Eiffel, that was taking pedestrians up from the Baixa to the busy streets of the higher levels. Far to the west, the slender ribbon of the Salvador bridge seemed suspended in midair on nothing at all. I waited for ten minutes, and then the ration truck passed by and picked me up, and soon I was with Fenrek again, down in the cheerful little cafe opposite the police station.

He said, accusingly: "You look impossibly smug, Cain, You look like a cat that knows where there's a big fat mouse."

I told him gently: "Just thinking about likelihoods; it's a habit of mine. I know the mouse is there, but I'm wondering where he might go. Do you know the Cafe Peseda?"

"Next to the house on Rua Vicente? Yes, I know it. Why?"

"Nice place?"

He shrugged. "Better than most of them. But you're thinking of going there, I shouldn't. You're too conspicuous to be seen so near Loveless' hideout."

I said: "I wouldn't dream of going there. What do they charge for a glass of wine?"

Again, those elegant shoulders raised themselves a trifle. "The same as anywhere else, I imagine. Not very much. Does it matter?"

I said politely: "Could you find out for me?"

"If you wish." He looked at me thoughtfully, "I wish you'd tell me what's on your mind. There's always something up your sleeve, isn't there?"

"At the moment, the price of a glass of wine in the Peseda."

He sighed. He went to the telephone at the back of the cafe, and in a moment came back and said with yet another shrug: "*Vint fstoes*, about three cents American, does that make you happy?"

I said: "Uh-huh. I thought I might take Astrid out to a *Fado* later tonight."

He glared: "Cain, you're impossible! And suppose we have to mount a raid on the Rua Vicente at midnight?"

I said calmly: "You'll know where to find me. We'll be at the Alentejano. You know where that is?"

"I know." He sounded fed up. "Twelve miles from where the action is going to be."

"Ten minutes in the Jensen. I'm going there now to do a small job. If you need me, just call me, right?"

He was very suspicious; that's another trouble with Interpol, they just can't believe a man does something for nothing once in a while. Cause and effect, or effect and cause, it's all they seem to think about.

But this was the waiting time, if only for a few hours. And when there's nothing to do but wait, then a little relaxation is good for the soul. As I paid the waiter and got up to leave, Fenrek looked at me with an air of the utmost distrust. He said:

"The action is going to be in the Rua Vicente, isn't it? Because, if you know something I don't..."

I said: "Bear with me, friend, we all have our little foibles. Meanwhile, go back to your Goethe."

"Goethe, for God's sake?"

I gave him the quotation: 'Cause and effect together make up one indivisible phenomenon.' I said: "Don't try and separate them, Fenrek, 'X' follows 'Y' as surely as night follows day."

He was shaking his head sadly when I left.

The police had thoughtfully towed my car away from the beach and left it where I could get at it again; Fenrek's idea. And he had someone following me as I drove out through Estoril and on up the road towards Sintra. I thought it was very nice of him to keep such a careful eye on me, a sign that our friendship was as good as it had ever been. He always said it was good to have a man around when you were heading for trouble. But he didn't know the kind of trouble I was heading for.

Come to that, neither did I, really.

I first became conscious of it just after I passed through Estoril, a Volkswagen bug that attracted my attention because it braked hard coming out of a side street and let me pass, then did the same thing again a few moments later when I was on the inland road to avoid the traffic. It occurred to me that the driver had been going up and down the cross streets waiting for me to pass: in other words, looking for me on that particular stretch of road. Through Lisbon itself, where I'd been driving circumspectly, there'd been no sign of it. But here it was on the open highway burning up the tarmac far faster than a normal Volkswagen can.

I let him get closer and listened to the sound of his motor; that's one of the advantages of driving an open car. It sounded like the Porsche 911S mill, the fat six-cylinder 1991 c.c. that can push a bug to a good hundred and thirty—if you can hold it on the road.

I wondered for a moment if perhaps it was not Fenrek's doing; but I discounted the possibility. The driver knew where to start looking for me, and only Fenrek knew where I was headed. Fenrek's man, all right. I wondered if it were Pereira.

I didn't want him to break his neck, so I made it easy for him and kept the Jensen down to a mere ninety on the straight, slowing to seventy-five on the curves and hearing the squeal of his tires as he tried to keep up. Then I thought that I was being unfair, so I slowed down when we reached the sandy coastal road again, then pulled in to the side of the road, and signaled him on. He sat there for a moment, a hundred feet behind me, then crawled forward and drew level.

Him? To my astonishment, it was a woman, a strikingly attractive woman, young to middle-aged, with close-cut black hair and a plump and lively sort of face. She wore what looked like a dark cocktail dress with bare white shoulders and a single diamond pin at the breast. Her eyes were large and black and intelligent, and at the moment they were looking at me challengingly, ready to smile, but not quite doing it.

I leaned across as she rolled down the window and said: "My apologies, Senhora. If I'd known how beautiful you are I'd never have allowed you to risk your neck quite so blatantly. But if you lose me, the Colonel will only be sad. Not angry; he expects it."

She said calmly, a low, melodious voice: "Don't count on it, Senhor Cain. You have got the power in that beautiful machine of yours, but you haven't got the maneuverability. On a road like this, I can beat you."

I was astonished, and told her so. "In that thing? You'll snap your half-shafts in two if you pull that round a tight bend at more than eighty."

She laughed. "You too, your tires are too wide. Believe me, I can take you any time."

There was nothing arrogant in the statement, just a plain matter of indisputable fact.

I said: "I'm tempted to show you."

She was highly amused now. She said: "You don't know me, Senhor Cain, do you?"

"To my sorrow, Senhora, no."

She said: "Estrilla da Gloria, does that mean anything to you?"

Estrilla da Gloria, Portugal's famous woman racing driver. She looked more like a fashion model off the front page of Elle, and it was hard to imagine her at the wheel of a Formula 111 Cooper, but I'd seen her lap 1:48 in Monaco, in the wet, and anyone who can do that deserves a second glance.

I said: "I'm honored, Senhora, I saw you giving them all a very bad time at Tobacconists' Corner last year. So what in the world are you doing working for Colonel Fenrek?"

She said: "It's a dull life, racing cars. I like a little excitement once in a while. And, come to that, what are you doing working for him?"

I said: "But I'm not. As a matter of fact, at this precise moment, I'm sort of working against him. Before, we were just on parallel courses. Have you ever driven a Jensen FF?"

Her eyes were gleaming. "No, I haven't."

I swung open the door and stepped into the road. I opened the driver's door of her little bug and said grandly:

"Why don't we trade cars, and then we won't have to race anymore."

Her eyes widened, and she said nothing. She stepped out quickly with a lithe, easy movement that seemed to rob her of her plumpness (and now I saw there was nothing wrong with the shape of her hips) and slid in behind the Jensen's wheel. She pushed the button, listened approvingly to the murmur of the big mill and said: "Fuel injection?"

"No, Carter four-barrel. And four-wheel drive, so it goes where you point it with a certain amount of alacrity."

"Red-lined at forty-five? That can't be right."

I said patiently: "At forty-five on the tach you're hitting a hundred in third, and you've got two more gears to fool around with. I'm going to the Alentejano, but calling in first at Fenrek's hideaway, you know where that is?"

It was a bit blatant, I suppose. She laughed and said: "Yes, I know where my own house is. I'll have drinks ready by the time you get there. Try not to break my half-shafts."

She slipped the gear lever into first, shot away at speed, and before I even managed to find a way of getting my frame into that dammed bug, she was out of sight. I followed the road for a mile, pushing up to ninety or so till I saw her tail light far ahead of me, then cut the lights at the next bend, dropped down to twenty, took the side track that led to the sea down the side of the cliff, and headed towards the Bocca do Inferno.

In the darkness, I bumped on over the sandy track and down to the beach. I parked the bug under an overhang of the cliff, and had to run for nearly a mile, moving very fast, before I found the fishermen's phone I was looking for, and I called the number of the house where Astrid was staying. I let it ring twice, rang off, and called again immediately, to let her know that it was official. This time, she picked the phone up instantly.

She said: "Uncle? I thought you'd forgotten all about me."

"Not uncle," I said, "it's me."

"Ah, Cabot! My dear, where are you?"

I said carefully: "A rather good-looking racing driver will be there shortly."

"Oh good, how nice."

"Give her my regards, and ask her to take you over to the Alentejano..."

"*Her*, did you say?"

"I did. That's her house you're staying in. Her name is Estrilla, and she is one of your uncle's men. She's driving my car, and she'll be in a flaming temper, no doubt. But you are to stay with her at all times until I get there, all right?"

"Which will be when? And I suppose you don't want to tell me what this is all about?"

I said: "A, in a couple of hours or so, and B, you suppose correctly. The less you know, the less your uncle knows, the better. You'll probably see him soon after Estrilla calls him to say she lost me, and he'll no doubt be in a flaming temper too. So, by and large, there'll be a few cuss words floating around tonight. But don't let them get you down. I'll be with you in a couple of hours, and then well have a perfectly marvelous time together."

I heard her sigh at the other end: "All right. I'll wait for you till midnight, but not a second longer."

"I'll be there long before then. Remember, stick with Estrilla till your uncle gets there. And then, stay with both of them."

Another long sigh. She said: "A hell of a love affair this is turning out to be."

"Good-bye now."

I rang off, and wondered about the weather; it had become a problem, and a serious one. The wind had swung round to the southwest, and it worried me considerably. This time of the year it's supposed to die down at dusk, and instead, it was beginning to blow quite a bit. Not hard enough to be called a gale, but hard enough to keep the Bocca performing unseasonably, which I didn't like at all. Even at this distance I could hear the roar of the waves pounding their way into the cave more than two miles along the beach there. I used the phone again to call the Meteorological Service, a very good one on this rocky, dangerous coast where there's a lighthouse every few miles. There was one of their posts in the lighthouse at Cabo Raso.

The voice said: "Cabo Raso."

I said: "I'm speaking from the west of Cascais. What's with the wind tonight?"

"Southwest, Excellency."

Everybody is excellent to the courteous Portuguese. I said: "Yes indeed, but isn't it supposed not to blow after dark?"

"Ah, Excellency, tonight it is blowing."

I sighed. "For how long? When can I expect it to die down?"

"A disturbance out at sea, Excellency. We expect it to drop before midnight, but we cannot be sure."

"An educated guess?"

"*Sim, Excelencia*, if you wish to call it that."

I said: "Thank you very much indeed. Tell me one more thing, has my brother already checked with you on the wind? He is setting out from Cascais in a small boat, going to take a look at the Bocca, and with this unusual condition...I wonder if he called you?"

The answer came back a trifle tolerantly: "We have had several inquiries, Excellency."

"He speaks with a strong Angolan accent."

"Ah, yes, about an hour ago, Excellency. Much the same question as your own."

"Good, then I won't have to warn him, Thank you very much."

"It is I who thank you, Excellency." He was about to put down the phone, but a sudden thought struck him. He said sharply: "Excellency? Did you say the Bocca do Inferno?"

"Yes, I did."

"Then you must warn him not to go near it till the wind dies down, Excellency. And you yourself...even from the land side, you must keep well away, you must obey the posted notices. I cannot stress too much the danger there now."

"I'll watch out, thank you very much." I rang off.

So Loveless—or one of his men—had called. It was all working out very nicely; the long shot was paying off, as long shots have a habit of doing when careful thought makes them not as long as they might have appeared.

I wondered how much time I had. In case it wasn't much, I ran fast for the two beach miles that lay between me and the Bocca; and when I got there, I stared in dismay at the huge spout of live water that was gushing up like a geyser way over the top of the cliff above me, a hundred feet up there over my head. Its sound was the sound of violent thunder, the awful fury of the gods that Loveless was fighting. It was obvious that I was never going to get into the Bocca from down here. The furious water was high over the only entrance. From the road at the top, perhaps? It was a terrifying thought.

I climbed quickly in the darkness up the track to the summit, stopping once or twice to stare at the huge spout that was exploding upwards with the force of a howitzer, not much more than a hundred feet or so to my left. I hurried along the clifftop with the help of the handrail there, closer and closer to the spout as it burst up every thirty seconds or so, and getting myself drenched with the falling spray. I hung onto a rail and waited, then dashed forward with the downfall of water and threw myself onto the top rungs of the ladder, grappling them like a limpet and waiting, tensing my muscles and hanging on with every degree of my strength, not a fiber of my body relaxed.

I braced myself for the next wave. It hit in thirty seconds, a great mass of water that came rushing at me from down below like an inverse waterfall. A stone caught up in it caught me a glancing blow on the side of the head and nearly knocked me out with the sudden sharp sting of it. I held on tight while the falling spout dropped back with a mighty, sucking pull, and then slipped down three more steps, counted the seconds, and waited for the next one. I wrapped my arms round two rungs and doubled up one leg round another, for this wave was going to be worse, far worse, than the last; I was in the chimney itself now, and could only guess at the strength of the mighty wave that would be funneling up there in a moment. I took a deep, deep breath, and bound the iron ladder to my body with arms and legs and will power. And it was a bad one.

It came roaring up at me again, preceded by a ghastly hollow roar that was a warning to hold on tight. I felt it going past me and sucking me up from my perch like a gigantic, wet, vacuum cleaner. The force of the water broke the grip on my left hand but not on my right, and twisted my doubled up leg round horribly. But I found the rung again, groping, and held my breath till the spout subsided, and then dropped down three more steps for the next one.

It was even worse this time. It broke the grip I had taken with my leg, and upended me violently, leaving me standing on my hands, gripping the ladder with both fists and with my legs flailing in the water above my head, sucked upward by a monstrous column of driven water. It was a gigantic serpent's tail, thrashing savagely. My arms were being torn out of the shoulders, and for a moment I thought I couldn't possibly hold on any more. For a moment, we held it there, the water and I, suspended in space as gravity slowly took over and the mighty waters began to fall again. I let go at just the right moment, as the wave began to suck me back, and I let it pull me down a bit more so as not to have my arms pulled out of their sockets, and then grabbed on tight to the lower rungs as they shot past me.

The wrench was painful, but bearable, and now, I guessed, I was out of danger. Four more steps, and I was under the overhang; the next wave was an impotent thing three feet behind me, with only the powerful wind of its passing to tell me that I'd never have survived in it. I stood at the bottom in the darkness for a moment or two to get my breath back, and then groped my way into the darkness inside.

The iron gate was still locked. Good. I clambered over it, squeezing painfully through the narrow gap and tearing my clothes on the barbed wire that surmounted it. It was pitch black now, and I wondered if I dared to use a light.

With the gate still locked? I thought I could. I switched on the tiny pencil beam of my penlight, and moved off down the long tunnel that led off deep into the recesses under the cliff. Here, somewhere, there was an underground lake, closed off many years ago when the Bocca's quirks and tricks had become too dangerous for mortals. I groped my way along, clambered over the wet rocks, past the sign that said, unequivocally: *Do not pass this sign; danger of death.*

The tunnel was still wide and high; good. I found the first of the barriers, a roll of barbed wire that had been firmly tied to iron stanchions at the sides; it was still in place, but one end had been cut. I opened it just enough, went on and found the second, more formidable barrier; cut too; good.

I switched out the tiny light now, sat down in the absolute darkness, and listened long and carefully.

The Serpent's Tail, Histermann had said; he had said too: *all day to get the boat in...*He couldn't have meant anywhere else, his conscious fighting in his subconscious and neither one of them quite winning out, a mind sick with psilocybin groping in the dark on his native Barrier Reef where the Serpent's Tail looks just like the fearful violent spout that blows up out of the Bocca; a mind groping around and trying to hide the truth, impressively, but not quite succeeding.

I wondered if Fenrek had ever been to Australia. Probably not. If he'd ever seen that Tail, he'd have caught on at once.

I listened a while longer; silence. I moved on.

There was a very narrow path along the dark underworld creek, so broken in parts that twice I had to enter the water, very deep here, and feel my way along. The rock had been carved by the constant wash of the waves into fantastic shapes, with weirdly molded boulders that were striped, in the thin beam of my light, in purples and yellows and sandstone reds.

I could smell the sour stench of bats now, and when I turned the light up to the high rock ceiling above me, I saw them there, a dozen, a score of them, clinging to protuberances in the rocky wall, upside down but still awake and waiting for the waters to subside and release them from the trap their home had become with the action of the Bocca. I could hear them arguing among themselves, squabbling angrily as they constantly maneuvered for space; one bat never likes to be touched at rest by another, and the space between them must be meticulously and mathematically accurate. I moved the light over and saw dozens more, a hundred perhaps, in the far recesses of the cave.

They were horseshoe bats, the *Rhinophulus ferrum-equinum.*

And then, to my surprise—and I must confess to a shudder as well—I spotted a little cluster of *Desmodontidae*, the blood-drinking bat that so many people call the vampire, drab colored and small, not more than three inches long, without the nose leaf that always looks so repulsive, even though it's harmless. The *Desmodus*, without that hideous leaf, is the one to worry about if you are sleeping in a damp cave by the beach. I wondered what they were doing over here in Portugal; they're supposed to be native to Mexico. But, you can't tell with bats; I once saw a *Machaerhamphus*, the Falcon Bat, in England, and that's indigenous to Asia and Africa and nowhere else.

And now, the creek made an abrupt turn, and at the same place the ceiling dropped down to no more than six feet or so above the water. It broadened out into a small lake, blocked off from the main channel by a passage only ten feet or so wide, a small circular lake of placid water with a broad shelf running almost all the way round it, the famous underground lake of the Bocca that had been closed off and unseen for so many long, long years.

And that's where, just as I anticipated, I found the boat.

It was rather larger than I had expected it to be, a twenty-five foot whaler with a raking stem and a sharp stern, with a powerful gasoline engine set amidships, rather further forward than it really ought to have been, close by the tiny cabin. The two masts, normally used for lug rig, had been removed entirely; whoever had done that had wanted a fast boat, and to hell with the delights of sailing.

The rock here was rock and nothing else, and it took me more than ten minutes to find any earth. But I found some at last, not much more than a handful; but sufficient for what I had to do. I wet the earth down thoroughly and pounded it into a reasonable facsimile of clay, mixed it up with my handkerchief, and plugged the engine's exhaust pipe with it. I found a stick that had been washed in by the tides, and wedged the plug in as far as it would reach. I didn't know how expert a mechanic Loveless might be (though I guessed he just might be very good) but I knew it would take him all the rest of the night to figure out why his motor wouldn't start. And he wouldn't be able to maneuver a craft that size out of the tricky cave with anything but engine power, even after the force of the Bocca had died down and opened up, once more, the channels that led to the open sea.

All night, and then some.

It was easier to go up the ladder with the water than come down against it, I took loose hold of the iron uprights so that the first of those terrible waves could shove me at least part of the way up to the top. But I underestimated its power.

With a fearful roar it hit me under my thighs, tore away my grip completely, and threw me up into the air like a ping-pong ball on a fountain spout. And when I came down and hit solid ground again, I was at the top of the cliff, dazed and bruised and wondering why every bone in my body wasn't broken by the strength of the water or by the force of my fall; but I was where I wanted to be.

I bent myself up double, found the shelter of the gorse bushes, smelling sweetly now on the night air, and raced along the top of the cliff till I was sure that Loveless, if he were anywhere around (and I was sure he was, waiting impatiently for the Bocca to stop playing up) could no longer see me. And then I ran fast to where I'd parked the little bug, and started up.

And ten minutes later I pulled in outside the Alentejano.

CHAPTER 9

The hell with the ladies present; Fenrek said coldly: "Cain you're a goddamn son of a bitch."

The waiter was frowning at my very disheveled clothes, but he pulled a chair out for me all the same, largely, I suspect, because he was worried about my size. It's hard to be six-foot-seven and not look as though you're going to tear the opposition apart at the slightest pretext. I watched him sidle off to the Maître d'Hotel and whisper with him, and in a moment the Maître came over and bowed to the impossibly elegant Fenrek and said, not even hesitantly:

"Senhor, I am sure you will understand...If I could find you a better table? Perhaps a more discreet corner?" He smiled neatly at Estrilla, and then at Astrid, as though he thought we might want to roll on the floor with them in the middle of the *fado*.

I looked at Fenrek and spread my arms. "How the hell can I look respectable when I've been spelunking all night?" I turned to the Maître and said: "I'm terribly sorry. I fell into the ocean. Too much of your splendid Antigua, I never could hold my liquor very well."

He accepted the lie graciously, and smiled with an expression that could have been called either benign or bloody patronizing, depending on your mood. But with the lovely Astrid there, and the lovelier still Estrilla looking so forgiving, I was in the best possible temper.

So, he smiled and said: "Then *o senhor* understands my predicament?"

"Of course. A table where I can't be seen and disgrace you will be fine."

People turned to stare as we moved. We were on the patio, the best part of the restaurant, and we found a dark corner in an angle of the wall, where the scent of the jasmine was delicious.

I said to Fenrek: "Why didn't you find us a dark corner to begin with? I'm surprised at you." I turned to Estrilla, looking absolutely charming now in the soft yellow lights here. "How did you find the Jensen?"

Her teeth were white and gleaming. I thought: what an agreeable looking woman Fenrek found himself this time! She said:

"I'll never drive a car again that has power to only two of its wheels. And those brakes!"

"Did you punch it?"

She said calmly: "Not really, until I realized that you hadn't the slightest intention of following me. I should have thought of that at once, shouldn't I? The Colonel told me you were a devious sort of character. He says there's always something up your sleeve."

I said: "In this case, I was playing it off the cuff. You just gave me an opportunity I couldn't resist. Am I forgiven?"

She looked at me shrewdly: "Of course, my own fault. I should have realized that no one hands over a car like that to a perfect stranger without an excellent reason."

I said gallantly: "Perfect, but no stranger. Your reputation was enough to assure me you'd take care of it. You didn't...er...bash anything?"

"Nothing. And where did you go once you'd lost me?"

Fenrek said tightly: "That's what I'm waiting to hear, Cain."

The waiter was hovering. We ordered the pork pieces hot-fried with dozens of tiny scallops in a rich Madeira sauce that they call *porco Alentejano*, and another two bottles of Dao, the dry white wine from Douro that deserves an international reputation it doesn't really have, and I said happily:

"I've been making sure that our Loveless friend doesn't leave the country quite as easily as he probably expected to."

There was a long, silent pause of the kind commonly called pregnant. Fenrek said at last, heavily:

"He's almost certainly not ready to leave the country yet. He's lost his chemist, remember, so it's a fair assumption that he'll try to find another. That might take a considerable time."

"He doesn't need a chemist. He's got enough botulin to take care of half Africa."

He said, protesting: "But he doesn't know that, isn't that the crux of the whole matter?"

I said gently: "He knows that now. Before, he didn't."

He said, incredulously: "Have you seen him? God damn your eyes, Cain, if that's what you've..."

I interrupted him: "Not yet. I just sent him a message. A couple of messages."

He glared at me.

I said: "The more I thought about it, the more certain I was that we'd never have trapped him in his Rua Vicente house. We were forgetting that Loveless is an animal, a man who's spent almost his whole adult life as a mercenary in Africa, keeping alive by the sheer competence of his wits, fighting against insuperable odds all the time, with a price on his head wherever he goes. How does a man like that stay alive?"

Fenrek shrugged. "You just said it. By the competence of his wits."

"And you expect me to believe he's going to run to his lair with a dozen men—or was it fifty?—watching it? You expect me to believe he wouldn't know that the house was being watched? In my opinion, a man like that would smell the danger. Physically smell it. And he'd run. Not in panic, but carefully."

"In your terms, it was at least a likelihood that we'd get him there."

"But not strong enough. The weak ones, you have to throw out. And there's another difficulty, a matter of mechanics. Not so obvious, but a very serious one. This really is an excellent wine, don't you think? I wish they'd export it to the States."

Astrid silently filled my glass, and the waiter brought the *porco* on a silver platter; for good measure, they had it *flambe*, with cheerful blue *conhaque* flames hovering over it. When he had served it and had gone, I said, taking advantage of the hiatus to make the switch:

"If you were a damn good soldier, much decorated in the field and with every prospect of getting a commission one of these days, how would you feel about a man who held you back deliberately? Merely because your competence also made you a very good servant?"

Fenrek sat up straight, staring at me. "We talking about Loveless now, are we?"

"No. About a sergeant named Nacimento. I was always worried that Loveless attacked the old General for the first time no less than a week after he realized that the General would be aware of his presence here. The big question was: why didn't he act at once? And the answer is a rather sad one. It took Nacimento a week to decide— hesitantly, I'm happy to guess, but none the less he decided—that here was a chance to get back at the man who'd kept him in servility all these years when he had a brilliant military career ahead of him." I shrugged. "He was too good a servant, the General suggested, to be let go and get the field promotion he deserved. Oh yes, the old man was very selfish here, but kind men can be selfish without even realizing it, it's very easy for them because they don't do it deliberately. Nacimento told the General he'd seen Loveless. And then, for a week, he worried about it, worried about whether he could pluck up the courage to pay off an old debt, a debt the General wasn't really very conscious of owing him, though he admitted to me that he'd been unfair. He just didn't know *how* unfair, or how that would rankle with a man like Nacimento."

He was ahead of me already, Fenrek. But he said stubbornly: "You couldn't have been certain of that."

"No. Not till Nacimento told me a quite insignificant little lie that he, really, needn't have bothered with. He told me he never used the cafe next to the Rua Vicente hideout because their wine was too expensive. Not the sort of place I'd go to, and not the sort of thing I'd check—if I hadn't already formulated a certain suspicion. But you told me yourself, remember? Three cents American, the same as anywhere else. That foolish little lie clinched it."

He grumbled: "Precious little to go on, if that's all it was." I shook my head, and he said sourly: "And now were back in Africa, aren't we?"

He could always read my thoughts, a most disturbing talent.

I said: "We are indeed. On that momentous occasion, do you remember the General's secret meeting with the rebels? With Ojugo? A meeting so secret that only the General himself knew about it. The General, Ojugo, and...one other man. The man who accompanied Queluz on his journey through the bush. It always worried me that Loveless and his mercenaries knew exactly when to hit the General's H.Q., knew exactly when the General himself wouldn't be there. He told me, the old man, that when he was at his H.Q., the security was tight as a drum, that he hated to leave his H.Q. because his overworked officers, Portuguese fashion, immediately relaxed. So somebody told Loveless just when to lead his mercenaries in. Why?" I shrugged. "Don't ask me why, but it's a likelihood that Nacimento was in cahoots with Loveless even then, wondering if perhaps he could pluck up courage to desert from the army and become a mercenary himself."

Fenrek said: "Now you're guessing, and nothing else. And the characterization is all to hell and gone."

"No, it's correct, I'm certain."

Fenrek sighed. "I say it again, Cain, you're a son of a bitch. So you let Nacimento volunteer as one of the stake outs in Rua Vicente. And if we lose him as a result..."

I said gently: "The problem of mechanics. I wanted to make damned sure that when we find Lovelace, he's not in the middle of a big city with four ounces of botulin in his pockets. Or, worse still, with the toxin hidden away somewhere where we'd never find it. Can you imagine the complications that would derive from *that?*"

"And so, we've lost him."

"No, we haven't. I also made sure that he'd learn that he already had enough of his new weapon, that he needn't bother with making any more. I even told him how to use it at maximum efficiency, in aerosol canisters. So now, he'll head for home, glad that we've made it so easy for him."

Estrilla silently reached over and filled my wine glass for me; Astrid threw her a look.

I said: "He's down on the beach somewhere, less than a mile from here, waiting for the wind to drop so that he can go aboard his boat. That's why I thought it would be nice if we all gathered together here. Comfortable, and handy."

Now, Fenrek was furious. He said angrily: "His boat? You know where it is?"

"Yes, I do. Histermann told me. He told both of us. If you go over what he said, and cast your mind around a bit, you'll see just *how* he told us."

"For God's sake..." Fenrek half rose from his chair, and then sat down again with an expression of utter defeat.

I said: "As soon as this unseasonal wind drops, he'll go into the Bocca do Inferno, which is where his escape hatch is. A twenty-five-foot whaler with a gasoline engine. The wind will calm down any minute now, and he'll have four, maybe five hours before daylight in which to get the boat, unseen, out of the Bocca and hit the high seas. He'll presumably land somewhere on the North African coast where, no doubt, there'll be a plane waiting to pick him up. And, of course, he'll be carrying his precious toxin with him, won't he? It won't be hidden somewhere so that when we pick him up we won't find what were really after. That was the danger in Rua Vicente, wasn't it, that we'd find him but not the botulin? And I couldn't allow that to happen."

Fenrek said calmly: "You are waiting for me to leap to my feet and order out the coastguard, but I'm going to spoil your fun by just sitting here and enjoying my dinner." He began to pick at his food, his heart not in it.

Estrilla said suddenly: "There's the singer."

A dark, pleasant-looking woman was moving towards the tiny stage, and soon she began to sing a low, melancholy love song, her whole body tense and emotional, her eyes closed, her dark eyebrows knitted in a frown, her head thrown back.

We listened for a while, and then Fenrek threw down his knife and fork and whispered angrily:

"All right, you bastard, what did you do to that boat?"

I whispered: "I blocked the exhaust with a handful of mud and one of my best cambric handkerchiefs. Before he finds out why the motor won't start, he'll strip it down to every last nut and bolt, and when he reassembles it, it still won't fire. And by then, it'll be daylight, and he'll have missed his only chance of skipping the country tonight. A twenty-four hour delay, with Loveless and his bacteria, which we'll separate from him, where we can safely get at him without endangering the whole of the city. That's all we want, isn't it? And I don't see why I should have to do all your work for you."

Some people nearby, absorbed in the lovely *fado*, turned and shushed us. Fenrek glanced at them, lowered his voice another tone, leaned forward and whispered:

"Separate him from his toxin?"

"Of course. I don't want him uncorking a vial as soon as he sees us and daring us to touch him."

"I know that, damn you! But how?"

I shrugged. "We just let him send the telegram he's got to send."

"Go on." The light was dawning, and Fenrek's tanned, handsome face had lost some of its anger; but not all of it.

I said: "A boat means he's either going to land further along the coast for a rendezvous, or else cross over to North Africa, which is most likely."

"Why?"

"Because, once he leaves the Lisbon area, which means danger to him because of you and me, he'd be a fool to land anywhere in Portugal for more danger if he could just as easily get to the North African coastline, where there's virtually nothing to stop him landing wherever he wants."

Grudgingly: "Right, I suppose. Even if it is a trifle tenuous."

"And if he intended a short trip along the coast, he'd have prepared an outboard motorboat, something small and easy to hide. Instead, he chose a damn great whaler, twenty-five feet of it, that must have been one hell of a job to maneuver into the cave at the Bocca. As Histermann said, it took all day to get it in there, right?"

"Go on."

"He is trying to get away tonight."

Fenrek said swiftly: "You can't be sure of that."

I said: "He called the lighthouse a couple of hours back, worrying about the southwest wind. He's planning on leaving tonight, there's no doubt of it."

He was getting impatient again. He said testily: "And so?"

"And on the North African coast, no doubt, someone is going

to pick him up by plane."

"Why?"

"Because he's taking his new weapon to Nigeria, Histermann told us that. And he's sure as hell not going to walk. Or do you think he might take a commercial airline? Of course not. One of his own pilots will pick him up."

"So far, so good. Perhaps. But a telegram?"

"Of course. Even on the deserted beaches of the North African coastline, where a plane can land and take off easily without too much official interference, the same plane can't just set down and wait for more than a few hours in safety. Certainly, within twenty-four hours someone is going to ask what the hell goes on, and I don't suppose for one moment Loveless and his men will risk that. He doesn't mind taking risks in the least; but that would be just plain stupid. Ergo, he'll send a telegram to his contact over there, telling him to delay the pickup for twenty-four hours."

For a long time Fenrek was silent while he tried to find a hole in my reasoning. They don't like working on assumptions at Interpol, they prefer facts. But personally, I always find that facts can be terribly misleading, while likelihoods seldom are.

I sat back and listened to the mournful plaint of the *fado* for a while; somehow it reminded me of the sad old *pibrochs* of the Scottish Highlands, the plaintive dirges they mourned the deaths of the fighting men. Here, the words were lighter, with a lilt of love to them; only the music was the same.

He said at last: "I hate it, but I'm forced to agree. Now tell me what a telegram's going to do for us?" Before I could speak, he raised a hand and said: "Yes, I know, he's got to use the post office in Cascais, or in Estoril, or in Guincho, and we can watch all three and take him when he shows. But, for God's sake, why do we have to go to all that trouble? We could have taken him just as well in that cave, once we knew he was there."

I said: "No. In the cave, he'll have four vials of his bacteria, and if it's the end for him and he recognizes it; what's he going to do? I'll tell you. He's going to bust them the moment he sees an unfriendly face, because he just doesn't give a damn. If he goes down, he'll want to take us all with him, and that means half the coastal population as well. Because that's precisely the kind of man he is. But the next few hours of daylight, for him, are just a waiting period till he can get that motor running again. He'll hurry into Guincho, at a guess. You want to bet on that?"

"I'll settle for Guincho, its the most likely."

"And he'll send his telegram, and then he'll hurry back to the cave where everything is ready and waiting; including the vials of toxin. In other words, chose to hit him when he's not carrying anything quite so deadly on his person."

Fenrek said sourly: "You've just lost us every chance we ever had of taking that man."

Well, that was an attitude I'd expected, and I told him so as gently as possible. I said: "I didn't think you'd go along with my reasoning, or I'd have invited you in on the deal. But take my word for it, a man like Loveless, a man whose fight is against everything you and I stand for...we've got to take him when he's defenseless, or we'll all go down in flames together."

"You're working on assumptions instead of certainties."

"On likelihoods instead of facts, they're always better propositions."

He looked worried and said: "I hate everything about it. Its so...so dammed..."

"Tenuous?"

"The only word for it. Histermann said he had four ounces of that toxin. Suppose he's got more cached away, that no one else knows about? We get Loveless with the stuff he's carrying, and unknown to us there's another little store of it somewhere. Then, one day, a child finds a hidden bottle and opens it, what then? It could be five years from now, Or fifty, even."

"Yes, I know that. That's the one hole left that's got to be plugged. At whatever the cost."

"And no doubt you know just how to plug it?" Thinking ahead of me again, he stared at me, shocked. He said quietly: "No. It would never work, not once in a million years."

I said: "It will. I've got to make it work, somehow. I'm going to talk to Loveless, undisturbed by a hundred policemen crowding the beaches and giving the game away."

Estrilla was toying with the stem of her glass, smiling quietly. I could feel Astrid's pale eyes on me.

Fenrek said brusquely: "Out of the question, Cain."

"I'm going to talk with him and find out exactly that—if there's any more of it lying around. It's something we've got to know because, if we don't...the whole thing, all the trouble we've gone to...it can all fall apart at the seams and put us back where we started, only more so. And this is the only way to do it."

For a long time Fenrek said nothing. I could hear the wheels turning over and over in his mind, agreeing with this, discarding that, checking something else, and finally coming up with undeniable truth that there was no other way about it. But he made a half-hearted attempt, none the less. He said:

"When we get him, sodium pentothal would give us the truth about that."

"Perhaps. But unhappily, pentothal is not absolutely infallible. Under the influence of *any* of the so-called truth drugs, there's one chance in a hundred that he'd be able to hold back just a little bit. His subconscious fighting against his conscious will and winning out. I really wouldn't like to take even that small chance. If he said: *no, there's no more,* while in a pentothal-induced coma, you know damn well that we'd never be absolutely sure, not as long as we live. We'd be worrying forever about that child reaching out for that bottle. But if he says it while he's wide awake and at his most alert, I'll know whether to believe him or not."

"And if you don't?"

"If I don't...then we're back to square one. But let's take one thing at a time. The stakes are too damned high for anything else. One careful step at a time."

"All right," he sighed. "Just one man on the beach to make sure you come out of there alive."

"No."

He pleaded with me. "On the top of the cliff then."

"No."

"God dammit, my men aren't going to show themselves, you know that!"

"To Loveless? To an animal from the bush? He'll smell them

if they get within a hundred miles of him."

"No he won't, he's cooped up in a cave a hundred feet below the road. If I'm to take all your goddamn likelihoods for truths."

"And there'll be a man on the beach, or at the top, just where you want to put your man, with a walkie-talkie, in contact with his commanding officer. We've got one of his men, but he's still got Van Reck, remember? And that's all he needs. He'll have Van Beck posted outside the cave to keep watch, he's bound to. He'll see me go in, but I'm damned if want him to see anything else."

"And Loveless will be waiting with a shotgun blast."

"No. He'll have to find out what I'm up to. He'll have to."

He was about to argue some more, but he gave up. The Maître came over and whispered in his ear, and Fenrek excused himself. I wondered if he had a couple of cards up his sleeve too, but I merely looked at him.

He said briefly: "The telephone."

"Do me a favor while you're on your feet. Check the wind for me, will you? It should be dying down about now."

He nodded and was gone.

Astrid said quietly: "If he really is down there, he'll never let you get away alive. He tried to kill us once, remember? Both of us."

"I remember. And he'll probably try again. But it's the third time that's always lucky, not the second."

Estrilla said somberly: "I hope you know what you're doing, Mr. Cain. I hope you've got a way picked out, a way to get out of there when the time comes."

I said glumly: "I haven't, as a matter of fact. But there's not really an alternative, is there?"

And there wasn't. I'd have to play it off the cuff again, but that's not as messy a business as some people think. If you keep your wits about you, you'd be surprised at the unexpected advantages which are liable to show themselves. And if your plan's too tight, you can't make those advantages pay off, because they're not part of the pre-arranged pattern.

Astrid looked at me unhappily and said: "He'll put you down among the lobsters again, and this time I won't be there to get you out."

Fenrek hurried back to the table, livid with suppressed fury. He said grimly: "Two more deaths at Loveless' door, Cain!" When I said nothing, he exploded: "Histermann. He's escaped. Two men guarding him, and he killed both of them. God damn their eyes, I told them..."

I looked at my watch. "What time was this?"

"Two hours ago. They've been trying to get me ever since, but the line was down with that damned wind. One of the guards unlocked the cell door to give him his evening meal, and both the men in the cell with him were stretched out on the floor with their necks broken. He says Histermann moved out past him like a bolt of greased lightning, and no one was able to stop him. He got clear away."

"And they're following him?"

"There's a dragnet out."

"Call it off."

He rubbed a tired hand over his narrow, aristocratic face. "And we're sitting here, listening to a *fado*...All right, I'll see they don't track him down to the Bocca, if that's what you want. Not that they're very likely to." He hesitated. "I suppose that's where he'll head for?"

"Of course. Even when he thought he was all set for a very painful death, didn't you notice? He was straining not to tell us exactly where the boat was hidden. Just the glimmer of hope that he might not be dying after all. They die hard, those men, and they never know they're dead until they're buried. Even then, I suspect, they are never really sure."

Fenrek said again impatiently: "For God's sake, I told them he'd try and make a break for it! I told them he was more trouble than they thought, and still..."

I said gently: "Hardly your fault, Fenrek. Two men in the cell with him, that's more than reasonable precaution. How was the wind?"

"Huh?"

"The wind?"

Even under the stress of the moment, he'd remembered to check. He said: "Dying down and veering to the west now."

I got up to go. I tossed Estrilla the keys to the little bug and said: "This is where we trade cars again. Hope you enjoyed the Jensen."

She gave me my keys. I finished my drink and looked at

Astrid. Her face was terribly lined and worried. I said: "It's all right, Astrid, I'll be back." I turned to Fenrek and said: "I'll be back by daylight."

"And if you're not?"

It was hard to tell him. But there was so much that could go wrong. I said slowly:

"If I'm not...it's no good waiting for that whaler to come out of there tomorrow night. He'll have the toxin on him, and God knows it it will be properly protected. So, if you sink his boat...you might have a major contamination on your hands, a seaborne infection that'll spread along the coast until...For God's sake, I don't even want to think about it."

"So?"

"There's only one thing to be done. If I'm not out of there by daylight, get the Navy to lob a couple of shells into the Bocca. Like that we'll know it's buried a hundred feet underground, the only safe place for it."

"And you, Cain?"

I said: "If I'm not back on time, I'll be quite past caring. I'll see you."

I went out into the cool, still night and listened for the roar of the Bocca. It was gone now. There was only silence, and that was all to the good.

CHAPTER 10

I drove down and parked near the Bocca; no attempt this time to hide the car; I wanted it to be seen.

I purposely parked below the skyline so that I would have to cross it on my way to the cave's entrance; a large sized man looms larger in the darkness, and I didn't want to be mistaken for a casual passerby. Not that there was much chance of that; anyone with any sense leaves the treacherous Bocca alone at night. I vaulted over the fence, hummed quietly to myself, and kept my ears peeled for any suspicious sound, like the slight click of a safety catch going off; I heard nothing. I didn't expect to, really.

Now the wind had swung round, and the whole character of the Bocca had changed. A matter of a few degrees was all that it needed to send those heavy seas funneling into the caves in Wagnerian fury; but now, it was a calm and silent place, as though the sea gods' had exhausted themselves and were resting, waiting for the next time.

I climbed over the precautionary rail, took hold of the iron ladder that had given me such a bad time a while back, and went down quickly to the cavern at the bottom. It was strangely quiet there after the tempestuous fury of the last time. The gate at the bottom was unlocked; so he hadn't had time to close it, even if he wanted to.

I switched on the big flashlight I'd taken from the Jensen, and went inside. The water was lower and quieter here, and the long and winding tunnel that led to the underground lake was easier of access, brightly lit now by the powerful beam of the light. It took me less than four minutes, walking quickly, to find the whaler. As I'd expected, he'd begun to strip the carburetor down; just the first step in the fault-finding process that would have gotten him nowhere anyway. I looked at it and sort of snorted loudly, and then there was a sudden bright light behind me, the beam of a very powerful searchlight, something like five hundred thousand candlepower, a quartz-iodine flood that turned the darkness of the cavern into brilliant day.

He said, quite quietly, very much in control and not even sounding worried: "Stand absolutely still, not a move of any sort, don't even put your hands up."

I froze correctly.

The light changed, and I knew that he'd flicked a reflector to give us overall illumination instead of a beam; a Richter Admiralty Light, then, the kind the British Navy uses; interesting.

He said: "All right, turn round very slowly, I just want to make sure."

I turned and smiled, and said: "It's me, Major Loveless. You must have heard the lobsters didn't eat me."

"I heard." He was holding a flat black box in his left hand, a compact affair like a walkie-talkie with a receiver and a mouthpiece built into it, the S-phone that the British Army uses. His ever ready, sawed-off shotgun was in the other. Speaking very quietly into the receiver, he said:

"Yes, it's him alright, let me know if anyone else comes along." He hesitated a moment and corrected himself: "No, on second thought, get out from undercover and take a look around. You'll probably find fifty of them scattered around the beach, waiting."

I said: "There's no one else, Major. Just me."

He said into the walkie-talkie: "Correction, there's probably a hundred of them."

Strange how some people will never believe the truth. The easiest thing, sometimes, is to tell them the exact opposite of what you want them to believe.

He flicked off the receiver and said lightly: "So we're in trouble, aren't we? Take your jacket off." I didn't particularly want to argue, so I did as I was told, and he said, reminding me: "The cave's only unstable at the entrance, don't think I won't fire this thing when

I'm ready to, no danger of a fall in here."

I said: "I know that. I just came down to see how you were getting along with the repair. You know you can't get out tonight now, don't you?"

He shrugged. "Tomorrow then, no problem." He thought for a while, and then said: "What did you do to it? I suppose I should have looked at the plugs. A pencil line down them?"

"Something like that."

He was smiling gently. "Are you aware that we're not alone?" He raised his eyes to a point above and behind me, and I looked round, moving quite slowly.

The other man was there, Van Reck, Histermann had called him, sitting high up in the cavern roof on a protrusion of granite, with his comic little bow at the ready. Among the stark shadows cast by the bright light, he might almost have been high in a tree in the dark jungle, and I was impressed with his choice of position; up there, no one was going to get at him without a gun, and Loveless was about to find out if I had one or not, and if so, to take it away from me. I thought it might be interesting to see how he was going to do that; he was looking at me very warily, as though he knew now that he'd underestimated the danger that first time, and was not about to make any mistakes now.

He said: "Throw your gun down, on the ground, right there, very slowly and carefully." His finger was crooked around the trigger of his gun, and I hoped he hadn't haired it up too much.

I said: "I don't carry one, matter of principle."

He grunted: "No? Lie down on the floor, on your back, with your hands crossed behind your back."

I shrugged. "You can take my word for it, but if you insist..."

I folded my arms in the small of my back and lay down, and he came over with the gun held in one hand, finger on the trigger, and the barrel under my chin. It was a Lames over-under with a single selective trigger and a point-to-point patterned walnut stock. He quickly patted me all over the sides and front, and said:

"Now, this is the danger point, isn't it? Roll over, slowly and carefully, to your right."

Again, I did precisely as I was told, and he patted the rest of my body till he was satisfied there was no weapon there. It was good for my ego to see how warily he moved, on the balls of his feet, ready to spring back instantly out of harm's way if I should make that initial move that meant I was going for him, though from that position on the floor it would have been a slow business.

He stepped back, satisfied, and I sensed that he was relaxing a bit, as though a truth that he wasn't very sure of had just been demonstrated. He looked at me with a very puzzled expression, and said:

"For a microbiologist, you're a very reckless man. I wonder why?"

Microbiologist? I'd told that lie only to Histermann. They'd already been in touch then; he was probably here too; the man at the top, no doubt, with the other end of the S-phone, standing guard while the getaway boat was being readied.

I said gently: "Where's the toxin, Loveless?"

He looked at me hard and long, and said: "Just sit there and do nothing, just sit quite still. You're a big, big man, and you've more sense than I gave you credit for, though not as much as you think, so don't kid yourself you can take us. Two of us in here and another outside, and each one of us could have you dead as mutton at the flick of a finger. So just—sit—quite—still."

Three of us...I thought: *and now abideth faith hope and charity, these three*...But there wasn't much charity showing.

As I sat on the ground with my legs crossed under me, he moved well away and leaned against the deck rail of the whaler, letting himself sway gently with it, his shotgun still very ready. He was puzzled, and he showed it.

There was an *intelligence*, a lively and yet somber intelligence that showed itself very clearly in those dark, brooding eyes, and something else too...He was a rough and uncouth man, and yet—there was something almost admirable about him, and I still couldn't place exactly what it was. I thought perhaps it might be just that air of competence that seemed to exude from him, the way you can almost see the halo over a saintly woman's head.

He was wasting time now, conscious that he had plenty on his hands and devoting it to finding out just what it was that brought me so carelessly into his lair; he *had* to know. There were a lot of thoughts going through his mind; jostling each other, seeking clarity and not finding it. I waited for him to ask the crucial question. Instead, he said at last:

"I've a feeling you're an intelligent man, am I right?"

I shrugged. "Events are soon going to show that, one way or another, aren't they?"

He laughed, a sad little laugh of repressed amusement, and then was very preoccupied again. He thought for a while and said: "And we've got time on our hands, haven't we? Time to find out just who you are and what you're up to."

I said: "It should be obvious to you, Loveless. If you want to think about it for a bit."

It wasn't at all obvious, but he didn't want to say so. He said: "So talk to me, I've a sudden craving for conversation, can you believe that?" He jerked his head towards Van Reck, and said: "Dummy up there can't talk, but I suppose you know that already?"

"No. How should I know it?"

"I just thought perhaps you might."

The pattern was emerging; he wanted to know a great deal more about me; good.

I said: "Dumb?"

He nodded. "Oh, only recently. He made the mistake of getting caught by the wrong people. Fellow called Asimulu or something, one of the non-people, a Captain in the Federal Army."

"Nigeria?"

He shrugged. "Nigeria, Mali, Angola, what does it matter?"

I said: "When you're fighting the way you fellows fight, you're always going to get caught by the wrong people. There's no other kind."

"Aye, you've a point there." He rubbed the barrel of his shotgun moodily along the side of his nose, with his finger still on the trigger. He said: "They caught him and tried to make him tell them where our hideout was, and he wouldn't, so they gave him an excuse not to talk anymore. Anymore, ever. They cut his tongue out. But he got away before they could do him any real damage. He never did talk much sense anyway, just a damn good soldier, a good man with any weapon you care to name."

"That's a comic little bow he carries. Homemade?"

"Homemade? Yes, I suppose that's one way of putting it. Custom-crafted, he used to call it, before he lost his tongue. He's pretty damn fast with it. But you know that, don't you?"

I remembered that back in the sixteenth century, when the Spaniards were wrecking the Aztec Civilization, Hernando Cortes had refused to use firearms, the old muskets of the day, because his archers were so much faster. They could fire ten well-aimed arrows in ten seconds, whereas it took ninety to load a musket and fire a single shot.

I said mildly: "Guns are a lot faster than they used to be." It seemed important to keep him talking, to let him have the conversation he craved. It's the easiest way to get to know a man, to talk, and talk, and keep on talking.

He grunted again. He said: "Aye, they're faster. And noisier. And you can put three, four, half a dozen bullets into a man, and if he's tough enough he'll still be coming at you. But put a hunting shaft through his guts and he's down for the count and he won't get up again, ever."

"And Histermann?"

Loveless said nonchalantly: "Did you know he escaped? Ah, I see you did." My face had been absolutely blank. He said: "Histermann's all right. He runs scared once in a while, but all right really, for a bloody Australian."

He was relishing the talking as much as I was. And now, that little muddiness in my evaluation of him was clearing itself up. What it was I'd seen in Loveless was a terrible kind of *loneliness*. And it occurred to me that I should have expected to find just that, except that I hadn't really looked for the intelligence that such a frightening loneliness demands. A mercenary? Fighting a savage war for anyone who would pay him, right or wrong, black or white, it didn't matter which?

He said to me irritably: "Talk to me, tell me what your name is."

"Cabot Cain."

"And you're a microbiologist? Who brought you into this? The Portuguese police? Or Interpol?"

"Neither. And I'm not a microbiologist either."

"A doctor then? You look more like a prize fighter."

"Not a doctor either."

"But you knew what to do when Histermann went down with that godawful poison. How come he managed to get over it so quickly?"

"He was suffering from a small dose of psilocybin."

"And what the hell's that, for God's sake?"

"LSD, mescaline—it's in the same field. He was just on a trip, only he didn't know it. It would have been a lot worse if he'd really been contaminated by that toxin you're carrying. There's no antidote to that stuff at all." I was waiting for him to ask me how Histermann had managed to get himself a dose of psilocybin, but he wouldn't. Pushing him hard, I said:

"Natural botulin is bad enough, there's no antidote to that either. But a manmade toxin is nearly always far more potent than the stuff nature turns out. More potent, and less predictable. The doctors can't always diagnose it, and they can never treat it with much hope of success. The patient just lies down and dies." Looking for an opening, I said: "You do know just how dangerous it is, don't you?"

"Aye."

"I wonder. You know that the island of Gruinard—that's not far from where you come from, is it?—is likely to remain infected for another hundred years because of an accident that took place there twenty-five years ago? With the same stuff you're toting around so casually? You know that half a dozen innocent fisherfolk were killed by it just outside this cave?"

"Aye, I know that too."

"Why, Loveless?

He shrugged. "The wrong people got killed, does it matter? It told me what I wanted to know."

"Its precise effect?"

"Roughly, yes. There was an Army unit landing on the beach that night, and I wondered what a pinch of that stuff in the water would do to them. My tame chemist had told me it would wipe them all out, but I wanted to be sure."

"A pinch? For God's sake, that's not salt you're fooling around with.”

He said calmly: “I know that. He said, my chemist, a pinch so small you can’t see it.”

“It’s in a glass vial?”

“Aye.”

“Then within ten minutes after you uncorked it, you ought to have been dead, you realize that?” It was true; he’d had the most colossal luck, part of that unpredictability.

He showed some uneasiness now, for the first time. In his mind it meant I wasn’t telling the truth; but he couldn’t be sure. He said angrily:

“How can you say that, you said yourself you’re not really a microbiologist. And I used rubber gloves anyway.”

I sighed. “I’ll explain to you one day just how they handle that stuff on Gruinard. I’ll tell you some of the precautions they use to keep it well wrapped up. The way you plan to use it, your mercenaries are going to be the first casualties.”

He grinned suddenly. “Maybe that was true a while ago, but not anymore. We were going to cut it with flour, but now” — he laughed shortly— “now we’ve got a better idea. And you know what? You gave it to me. I told you, you weren’t as bright as you thought.”

I said, looking puzzled: “I did?”

“Aye. We’re going to use aerosols, your own idea. And it was you who told me too that I didn’t have to hang around here with every cop in the country looking for me while my tame chemist made up some more. I didn’t realize I had so much of it till you told me. And how do you like that, bright boy?”

I’m not very good at looking aghast, but I had a shot at it anyway. I said: “Nacimento!”

He laughed again. “A pity you’re not on my side, isn’t it? Between us, we’d give the non-people hell.”

I said calmly: “Exactly. A new weapon is all that’s needed, except for someone who knows how to use it. You need that too.”

Now the seed was planted. Either he didn’t see it at once, or wanted time to think about it a lot more. There was a veiled look in his eyes as though he’d just had a brilliant idea and wanted to hide it from me. And so, he kept talking.

He said: "Aye, I figured you'd found out just what I was up to. We're fighting organized armies now, the old days have gone, and...Cain, was it?"

I said: "Aye."

"There was a time when the non-people had beat-up old rifles they didn't really know how to use, and they weren't very much opposition for us. But now, it's America, or England, or Russia, or sometimes China were fighting, and when those bloody non-people lose their rifles, the major powers are in there quick, fixing them up with bazookas and flamethrowers instead, and a hundred more rifles thrown in for good measure, just in case they feel like losing them all over again. We're fighting tanks and aircraft now, and the odds are getting too heavy against us. So I took a quick look at the arsenals of the big boys and came up with something they've got but are afraid to use in any of their bloody fool little wars. They're scared of their own products. But I'm not, Cain. I'm not. I've got something now that's going to turn the scales, all over Africa. Anywhere I want to fight, they'll hire me, and I'm going to win hands down, overnight. Do you realize that with a few ounces of this stuff in Katanga I could have wiped out the United Nations Force in the space of twenty-four hours?"

I said quietly, making a question of it: "And you'd have done that?"

He thought for a while and sighed, and said: "No, probably not. I'd not take on a serious army, they'd have been backed into a corner and they just might have used the same weapon on me. No, I only fight the non-people. You'd be surprised how many of them there are around."

I said: "It's a word you're very fond of. What's the definition?"

"Of non-people? Hell..." He thought for a while and said at last, with a wary sort of grin: "I suppose you could say anyone excepting present company."

He jerked his head at Van Reck. "He's non-people because he can't talk even if he had anything intelligent to say, which he doesn't. Histermann's non-people too, really, though he doesn't realize it. But the real non-people are the blacks. There's not one of them knows his arse from his elbow, or knows what he's fighting for. If I'm on their side, they just do as I tell them. If they're on the other side, they just listen to someone who tells them to go out and get the mercenaries, and then they walk into my ambushes and get killed off, and there's another little victory, chalk it up on the board. And when there are no non-people left in Nigeria, or Ghana, or Mali, or anywhere else, it'll all be starting up again just over the border. Any border."

"And you work for the highest bidder, is that how it goes?"

He was enjoying the opportunity to talk. I thought: what does a man like that do in the bush, with no one to vent his spleen on? I knew the answer; he goes mad, it's a common enough occurrence in the bush not to excite comment:

He said, very thoughtfully: "No-o, that isn't strictly true except in theory. But sometimes...Take Tshombe, for example. Back in those days, Lumumba was offering us a lot more than the Katangese could ever have paid us, but I didn't trust him, and I always half-thought that Tshombe was right, and he was, dammit. But the U.N. drove most of us out of there; we had to cross over into Uganda. There, it's a tossup, all of them at each other's throat and none of them in the right, so we went with the Banyankole tribes. They were at the throats of the Batoro, non-people like all of them; only the Banyankole had the diamond mines, and so..." he shrugged, "that threw us into their camp. We did pretty well, too."

Now was the time. I said: "Is it just money you want? For God's sake...."

He looked at me shrewdly, and waited. I waited too. He said at last: "What's on your mind? Cain, did you say?"

Well, there it was at last, and the idea was his, not mine; he was sure of that.

I said: "Cabot Cain, and what's on my mind is a deal. I'm surprised that it didn't occur to you." The friendliest fellow in the world, I said earnestly: "I could get you a round million dollars, American, for every ounce of that culture you've got. That's a pretty damn good price for a commodity that costs fifty cents an ounce to produce."

He was smiling gently. "Four million dollars." Question answered; I was watching his face as carefully as I've ever watched anything in my life. He said dreamily: "I'm almost tempted. With a guaranteed passage to South America, that sort of thing?"

"Something like that"

"And who'd put up the money?"

I could see what he was thinking. He'd been too long with no one to talk to, no one except his non-people. He was disappointed that the deal I had in mind wasn't the one he'd hoped for; or wondering if he'd hoped for too much; or perhaps calculating the risk of that better deal and wondering if it was worth it.

I said, making it sound as though this wasn't what I was after either: "I'll get the money somehow. A lot of people would pay handsomely to avert the danger of plague in Africa."

"The do-gooders?"

"If that's what you want to call them."

"A bit dicey, isn't it? I mean, there I am sitting around a police station while Cabot Cain—that's a hell of a name! American, aren't you? Where from?"

I said: "San Francisco. You were sitting around the police station."

"Och, I was too, and Cabot Cain is passing round the hat asking for benevolent contributions to get this mass murderer on a ship to South America with four million dollars in his pocket."

I didn't like that repetition of the *four*. I thought about it for a while and decided it was merely fortuitous, not thrown at me deliberately. Loveless had many virtues, if that's what you want to call them; but a chess-player's mind wasn't one of them.

He said again: "It's a bit dicey, isn't it?"

"I could manage it." I hoped I sounded unconvincing enough, and was sure that I did.

He shrugged. "It's an academic question, anyway. I don't need money that badly."

"What do you need, Loveless?"

He sighed, and thought for a while, staring moodily at his feet. He didn't look a bit like the villain of the piece now. He was a sad man with a terrible dream that perhaps he knew could never be realized. A vicious, unholy dream; but none the less I couldn't bring myself to hate his guts as I should have done. I found myself hoping that his killing would not be at my hands.

He said, and he sounded troubled: "I don't know, really, and that's the truth. I only know that when I'm at work, I'm a kind of...a kind of king. There's nobody does my job better than I do; Cain. Nobody. There's a thousand mercenaries, five thousand perhaps, fighting all over Africa. Most of them are bums, but not all of them. Some of them fight for money, some for the left against the right or the right against the left, because that's what they believe in. Some of them fight for one tribe against another just because they just screwed some pretty little virgin in tribe 'A'. Some of them fight for whoever's losing, just on principle, and some of them fight for whoever's winning for the same reason. And some of them fight just for the hell of it, because that's the only thing they've ever learned to do. I guess that's my reason, really. But to tell the truth, I'm not too sure of it."

I said, very quietly: "You are not fighting against non-people, Loveless. You are fighting against God."

He snorted: "Him too, I know, He killed my..." He broke off and took a deep, unhappy breath.

I said: "Your mother."

He looked at me with a strange expression in his eyes: not angry, not surprised, not hurt. He said: "You know about that? You've really done your homework, haven't you?"

I said: "I know the progression."

"Progression?" He sounded irritable. "I wish you'd talk more clear."

"Progression's the only word. A red tide that killed your mother with mussel poisoning. A disastrous epidemic in Scotland that looked like the same without the red tide, and finally, your own red tide to make it look real when we had more mussel poisoning here. Yes, I've done my homework."

Now, he took the plunge. He said: "Ever been in the bush, Cain? Or are you a city man?"

"I've been in the bush."

"You don't carry a gun, that means you don't know how to use one."

"It means nothing of the sort, I am a crack shot."

He said carefully: "If I invited you to come in with me...?

Maybe I need someone who knows about this stuff. What would you say?"

I had to be careful not to leap at the suggestion, not even to let him think it wasn't entirely his idea.

I said: "And if I ever got in your way?"

He shrugged. "I'd stamp on you, big as you are, you must know that." He looked at me broodingly and said: "Well, it was just a thought."

He was suddenly very alert again, alert and suspicious. He looked at me in utter astonishment, and said: "Och, is that what this is all about? I was trying to figure out how you had the guts to walk right in here, and there it was laid out for me to see, and..." He broke off, angry and puzzled. "But you couldn't have *known* I'd make you an offer like that? Were you just...just waiting and hoping I would? You'd better tell me that fast, Cain."

Play it off the cuff, I'd said. And there it was, written in red ink all over the white starched poplin. Not the best crib in the world, but in the moments thought I gave myself I couldn't think of a better one; and if there was a more promising way out of that cave alive, I should have found it by now. I sort of smiled slowly, and said:

"In the course of time I'd have made you an offer. When I was sure I could trust you."

Now, that wariness was suddenly honed to a razor edge. He put the S-phone slowly to his mouth, flicked it on, and said:

"Still all clear, Jerry?"

Histermann must have told him it was; and he must have sounded puzzled about it too. Listening to the answer, too faint for me to hear, Loveless laughed. "No, I didn't know either until ten seconds ago. And I'm still not sure that I know. But we might just have a major development on our hands." He stared at me thoughtfully as he listened and then spoke into the receiver again: "No, a very interesting development that I want to think about a bit. Keep your eyes skinned, Jerry, this is the crucial time."

He put the instrument down and looked at me long and hard, and said: "I'm an evil man, I suppose, if you want to call it that. I'm alone in the world, and I'm an uneducated sort of bastard by your standards. But one thing I am not, Cain, I'm not a fool. Now, tell me why the hell I just shouldn't blow your head off right now."

I said: "If you were going to do that, you wouldn't look for a reason, would you? You said just now that maybe you needed a man like me, isn't that enough?"

"No. It's not."

"You mean that remark was just squeezed out of you? A slip of the tongue?"

"I mean that maybe I got carried away. Aye, you'd be useful, there's no doubt about that at all. Maybe I'm thinking that you're even indispensable under the circumstances; you, or someone like you. Someone like you, Cain. All I really need is another man who knows a bit about this botulin stuff."

"Try and find one who's willing to go along with you, or not scared stiff of it. Why do you think no one ever used this stuff in warfare? It's just too damn dangerous, that's why. And you haven't got the brains to use it properly."

"All right, and it's still not enough."

There were plenty more arguments, and it didn't take long to think of the one that would appeal to him most.

I said: "Then there's more. Plenty more."

"Talk."

"All right, I will. You know that the Egyptians are busy wiping out the Sudanese as fast as they can?"

He shrugged. "Common knowledge. Go on."

"Did you read last Friday's *Jeune Afrique?*"

He shook his head. "I don't read French. Just German and Portuguese."

I said: "The Sudanese have put out a call for help. They want some mercenaries."

He was a commander carefully examining each side of a problem, testing it for possible loopholes. He said: "What's the rights and wrongs of it, I don't know about the Sudan, not at the moment."

I said: "You should, that's also common knowledge. It used to be the Anglo-Egyptian Sudan. When the British pulled out, it became the Egyptian Sudan. Now it's trying to be the Sudanese Sudan. They want autonomy, and the easiest way for the Egyptians to put a stop to that is just to wipe them all out, and that's what's going on there at this moment; genocide. It is casually reported once in a while in all the newspapers, so how come you don't know about it? You want *Jeune Afrique's* latest figures? A hundred and thirty-five thousand Sudanese slaughtered in the last three weeks, and it's been going on now for almost a year. Interested?"

He said: "Weapons?"

"The Egyptians have sophisticated modern weapons, the Sudanese have spears. Their army, such as it was, was practically wiped out in the first few weeks, only nobody in the civilized world bothered to notice that. Now they're just about down to bows and arrows and spears."

"And who's got all the money?"

"The Egyptians, of course."

"So I'm expected to fight for the poor bloody Sudanese and get paid off in cotton, is that it? That's about all the Sudan is good for."

I said: "And peanuts. They grow a lot of peanuts."

He was angry now. "You're not out of the woods yet, Cain." (I was, for the moment at least, obviously). He said: "And I don't like men who make jokes, life and death's a serious matter. Who's going to pay me?"

I didn't want to offer him too plausible a possibility. I sort of shrugged, and said: "According to *Jeune Afrique*, they can raise the money. But more important, they're offering concessions."

"For cotton? Let them rot."

"For gold."

"Gold? In the Sudan?"

"Three fairly productive mines, two very good ones, and six or seven that might turn out very well indeed."

"Who's working them now?"

"A bunch of Frenchmen and Belgians, but they're mostly in Egyptian-held territory now." Time for the clincher. I said: "The upper Nile Valley, an ideal place for bacteriological warfare, wouldn't you say?"

Now he took a long, long time to think about it. More on principle than anything else, he asked idly, trying to mask the urgency: "Who else knows you're here, Cain?"

I said promptly: "Nobody."

He shook his head irritably: "I don't believe that. I *won't* believe it: It doesn't make sense. No sense at all!" He threw his head back and peered at me. "Just who are you, Cain?"

"An adventurer. Just as you are. Only perhaps I'm better at it."

"And what do you expect to get out of this?"

"Money, what else?"

"There's easier ways to make money. Lots of them."

I said with just the right amount of eagerness: "And maybe I'd like to be a sort of king too. You know the fear of plague in Africa, and man with a few vials of that stuff in his pocket can rule the whole goddamn continent. How much toxin have you got?"

"Four ounces." Check.

"Any man with four ounces of that stuff, in the Nubian desert, is a king, an emperor, with all the power in the world."

"You're pushing me, Cain."

"Sorry. I guess I'm just eager."

The irritation was coming back again. He said, his eyes angry: "I know better than to trust *anybody!* Particularly someone with as smooth a tongue as yours."

I said: "You trust Van Reck, don't you? And Histermann?"

He said coldly: "No. They'd either of them sell me out if you made it worth their while."

"I doubt it. Histermann held back a few things even when he thought he was about to die, horribly."

"Yes, yes, I guess he's all right, really." It was a grudging admission.

I looked up at Van Reck. He was still sitting there as immobile as a statue, his bow ready still. I said: "Does he really find that thing more efficient than a gun?"

Loveless shrugged. "Every man to his own favorite weapon, it's one of my rules" He laughed. "That's what started all this, really. Do you realize that's the oldest form of chemical warfare there is? The poisoned arrow? All I'm doing is refining a process that Africa's known about, and used, for three thousand years. They used strychnine—I use botulin."

"Ironic, isn't it?"

He said grumpily: "If that's all you've got to think about..."

"I was thinking it's about time you made up your mind. I don't want to stay here all night."

He looked surprised, "All night? Till we pull out of here tomorrow, Cain. Till then, I'm not letting you out of my sight, or Van Reck's either. I've got a lot of thinking to do, about you, and until I make up my mind you stay right there, where you are."

I shrugged. "All right with me."

Maybe it was a little too casual. He came quite close to me (with a quick, reassuring glance up at Van Reck), and said carefully:

"Just know this. If Histermann says there's no one up there watching this place, then I know that's how it is. It'd take more than a Portuguese cop to hide from him, I can tell you."

It had to be constantly difficult, all the way down the line.

I said: "Not police, Fenrek's men from Interpol. Only there aren't any of them up there, not a single one. I told you."

He said smoothly: "I keep telling you, Cain, don't try to be too bright. Interpol only has one man here, and he's a banker or something. Now there's that Colonel Fenrek from Paris and nobody else. If they want a dozen men to prowl around the beaches in the dark, they have to use the local talent. Flatfoots."

But not too constantly difficult. I gave way.

I sighed. "Yes, you're right there, I suppose."

He said unexpectedly: "Who was the girl you were with that night?"

Did he know already? I thought perhaps he did.

I said: "Colonel Fenrek's niece, she's here on holiday from the States. Why do I have to stay here all night? If I'm coming with you, I'd like to do a few things first."

"I'll bet you would." He said angrily: "*If* you come with me, I don't let you off the leash till we're there. Everything you've got that I need, you've got it with you, in your head."

I shrugged.

He said: "There's less than an hour to daylight, and it takes longer than that to get this boat out of here, so we have to wait till dark tomorrow night. Say, another eighteen hours or so. I've just got one small job to do in Guincho, or maybe I'll send Van Reck to do that. But meanwhile, if there's the slightest sign that anyone's coming looking for you, you know what I'm going to do, Cain?"

He reached down into the cupboard where the whalers sheets were stored and pulled out a small steel box, a box of finely-machined stainless steel, not much bigger than a pack of cigarettes. He opened it and took out a small glass vial. He held it up and let me see it. "I don't have to tell you what this is, do I? I've got four of them. And somehow, anyone shows his face anywhere near this place, one of them's going to get broken, and the hell with everything and everybody. I just don't give one damn anymore."

I didn't like to mention to him that in less than an hour, Fenrek's men would be blowing up the cave and everybody in it anyway, so I said nothing.

He put the vial carefully back into its box and said: "Now, you fixed that motor for me. Unfix it."

I said: "Gladly. It'll take a little time."

"And watch your step." He spoke very clearly, "Just—watch your step. Every inch of the way."

He flicked the switch of the S-phone. "Jerry? We're here for the rest of the night. At daylight, come on in. There'll be people coming and going around the *lagosteria*, maybe. But anyone looks like he's headed this way, into the Bocca, even looks like it, I don't care who he is...you just let me know, man. Right?"

I shuddered at the way he tossed that box back among the ropes in the cupboard.

He sat there and stared at me moodily while I went to work on the exhaust.

An hour to daylight. An hour before the Navy would start lobbing shells in on us. It wasn't a very happy thought.

CHAPTER 11

I said: "You don't know much about motors, Loveless. That's no way to strip a carburetor."

He said impatiently: "I'm a soldier, not a bloody mechanic. But I know enough about engines to strip down a Weber."

It was seven o'clock in the morning, and we were still both there, all in one piece. I wondered if the Navy was out there waiting, lining up the sights of its heavy guns. It occur to me that Fenrek might want to try something else, before taking such drastic action as I'd suggested. I hoped he would; but there didn't seem much else that he could do.

Loveless was looking at the spark plugs suspiciously, still keeping ready for instant movement, still with that damned sawed-off gun held ready for immediate action. I didn't expect him to trust me, yet, though the more he thought about our collaboration, the more reasonable it must have seemed to him. It's hard for the twisted to realize that most people are fairly straight.

But he was still brooding about it, all the same. He said, scowling: "How come you were working with the police?"

I told him the truth, it was easy enough. I said: "General Queluz hired me to find you. He was hoping you might clear him of that trouble back in Angola."

"Hired you? So you work just for money, is that it."

"Doesn't everybody?"

"No. With some of us, it's...it's something more than that." My

God, he was getting patronizing. He threw down the plugs and said: "So you didn't pencil line them after all?"

"Nope. I put a wedge in the exhaust system. You'd never have found it. All we have to do now is take it off at the manifold and worry it out again, that won't be hard. If you'd left the carburetor alone we could have been out of here in an hour."

He said sullenly: "Time, we've got. Plenty of time." He was still wondering just how far I could be trusted, and knowing that it wasn't very much.

He got on the S-phone and said to Histermann out there: "Get down to Cascais and send a telegram, tell them to hold the plane up for twenty-four hours. Same time, same place, but tomorrow." He listened for a while. I knew what Histermann was protesting about. He said at last: "All right, all right, so they're out looking for you. So go to Guincho instead, they're not likely to be out as far afield as that." He listened again. "What? Aye, that might be true. What? At this time of the morning?" There was a worry creeping over his face. He flicked off the switch and looked at me and said softly:

"It's nearly daylight out there, and there's no traffic on the road, none at all."

I shrugged. Just as he had done, I said: "At this time of the morning?"

"There ought to be a few fishermen coming in, the shrimp trucks, a couple of bicycles at least." I said nothing, and he went on: "Unless they've got the roads blocked off."

That's what I'd been afraid of. The first step if Fenrek was doing what he was supposed to do; he'd have had the early traffic diverted to the inland road, with the fisherfolk held up five miles back and told to wait. A destroyer would have been standing offshore too, ready to lob its shells into the cave. It could only mean that Fenrek really was ready to blow us all up, unless he could come up with a better idea in time. And I hate relying on other people's ideas, even Fenrek's.

I found an excuse. I said: "Well, obviously you haven't heard."

"Heard what?"

"They found out that the red stain in the water wasn't just a red tide, they found out it was cochineal. A bright move that, incidentally."

He shrugged it away. "It seemed necessary to fool them just a little longer. So they found out?"

"Of course. And since they weren't worrying about a simple case of mussel poisoning, they performed autopsies on those people who were killed, and found it was botulin. So..." I shrugged, "as far as they were concerned; it was Scotland all over again. They closed the beach off for five miles each way."

It made sense, and I didn't expect him to reject it, and he didn't. I pushed the point home. I said: "If Histermann's going into Guincho, he'll be stopped. Not because he's an escaped prisoner, but just because he's moving on a road that's been put off limits."

His face was getting very tired. He said wearily: "It was all so easy, Cain, before you happened along."

I thought I'd better needle him a bit, to help him make up his mind, if it wasn't already thoroughly made up. I said:

"The mistakes were all before I happened along, not after." He said nothing, knowing there was more to come. I said: "If you'd put a few drops of dimethylarsenous acid in with the toxin, you'd have fooled them completely, they'd never even have started looking for botulin. And you can buy that in any drugstore at fifty *escudos* a pound."

Dimethylarsenous acid is the term you use when you can't remember weed-killer, but I didn't suppose he'd know that; he didn't have the looks of a gardener. He wasn't really very interested, but he said:

"Oh? And what would that have done?"

I gave him a little more misinformation, to show how knowledgeable I was in the things that mattered most to him.

I said: "It would have made them suspect an underground seepage of poison gas. It's fairly common."

"That's as it may be, but I never even heard of such a thing."

Bolting the carburetor back into place, I said: "But you're not a microbiologist, are you?"

I waited for his reply. It came very quickly: "And you said you weren't either."

"No, I am not. I'm not even a psychopharmacologist. But I'm a very erudite sort of fellow, Loveless, and I know a lot about the neurotoxin poisons, and you're fooling around with one of those like a three-year-old child with a live grenade. You need expert help, you'll get nothing but an early grave without it, and that's why you and I together can make this thing really work. My brains, your guts. In a year, working together, we could be kings, both of us."

He laughed, a dry, humorless laugh. "King of the non-people, what a bloody prospect."

I said: "That's what you've been fighting for all these years."

"Aye, I suppose it is, at that. How's the motor coming?"

"I've undone the damage you did, now I've got to undo my own. Give me a hand with this manifold."

"No, you'll have to get it off yourself. You've got the muscles, by the looks of it."

He still didn't want to get too close to me, but he was fast becoming convinced that maybe after all we really could get along together. Wishful thinking, some people call it; they wouldn't underestimate it quite so much if they called it autosuggestion instead.

I said patiently: "It's not a question of strength. I've only got two hands, so grab hold of that induction box, or it's going to snap off."

He hesitated, looked up at his tame archer, decided to risk it, carefully unloaded his shotgun and put it down, slipping the cartridges into his pocket, and said calmly:

"You're big enough to take me pretty easily, is that what you're thinking?"

I said calmly: "I could, no doubt about that at all. But why should I?"

"If you'd seen a bit more of Van's work with a bow and a poisoned hunting head you wouldn't even think about it. He can hit a mosquito travelling at speed."

"Grab hold of that box, for God's sake."

He came over then, and did as I asked him. A little more trust, it was growing slowly...

He said: "If the road's blocked, how did you get down here by car, and that's a question you can answer without stopping to think too long."

I said: "I came over the dunes."

"In a car?"

"Four-wheel drive. A Jensen, it'll go anywhere a mule can go."

"Oh." That made sense too. He said: "I've heard that's a pretty expensive car."

"It is. Have you got any penetrating oil?"

"Aye, in the toolbox."

I found it and squirted some on the bolts of the long exhaust. They came off easily enough, and I found the mud plug I'd rammed up there and removed it, and in ten more minutes the motor was ready to go. I said: "All right, now we'll start it and make sure."

He said sharply: "No."

"Then you'll have to take my word on trust."

Was he ready to do that? It was a good sign. He looked the motor over carefully, though I knew he wasn't sure what he was looking for. He said: "How good a mechanic are you?"

"I have a degree in Automotive Engineering."

"That too?" He sounded sarcastic.

I said: "And a good many others besides."

"Then we'll take it on trust. We don't start up till we're ready to go, just in case someone's listening for the sound of it."

I sighed. "You're determined not to trust me, Loveless, aren't you?"

He looked at me with that somber, brooding look for a very long time. He looked away at last, as though he didn't want me to see the doubt in his eyes; but he said sullenly: "*Major* Loveless, to you." It told me all I wanted to know.

The cave was still brightly lit with the Admiralty lamp. But on the water at the entrance, there was a faint glow of copper red where the early morning sun was playing games with the red and blue rocks that stood at water level there, washed bright and clean by the receding tide. It was a strange feeling, being cooped up there a hundred feet below the smooth green hills and the lovely pines so high over our heads. I couldn't help thinking of the peace and quiet up there, with the earth warming up again after the cool of the night, while down here...It was sort of Hades, with nothing but peace and quiet here too, but a calm that was only temporary; the most terrible things could be happening at any minute now.

He said suddenly: "How did you find out where the boat was hidden?"

It was a shot out of the blue and meant to surprise me, but I'd been wondering when he'd get around to that.

I told him the truth, why shouldn't I?

I said: "Histermann spoke about the Serpent's Tail. He was in a coma, trying hard to hide any thoughts of the Bocca. But I've seen the Serpent's Tail, and I got the association at once."

"Which is?"

"A waterspout in Australia, on the Barrier Reef."

"Oh. And who else knows we're here?"

"Nobody. That was a piece of information for keeping to myself, obviously." I was sure that he believed me.

I was desperately waiting for someone, anyone, to pursue the matter of the telegram; but there was no way to do any urging along. After all, I'd done what I came here to do—or at least, part of it. I knew, most important of all, just where the toxin was, and Loveless was partially separated from it, far enough away not to make a grab and kill us all if I gave him more than a split second. A rapid leap at him? Van Reck had demonstrated his prowess with that damned bow just a little too well. I didn't want a dose of the world's simplest poisons while I was trying to stamp out one of its most sophisticated. And he didn't look, Van Beck, as if he had any intention of moving from his high perch, where I couldn't get at him. Bush training again, a solid defense is the first thing a guerrilla thinks of before he mounts an attack; he won't show himself unless he's invulnerable. In the time it would have taken me to get up there to his perch, he could have loosed off fifty of his deadly shafts. The leopard has his camouflage coat, the eagle his height, and Van Reck had working for him the sheer impossibility of my getting close to him quickly enough.

Loveless eased the strain for me. He said: "In your car, can I get to Guincho over the dunes?" He must have already known the answer, but it was desperately important to mislead him now, to make it seem easier than it could possibly be.

I tossed him the keys to the Jensen and said: "Histermann presumably knows where it's parked. Just head straight for the dunes where the big pine tree is, it's a *Pinus caribaea* if you're fussy about detail. Keep going straight, keep the tree to your left, stay all the time under the lea of the cliff. And you'll come out of the road about a mile west of the roadblock."

Surprisingly, he asked: "What's the tire pressure?"

I reflected that traveling all over the African bush as he was accustomed to, that's one of the first things you think of.

I said: "Twenty-five pounds fore and aft, low enough for four-wheel drive, you won't get stuck. Not unless you over-rev the engine. Keep her in third all the way over the soft sand and don't stop..."

He said impatiently: "I know about that, I've driven in soft sand before."

And now was the moment he had to make up his mind about a very important matter. If he took that damned toxin with him...I hoped he'd been impressed by my very true explanation of the dangers. But would he leave it here in the cavern, with the problem I posed to him not entirely solved to his satisfaction? I dared not warn him to leave it there; I could only hope that I'd done enough already.

He scratched at his chin for a while, thinking hard. And then he made up his mind. He went to the cupboard where the toxin was, took out the box, looked at it reflectively for a moment, and then went below into a tiny cabin. He wasn't gone long, just long enough to hide it away down there somewhere, and when he came back he looked up at Van Reck and said distinctly:

"If he tries to go below, if he even makes a move for the door...You understand?"

Watching, I saw Van Reck nod slowly. The expression on his face had not changed a bit, still the same stolid look of absolute impassion. And then he made a queer, strangled sort of sound, as though he were trying to catch our attention, to make sure we'd both be looking at him for one split second longer. He held my look, and then, with incredible speed, drew back a strong right arm, not bothering to aim, and loosed the shaft that was in the string. Even before it hit, not more than an inch from my head, there was another arrow ready, notched and pulled back. The shaft had embedded itself in the sternpost, a target no more than two inches across and so close to my scalp that if I'd moved the merest trifle it would have gone through my head. I looked up at it and saw that it had split the hardwood dowelling, the steel point coming out just a fraction on the other side; dead center, an impressive shot.

I said sourly: "All right, all right, I know you can shoot straight."

Now, the expression was changing; Van Reck was grinning to himself, enjoying the joke.

Loveless said to him: "All right, just keep your eyes open, he's not as big a fool as he looks." He switched on the S-phone and said: "Jerry? I'm going down to Guinco myself. Stay out of sight, stay at the entrance. Van is standing guard down here. If anybody shows his nose near the cave, or comes out of it while I'm away, you know what to do. And if I'm not back in an hour, you know what to do then too. I've put the stuff..." He looked at me and said into the receiver: "You remember where we hid the money that time? There."

He switched off and, not taking his eyes off me, trying hard to find out what I was thinking and not succeeding, he said slowly: "This just might be the biggest mistake I ever made in my life. But risks— you have to take them sometimes, don't you?"

I said politely: "Indeed you do."

"And to tell you the truth, I just don't give a damn. Maybe if you think about that enough, it'll slow you down. We can all go to hell and I just don't give a damn, Now start the motor."

"I thought you didn't want the sound of it."

"Start it."

I shrugged, leaned over and pushed the button. It roared into life immediately, a muffled roar that sounded, in the confines of the cavern, more than it really was. I knew that we were too deep in the bowels of the earth to be heard out there where the bright sun was.

He said at once, shouting: "Cut it!"

I switched off, and he looked at me and half laughed, and walked away to leave me there alone with a madman perched up on a ledge twenty feet above my head, with a poisoned arrow ready to loose off if I even wanted to scratch my head.

At the entrance to the cave, Loveless turned back. He looked the cave and the boat over thoroughly, looked up at Van Reck and said: "Don't let him get behind the boat. If he does, just wait for him to show his head again. He can't get out, you've got a clear line of fire to the entrance."

I saw Van Reck nodding slowly. The grin had gone, and he was his own phlegmatic self again. Loveless turned on his heel and was gone. I thought I'd give him ten minutes.

I looked up at Van Reck and met his eye. I said: "Don't get excited, no one's going to get hurt."

Very slowly, I put my palms out and bent my knees, and leaned on the deck with my hands and slowly straightened my legs. I started doing push-ups, quite slowly, not to get the archer up there too worried. Not that I thought he would be. There was a clear field of fire to every point in the cave except behind the boat. And there, as Loveless had said, there could be no safety either—all he had to do was wait for me to show myself again as I'd have to if I were trying to get out of there. At thirty push-ups to the minute, I thought three hundred would be about right, and it was good to feel the blood coursing through my shoulders.

And then, when I'd counted a hundred and forty-seven, there was a very slight sound, and Loveless was there again, standing in the entrance and staring at me in surprise.

He said: "What the...what the hell goes on?"

I turned my head and smiled at him, not stopping.

I said gently: "Just getting my exercise, Major. I'm a nut about keeping fit. Too easy to get fat and flabby, isn't it?" Moving up and down, I said: "And I didn't expect you back quite so soon either."

I saw him shrug. "Just checking."

I'd half expected it. Ten more minutes then, another three hundred. He turned on his heels and was gone again. I went on pushing.

And then, at the count of two hundred and nine, my timing was forced up a bit, fortuitously. A shot sounded out there; or was it two, impossibly close together? I knew that Van Reck must have been as startled as I was—perhaps startled enough to loose off a shaft in my direction; or perhaps, with luck, startled enough to look off at the entrance where the sound of the shot came from.

I didn't check to see what he was doing; I knew there wouldn't be time. I did at once what I was preparing to do two or three moments later. I shoved hard with my foot against the deck rail and threw myself backward at the same time. As I went over the side and hit the water, I heard the arrow thud into the deck where I'd been; the sharp steel had pierced the sleeve of my jacket and I tore myself free and was under the water even before the second shaft hit close beside the first.

And I knew that he still wouldn't leave the safety of his defensive perch; he didn't have to. I dived deep and went under the hull, going as deep as I could while I was about it, killing two birds with one stone by checking the depth of the water at the same time. It was a good twenty feet or more, to judge by the feeling of my ears. Deep enough, at any rate. I came up at last on the other side, where at least for the moment it was safe, knowing that Van Reck would be on his feet now, waiting for me to reappear, as I must, or merely hold me there till his boss got back. I pulled myself silently up, hidden from him by the superstructure of the cabin's top, slid over the scuppers on my belly, and rolled down the four steps into the cabin.

I decided that I had plenty of time now, and I searched long and carefully. There was no danger unless I showed myself again. *A trap*, Van Reck would be thinking, *and the idiot's put his head into it, let's see what happens when he pokes it out again, as sooner or later he's got to do.*

It took me less than a minute to find the small steel box, hidden away in the bottom of a large can of coffee. It was empty, of course, and it took me another three minutes to find the vials, wrapped in oily rags and stashed away in the pipe berth, wedged in the bottom section near the inner cover of the bilges. Thinking of the terrible, indiscriminate death they represented, I couldn't help shuddering; a little play in the pipes as the boat swayed, and one of the glass vials, armored or not, might easily have cracked. I thought grimly: by God, he really does need someone with a little more respect for the most deadly toxin in the world's whole alarming arsenal. I replaced them carefully in the box and wrapped a length of stout wire round it to make sure it stayed good and shut.

But it took me longer to undo the seacocks with my bare hands. With a good heavy wrench I'd have opened them up quickly, but they were fastened down tight and not oiled. I used my belt as a sort of wrench, tightening it round the four-inch lugs and twisting till they came free.

There was a pleasant gurgling sound, and the water rushed up into the cabin, flooding it in less than a minute. I slipped the steel box into my pocket, not without certain qualms which I knew to be foolish, and soon there was only a foot of headroom above the level of the inrushing water.

Where would he be now, Van Reck? Would he have come down at last, knowing what I was doing and peering down into the water, not here, but at the entrance? That damned reflected sunlight on the water wasn't going to be much help; or was it? Would he see me ten feet down swimming strongly past him? And if he did, would he accurately gauge the effect of the water's refraction, and get at least one good shot in? One was all he needed.

The boat was keeling over now, the water on one side reaching the roof. I took in the last few gulps of air before she went down, then eased my way out of the cabin. I'd dearly have liked to come up just once for one more breath of air, but the risk was too great. Instead, I struck out hard along the channel, swimming down as well as along, getting deeper and deeper till my ears were bursting. I felt bottom and kicked my way hard along, then turned over on my back when I calculated that I'd reached the overhang where there'd be light. Could he see me here, I wondered?

My lungs were bursting now too, but there was still a long way to go and no hope of more air till I was clear out in open water, I swam hard and fast and deep. I heard a rush of sound as a shaft went spinning through the water four feet or more ahead of me.

He could see me, then; but the refraction of the water was worrying him. It's a simple enough equation if you've got any sort of an education at all; the sine of the angle of incidence above the water (or any other isotropic medium for that matter), bears the same ratio to the angle of distortion below as the speed of light in air does to the speed of light in water, and all you have to do is work it out. Simple. But I didn't really expect him to know much about the formulae for refractive indices, and to be fair, the water was turbulent anyway, which meant that the index was constantly changing.

So he was just guessing how far behind me he should aim, and being thrown completely out of kilter by a mathematical problem he knew nothing about. He wasn't even sure whether he should be aiming where I was going or where I'd been, and was trying to find out by trial and error, which is always a slow process.

I could almost sympathize with him. To a man of his proved expertise it must have been very frustrating to see those expensive broadheads so widely missing their mark.

Another shot went very wide. He was aiming ahead of me now, quite wrongly, with only a vague, refracted shape for his target, deep under ten feet of pounding waves. But the next was terrifyingly close when he realized his mistake and was lucky enough, perhaps, to shoot through a pool of momentarily-still water; it was no more than a few inches to my side. I went deeper and turned hard to the left till I bumped my head savagely into the rock wall. I could feel the turbulence of the sea now, with the water above me lighter in color, a blinding blue-white, and the waves dashing onto the rocks there. But I still did not dare to surface.

Another shaft went by me, and another, so fast on its heels that it was hard to believe they had both been loosed from the same bow. I wondered how many more he had left, and remembered the quiver I'd noticed the first time I'd seen him, in the *lagosteria*, a quiver with ten, twelve, maybe fifteen or more of his deadly red-tipped arrows. I tried to get deeper and couldn't; there was a steel bar bent around my legs, a steel bar that was cemented into the channel's bottom with a heavy rope tied to it and leading off to the right. I knew at once what it was.

I hauled hard on the rope and pulled myself into a narrow tunnel, so narrow that my shoulders were brushing on both sides, I thought: What happens if I take a deep breath now? The pain in my lungs was almost insupportable. The passage went on and on and on and on as I hauled fast on the rope; it was too tight a fit for swimming now, and the claustrophobic feeling added very considerably to my worries. But I knew the rope led to the *lagosteria*; it was the guideline for the baskets that would be hauled in there from the open sea.

And then, suddenly, the rope swerved upward over a cluster of big smooth boulders, and my head was up above water in cold, musty air, bumping against the heavy concrete upper floor of the lobster beds. There was a moment of panic when I wondered if someone had closed the trap again, but there it was to one side, wide open and inviting. I treaded water for a moment while I got my lungs filled up and working once more, and then swam slowly towards it and pulled myself up. I rolled over on my back and lay there, gasping for air and knowing that it was all over now, that there was air to breathe once more...

In the semi-darkness, a shadow stirred; and a sound disturbed the silence. Someone said, a hollow little voice: "Cain?"

I rolled over fast and was on my feet at once.

It was Astrid. She stood there, staring at me, her face white, her eyes startled. Close behind her, Estrilla was crouched as though she were ready for some sort of action, and I saw that her eyes were filled with tears.

I said: "For God's sake. How did you get here? And why?"

For a moment, nobody spoke. I said, a wave of sudden fear sweeping over me: "Where's Fenrek?"

Estrilla suddenly started to cry, quite uncontrollably, hiding her face in her hands, her shoulders shaking. She was no longer the calm and cool and competent young agent from Interpol; she was, instead, a broken, shattered woman for whom the end of the world has suddenly come, terribly and unexpectedly.

Astrid said, her voice low and soft and infinitely sad: "My uncle is dead. They shot him."

CHAPTER 12

Astrid was suddenly in my arms. I could feel the sobs she was trying to stifle. She said nothing. There was nothing to be said. The shot I had heard? I just held her to me for a while, her face buried in my chest.

I saw Estrilla sink to her knees on the hard floor, as though now that I was there with them there was no need for any support of her own anymore; it was as though the foundation had given way, completely, and the dam was about to burst. It was already bursting. Her grief seemed to well up inside her, almost bloating her as she sank down, quite helplessly. I wondered if Fenrek had loved her as much as she loved him...He was always extricating himself from some affair or other, getting close, too close, to an attractive woman and then pulling away from her, always too late.

I asked gently: "What happened? I heard a shot."

Astrid pulled away from me then, and dried her eyes. She looked at Estrilla and knew that it was up to her, to Astrid herself, to tell me. She took a deep breath and said, haltingly:

"He was coming down himself to find you. As soon...soon as it got light."

"Alone?"

"Alone except for the two of us, but that's really the same thing, isn't it? For all the good it did him. He wanted to take Estrilla in case...in case she could go for help when he found out whatever it was he hoped to find out. And I couldn't...couldn't stay there alone, and he understood that."

"No shells from the Navy, then?"

"No shells. He refused to have anything to do with it. He said...he said there must be another way, and we came down here to find one. Everyone had gone from the Alentejano, there were just the three of us there, and when it became light, he couldn't wait anymore. So we came down to the beach, taking a long way round. There was nothing we could see, of course, and...in a little while, he told us to stay among the rocks down there, below that abandoned shack, you know where I mean?"

"Yes, I know where you mean."

"He told us to hide there, not to move at all, while he looked for a way into the Bocca through the *lagosteria*. There are a lot of interconnecting tunnels, and he knew about them."

It was a small point, but I had to know. "How did he know about them? He doesn't know this coast as well as all that."

"No...Estrilla does, though. She'd told him about them and get through to you without being seen."

He would have had his head blown off the moment he'd gotten within a hundred yards of us, but I didn't tell her that.

I said quietly: "And then?"

"Then...he was crawling along a ledge above the cave. From where we were, we could see him quite clearly, and...and... and then...Estrilla was a little higher up than I was, and she said suddenly: *there's someone below him!* And I ran up the rock to look, and just at that moment my uncle turned around and fired his revolver, and this man below him fired too, at almost the same moment. If I hadn't seen the flash of his gun..."

"A shotgun?"

"I think so. A shotgun or a rifle, I wouldn't know really, not at that distance. But Uncle fell, and it was...Oh God, Cabot, it's a hundred feet down to the rocks below there. He fell, and..." She was crying again, very quietly, trying to hold herself in check and not succeeding. How can you hide such pain?

There was a long, low moan from Estrilla. She was out of it all, lost completely in the depths of her anguish. I knew it would be a long time before she'd recover; a girl from northern Portugal, where emotion is the strongest, the most vital of all the senses, a passion so crippling in its intensity that only death can put an end to it. Up in the north I've seen a *fado* singer break down on stage and have to be led away in hysterics, quite carried away by her own imaginings. Estrilla knelt there now, with her hands down at her sides, her eyes glazed, as though she weren't part of us anymore.

I went to her and lifted her to her feet I said: "You'll have to pull yourself together, Estrilla. You must!" She just stared at the ground as though she hadn't heard me. I sat her down on the heavy cover of the hatch; I wished I had some cognac, not only for her. But there was something else I had to know.

I said: "When he fell, did you see where he landed?"

Astrid shook her head. "No, it was too far down. We ran towards the place, both of us, and we found...we found the other man there, and he was dead. There was a bullet hole in his shoulder, just...just here." She touched her own shoulder, close by the neck. From where Fenrek had been, high above him, it was straight down and into the heart. Fenrek was the best snap shot I'd ever met.

I asked: "You searched? And found no sign of him at all?"

She shook her head again. "Nothing. Just rocks and deep water, and...and heavy waves breaking over them. But...he's down there somewhere, and he's...he's dead."

I said: "We can't be sure of that, can we? Not till we see for ourselves."

"I am sure." There was no sign of any hope there, just a statement of fact. She said: "We were trying to get down there, down the cliff, but there's no way down, and then...then we saw this other man at the bottom, close by the entrance to the big cavern. It was the man with the bow and arrow, and he was shooting into the water, like a bow fisherman. But I don't think he was fishing."

I said: "No, he wasn't. Van Reck his name is. Perhaps the most dangerous of all of them."

"So we came into the *lagosteria* to hide from him."

I said sharply: "Oh? Had he seen you?"

"No, I don't think so."

"Don't think so isn't good enough."

She hesitated. "No. He couldn't have seen us." She looked to the other girl for confirmation. "Could he? Could he have seen us, Estrilla?"

But Estrilla didn't hear her; she was out there somewhere in the distant past, living over the long days and nights again with a man she had loved, seeing his broken body now down there on the rocks.

Soon, the shock would leave her and the real pain would come, and that would be the danger time, when anything could happen.

But there was an elation creeping over me, entirely emotional and having nothing whatever to do with the logic of the intellect. Somehow, it was too hard to imagine Fenrek dying so easily. I was positive, as positive as I'd ever been about anything, that somehow or other, *somehow*, Fenrek was still alive. He just wasn't the kind of man to die, at all, ever, from any cause. He'd lived through assassins' bullets, and murderers' guns, and the knives of a dozen assorted hooligans and villains and if his time had come now, at last...Well, I wasn't ready to believe it. I thought it would be cruel to voice my hopes, but Astrid saw my face and said:

"Do you think...perhaps...you think he could survive a fall like that?"

I had to be very careful now. If we found him there, dead, the letdown would be too savage.

I said: "There is a chance, a chance in a hundred. He might easily have landed in deep water. The shot may have missed him after all. Perhaps he just lost balance when he turned to fire. We'll never know unless we go and see."

She was already halfway to the steps that led to the upper exit.

I said urgently: "Wait! Van Reck's out there somewhere, the man with the bow and arrow. And there's Estrilla."

I went over to Estrilla and pulled her to her feet. I held her by the shoulders and said, very distinctly: "He may not be dead, Estrilla, we've got to find out. He may be down there in the water waiting for us to come and help him."

For a moment, the life came back to her eyes; and then, just as quickly, it was gone. A moment of clarity, and then darkness again. She said dully: "*Nao, e morto,* he's dead, I know it." The eyes were glazing over again.

I shook her roughly. "And if he's not? If he's wounded and

waiting for your help? Are you going to let him wait out there till he is dead, is that all you can do?"

The light came back once more, flooding her face. The moment of hope went as soon as it had appeared, but it was enough. She shook herself free and said, her lips tight and angry: "We will go and see."

I held her still. "Do you have a gun, Estrilla?"

"Yes." She fumbled briefly, a vague sort of gesture, and then said: "No...no. In my purse, I left it over the rocks there. When we ran..."

"Well, that's useful."

Astrid said impatiently: "Come on then."

I told her to take it easy. There was a major question now. Should I leave the two of them here together, or not? What if Van Reck came in while I was out there searching for him? He could have guessed why I hadn't come up in the open water, where he would have been waiting for me, that deadly little bow ready. I looked at my watch; Loveless had been gone just over forty minutes, and he had expected to be back within the hour. I knew that it could easily be a great deal less.

I said to Astrid, urgently: "Did your uncle call off the men who were looking for Histermann?"

"Histermann?"

"The escaped prisoner, the man who is lying dead on the rocks there now. Did he call off the hunt as I asked him to?"

"Yes, he did. He called Lisbon to do that just after you left."

"Well, thank God for small mercies. If they tracked him down here...Van Reck's the kind of man who'd sit there calmly and pick them off one by one till he ran out of shafts, one by one and the hell with everybody."

It had always seemed to me to be the crucial aspect of this case, that we were dealing with men to whom the ordinary kind of risks meant nothing at all, to whom the most terrible gamble was nothing much more because they spent all their lives in an even bigger one. It was an aspect that had clearly shown itself on Loveless' face, in his eyes, in his manner of talking and in his behavior as well. When the odds are too great, most men will give up, even the best of them. But not these mercenaries.

For them, it was devil take the lot of us if that's the way it's got to be. It was a philosophy that was perhaps alien to Europe or the States; but not to Africa, to Africa in arms, where there can be an unbelievable savagery lurking in every unfriendly bush.

I said, to no one in particular and surprising even myself: "They cut out his tongue, Van Beck's, he can't talk." Trying to make some sense out of the comment, I added: "Another man who's got precious little to live for, and that's what makes them dangerous. Loveless and Van Reck, and we've got to find both of them, soon."

Estrilla was in command of herself again. Brooding and angry, and no longer as alive as I'd known her before, but still very much in command. She said: "First, we find my Colonel."

It was no good explaining that I couldn't leave them behind; they'd neither of them have stayed there, anyway.

I said: "All right, you follow me, in absolute silence, ten paces or so behind, and, so help me, if either of you makes a sound that even I can hear..."

Estrilla said clearly: "No." Her voice was very steady now. She said again: "No. I will go first."

It took me a moment to see what she was driving at, and while I was thinking about it, she said, just as deliberately, very proud and reserved: "My Colonel is dead, Mr. Cain. Now you will take your orders from me."

It wasn't worth explaining that I'd never been under Fenrek's orders; and what she had in mind made sense anyway. I said: "All right, so go down towards the beach from the concrete steps, but not all the way to the bottom. Take the ledge that you'll find about two thirds of the way down, it'll bring you out right below the mouth of the Bocca, among the oyster rocks there, you know where I mean?" If she insisted on playing the part of the cheese in the rattrap, I thought it only correct to make it as easy as possible for the rat to smell her out. She nodded.

"And you? Where will you be, Mr. Cain?"

"Above you, of course, every inch of the way. Don't ever look up, just take it for granted that I'm there. Keep your eyes open for the man with the bow, he's faster with that than you or I with a gun, make no mistake about it."

"And Astrid?"

"Right behind me. And, for God's sake, keep out of sight as much as you can, keep well under the lea of the cliff."

"I know what to do."

I said sharply: "No, you don't! The state you're in now, you're just going out to get yourself killed. That's not what we want, any of us!" More gently, I said: "If there's a complex of desperation, Estrilla, get rid of it, slough it off. Even if he is dead, we want the men who killed him. And for that, we need your help."

She stared at me, and I said, very, very quietly: "I don't believe that he is dead, Estrilla. I swear to you, I don't believe it. Try and take some of my hope, I have lots of it."

For a long, long time she held my look, trying to gauge the depth of my feelings, trying to find out how much of that hope was a lie. And then she suddenly put out her hand and touched me once, quite quickly, and she said: "I'll be careful, I promise you."

I was suddenly very impressed with Estrilla; I saw some of the qualities in her, perhaps for the first time, that must have attracted Fenrek to her. He liked good looking women, but his difficult and trying job had conditioned him into demanding something more than good looks, something more than intelligence too. I'd never known quite what it was he was always searching for and never quite finding; I thought now that it might perhaps be *ruthlessness,* a sort of inexorability to match his own.

I said: "Just let me take the first look." She nodded.

We went to the upper entrance together, conspirators in the semi-darkness, moving quietly with the huge empty cavern a kind of symbol of what we were leaving behind us. At the upper exit, I stayed close to the sandstone wall and looked out over the broad blue sea and the hot sands, brilliant now in the sunlight, watching for any sign of movement; there was nothing.

I examined the broken rocks down there where the waves were breaking; nothing there either. I tapped Estrilla on the shoulder and said quietly: "All right, go."

We waited a while, Astrid and I, while we watched her move easily and lithely along the wide path to the concrete steps. She went down them quickly, not hurrying, not yet trying to hide herself, because there was no place here to hide. And then, she moved off along the weed-covered track where the dense bushes were and we lost her. She was concealing herself carefully now, moving, I knew, bent double, swiftly, half running along the narrow track that was never used now because most of it had fallen down onto the barnacle-covered rocks far below.

I whispered to Astrid: "All right, keep behind me all the way. If I drop, drop too, fast, you understand? And I mean fast."

She nodded. As I began to move off, she put out a hand to stop me, and whispered, pleading: "You really believe that? That he might still be alive?"

I said: "I know it." Even to myself, I couldn't explain the certainty in my voice.

I began to slip down away from the steps, moving carelessly here where there was no cover. If anyone was watching, watching and waiting for me to get close, I wanted him to think we were on our way down to the beach too. And when we reached the bushes where Estrilla had disappeared, I whispered to Astrid: "It's harder now, we go up. Watch out for falling sand, it'll give us away." She nodded. I could hear her breathing, though her feet made very little sound on the soft sand.

I moved on a few paces, then reached up for the overhang of rock above us. I found a handhold there, a tangle of roots, and pulled myself up, then waited for Astrid to follow. We crawled on among the gorse bushes and the tall grass, moving steadily up, then down again, and up once more, edging along in parts, where the remnants of the track were less than two feet wide. Far below us, the sea was pounding, the white surf breaking and swirling and sending up its friendly, warning sounds to us.

In a little while, the goat track, which is about all it was, dropped away at a deep fissure in the rock. There was some wild anemone growing there, pale blue and pink in the morning sun. And the sheer side of the cliff fell straight down to the water. I felt Astrid's hands groping at my back, feeling for the comfort of a touch of another body, and when I looked back, she was staring down into the cleft with a look of horror on her face. It seemed that we had come as far as we could, that there was no room on the narrow shelf even to turn; we clung there like ants, suspended on the face of the cliff with no place to go.

Far, far below, the differing shades of color in the boulders that lay among the barnacles showed where the track had collapsed, leaving a twelve-foot gap and no way to cross it. But this was where we had to go.

Far below, I could see Estrilla moving steadily along. To go back now and leave her unprotected? Out of the question.

Across on the other side, the cliff seemed sheer too, till I searched it well and found a tiny outcrop, not much bigger than a doorknob, but granite-colored and therefore strong. Below it was a narrow horizontal fissure, quite small and deep, a transverse scar in the red sand wall. And above it, high above it and well out of reach, was a jutting piece of iron at the top of the cliff, a bent and rusted piece of angle-iron.

I looked back at Astrid and whispered: "Once we cross over, the worst is behind us." There was plenty of broken rock further on, on the other side of the fissure, broken rock and bushes to hide in, and great friendly clusters of golden boulders, all streaked with blue and purple and covered over with yellow creeping plants. I whispered: "Piggyback."

She stared at me, and I said: "Arms round my neck, legs round my waist, and close your eyes. And then, hang on tight for all you're worth."

She did not hesitate. She clambered up onto my back, locked her legs around me just as she had done that day in the lobster trap, and I smiled at her over my shoulder and said: "Trust me, it's not as bad as it looks. And for God's sake, don't open your eyes, you'll have kittens."

Her face was white, but she managed a half smile and a nod. I saw her screw her eyes up tight; I almost waited for her to start praying.

I put my feet together, slowly and carefully bent my knees and then...then I leaned forward. I toppled slowly over till Astrid's fragile weight was just so on my back, and the bottom of the gorge, whitewashed with the breaking waves, was directly below my eyes, and then I pushed hard with my legs and jumped, reached out with my arms, and grabbed with both hands at the granite protrusion. My fingers closed over it, and one foot and then the other found the niche below it, and we hung there for a moment, like a baboon on a cliff face with its young on its back. I thought: this is a hell of a time for Van Reck to spot us, suddenly.

I looked back and whispered: "We're over, you can open your eyes, but don't move a muscle."

She said: "I'll keep them...keep them closed if you don't mind."

"Good. Hold tight, we're going up."

I let go with one hand and groped for a better hold, but there just was none. I reached high above my head, as far as I could reach, wondering if I could find that hunk of iron, up there somewhere but out of my sight. Curving my hand over the top, I could just brush it with the very tip of my finger, but it was quite impossible to get a hold on it. I eased my body back and hung onto the lump of granite with one hand, my feet wedged tight in the fissure for security.

I said: "I always wanted to be a contortionist. Just hold on tight. Wherever you feel my hands groping, don't unwind yourself, it's a long way down to the bottom."

I slipped my free hand under her warm thigh and found the buckle to my belt, a good strong piece of two-inch cowhide, oil-tanned and supple. My fingers worked at it till the buckle was undone. I heard Astrid catch her breath, and I said: "Just about through." I pulled hard on the belt and felt it unwinding, and when it was away from my waist, I wrapped it tightly round my fist into a loop, reached up again, and slipped it over the bent piece of iron. I pulled hard on it and felt the belt wrapping itself tighter round my hand.

I said: "What do you weigh?"

She answered, whispering: "A hundred and ten pounds."

"And I'm two hundred and ten, give or take a dinner or two. That's a good belt, but whether it will support both of us together..." I've got figures at my disposal for almost everything, but the breaking point of a two-inch leather strap isn't one of them, because too much depends on the curing. I said: "Hold on tight round my neck with both arms, unwrap your legs, and feel for the fissure I'm standing in."

She said: "My God, what are you going to do?"

"Do as I tell you, for God's sake!"

I waited while she slowly, very slowly eased herself into position, her arms almost strangling me. I said: "Feet firmly in place?"

"Yes, I think so."

"Good. Now, hold onto this piece of granite. When I let go, slip your hand under mine and grab tight with it."

"All right."

"Ready?"

"Ready."

Her right hand was hovering. I let go, trying to keep my balance without a handhold momentarily, and grabbed fast again, over her hand and the rock, as soon as she'd taken a hold. I said: "Same deal, the other hand. And then, for just a few seconds, you're on your own. Ready?"

"Ready."

I let go and she grabbed hard, and I put all my weight on that belt and tested it for a moment. I could feel it stretching a trifle, which was all to the good; if it was going to snap, this was the moment.

I said: "Hold tight, I'm going past you. Just clutch on with both hands for all you're worth, it's not too difficult. And, whatever you do, don't look down."

"My eyes are shut tight."

"Good."

She said, her voice horrified: "Did you say...past me?"

"Yes, that's what I said. There's a bit of ironwork up there, all that's left of an old bridge across here, or a handrail or something. I'm hooked onto it now. Hold tight."

I swung up and over her, and heaved my body onto the broad green swathe above us. Before I even rolled over I had hold of her wrists with my left hand, and only just in time too. A hundred pounds or a thousand, she couldn't hold it, and she lost her grip; but I had her arms firmly and let her dangle there just for one minute to collect her wits. I said: "Don't worry, I've got you. Now."

I pulled hard and swung her bodily up, clear off the overhang, and plonked her down beside me. We lay side by side for a moment, panting, and she looked at me with something like amazement and said:

"I'd never have believed it possible. Any more of the same?"

I whispered: "I think not. It should be easy going now."

"Thank God."

We were on a broad plateau now, not much more than twenty or thirty feet below the top of the cliff. It was sheer and steep and quite unscalable above us, and I knew that from up there, there wasn't likely to be any danger. Below, the ground sloped quite gently for a few yards, and then dropped down abruptly for the remaining seventy or eighty feet to the sea.

I whispered: "I think not. It should be easy going bushes."

Together, we crawled on, feeling every inch of the way for loose rocks that could betray our presence.

Far down below there, below and to my left, I could see Estrilla. She was running swiftly along the sand in the lea of the cliff, climbing quickly over the jagged, broken rocks, splashing in and out of the surf and not stopping. And there was something wrong; she'd gone much further than I would have expected.

I whispered to Astrid: "Where, precisely, was the Colonel when he fell?"

She pointed: "That pinnacle there."

"Then she's passed the point where he would have landed."

Puzzled, Astrid watched for a moment. Then: "She has, too. Why?"

I said: "She's going for her gun. And that means she's seen something we haven't. She's seen Van Reck, and she's going for the purse she left in the rocks. Over there, wasn't it?" I pointed.

"Yes, there by the little hut."

"God damn her eyes, she's committing suicide."

"She's...she's *what?*"

I said: "Van Reck's out there searching for me, without a doubt. And, without a doubt, he's seen her purse lying among the rocks there with a gun in it. And it's equally certain that he'll know she'll come back for it, sooner or later. Come on!"

I jumped up and ran, and heard her following me, falling behind and trying to catch her breath. It wasn't far, no more than a hundred yards, to bring us directly above the broken-down shack, and I covered it over the rough ground in a little under ten seconds. I threw myself flat on my face with my head close to the edge and looked over. Estrilla was running more or less below me now, getting close to the high-piled rocks where the two girls had sheltered. I saw her climb quickly up over them and down, out of my sight, on the other side.

I had a dreadful foreboding. I felt for a moment the keen need for a gun, the need that drives a man who gets into as much trouble as I sometimes do to carry one with him always, and then do all the wrong things with it. It's one thing to be able to protect yourself without one, but it's something else again to stand helplessly by and see someone you like being murdered.

I groped around for the oldest weapon in history—for something to throw. My fingers closed on a stone, a smooth round stone the size of a grapefruit. It weighed about ten pounds, I judged, and though I'd have preferred something a little heavier, this was not the time to be meticulous. It was the kind of stone you can crack open with a sharp tap from a sledgehammer, to produce pretty pictures of the strata inside for kids. I moved over quietly a distance of twenty feet or so to see if I could relocate her; and I could. I saw her bend double and pick up something from among the rocks, a black silk purse with beads on it that caught the light brightly, just the kind of thing to give your position away if you wanted someone to take a shot at you.

I realized that she was up to exactly that; she'd seen him, then, seen him and ignored him, running on to make him wonder what she was up to, knowing that he didn't have to fire until she was almost out of range, if she ever went that far. She'd have been in the sights of his deadly little bow for...how far now? It didn't matter at all.

What mattered was that she'd seen him. She was shaking that damned purse about in the sunlight, letting the reflected light shine all over the place, just in case he couldn't see her clearly; she didn't know him as well as I did!

I moved again, just a few feet, out from under cover, signaling Astrid for absolute silence. I stood up slowly, my age-old weapon in my hand and ready, and I covered every inch of the view.

And there he was.

He was standing well away from the face of his particular piece of cliff, his back towards me, not more than fifty feet away and twenty feet or so below. That put him roughly the same distance from Estrilla; she was below him, and he was below me, both of them at a three-quarter angle to the watcher above. He was holding his bow loosely, watching her as she delved into her bag and came out with the gun. And I knew then that she was absolutely certain about precisely where he was.

It was all so unbelievably casual. At one moment, she was rummaging through her bag, a housewife who's lost the keys to the station wagon, waving it around in impatience. And then, suddenly, she dropped the bag, swung round, aimed the little gun high at the end of a straight arm, all very professional, with her feet firm and wide apart and her body slightly crouched; and she fired.

Or rather, she pulled the trigger; but nothing happened. I didn't expect it to.

Either he'd removed the shells already, or more probably (because of the delicate question of the difference in weight), had merely snapped off the firing pin. And now, as she stared in disbelief at the little gun, standing there in her professional stance, a sitting duck, I saw him raise the little bow quite slowly and pull back on the string. He didn't have to be so slow; he was fast and accurate, and she was only fifty feet away from him, a target so easy as to be practically unsporting.

But he wasn't thinking of the sport. He wanted her to turn and run, so that he could let her sweat it out for a while till she was sure that she was out of range. And then, then, then he'd use his expertise and revel in it. Out of range? How far did she think that might be? I'd seen how he used the Mongolian draw for maximum strength, a thumb-powered draw that's necessary with a bow so strong it can't be pulled back with the fingers. The unofficial record range for a handheld bow has been unbroken, even by modern methods and with modern equipment, ever since 1798, when the Sultan of Turkey sent a shaft for the incredible distance of nine hundred and seventy-two yards—a hundred yards more than the half-mile. And he used the Mongolian draw too.

I didn't suppose for one moment that Van Reck, with his three-foot steel bow, could come anywhere near that figure; the official record distance, handheld and bare bow, is still under six hundred yards. But that was of no importance. The only thing that mattered now was Estrilla.

She must have realized that her gun had been tampered with. She clicked the trigger again, twice, and then lowered it and just stood there, facing him, standing straight and solid and well in command of herself. I could see the angry, contemptuous look on her face. She knew I was there; but her look did not shift from him.

I saw Van Reck pull further back on the string. I saw him raise the bow the last few inches. But his sadism had betrayed him, he was too late. The moment Estrilla swung round and pointed that useless gun, I was up with my arm pulled back and already throwing that smooth round stone. I was once pretty good at putting the shot—or putting the stone, as it used to be called. Jimmy Fuchs, at Yale, gave me a few pointers in the old days, just before he gave the world a new record of fifty-eight feet, and that's a sixteen pound shot. I had only ten pounds or so to fool around with, and I didn't have to worry about form either. I just pulled back my arm and hurled it.

He heard me, Van Reck; he would, of course. But I hadn't taken the time to shift my weight, or bring in my right knee, or bend my left. I just threw. He'd already swung round and his right arm was going back, the thumb curled round the string in his Mongolian draw. But he was too late, or I'd started too early; the bow was barely in line when the heavy stone hit him like a cannonball in the middle of his chest. I'd aimed at the small of his back when he was facing the other way.

I heard a sort of yell somewhere, a sound that might have been the cry of a gull or perhaps, more likely, the shriek of the *Guincho* bird that's supposed to come along these shores once in a while; a strange, unearthly croak that could have been anything under the sun except a man calling cut. But there was no time to find out what it was, or even to let it do more than impinge itself upon the awareness. I was too busy watching Van Reck. The little bow flew out of his hands; and the shaft, at half pressure, made a graceful carve in the air and landed at my feet.

But Van Reck himself...He doubled up and seemed to fly back, leaving the ground completely with all his limbs spread-eagled, and a terrible sound came out of that speechless mouth, half scream and half roar. He sailed through the air a few feet and fell, and his own momentum carried him down the steep slope, rolling over and over towards the water. I saw the leather quiver that was across his shoulder break open, and his shafts were scattering in all directions as he rolled over and among them. He slid a little, and rolled again, and dropping down the last ten feet or so with a crash onto the rocks, where the water lapped at him hungrily.

Estrilla was already running towards him, the useless gun still in her hand, I didn't wait for Astrid and I was there first, ready for him because this, like Fenrek, was the kind of man who never really died. Like a shark that's been so long out of the water that it's dead; unless you take a belaying pin to those razor toothed jaws first, you'd better not put your foot anywhere near them unless you want to lose it. I half expected him to rise up out of the water and go for me, with a knife in his hand, perhaps, or the strangling wire that is the favorite nighttime weapon.

But he didn't.

I imagined that his neck might easily have been broken, but that didn't matter very much, really. One of his own steel-pointed shafts was under the armpit, just the point of it entering the flesh at a very acute angle and passing out again the other side, like a skewer in a fold of white chicken meat, twisting the white flesh round and tearing it a little as well.

The red on its tip was a mixture of blood and strychnine. They make the poison out there by boiling the roots of the *strychnos* tree and straining the pulp through a crab shell. When it is good and thick and ripe and red, it's ready.

It takes something like five seconds to kill.

And then, from somewhere behind us, Fenrek said:

"What a nasty business."

CHAPTER 13

We stood there for a moment, staring at him like idiots.

He rose up out of the rocks and the breaking surf, Fenrek, half lying, half rising, and half falling over himself. There was a great red gash on his forehead, and he was still wearing his nice silk suit but without the shirt. He stumbled and fell flat on his face in the sand, and as I ran forward I saw what had happened to his shirt; it was all torn up and bound around his leg, binding a piece of sea-weathered cedar to one side and a round stick of what looked like Eucalyptus to the other. If it was meant to be a splint, it was a pretty lousy job. I ran to him fast.

But Estrilla was there before me. She flung herself down on top of him on the wet sand, her arms tight around his neck, half strangling him. Astrid came running up, crying now, and between the two of them they helped him to his feet as I stood there and watched. Estrilla was in a mild state of hysteria, and Fenrek put his arms round her and said:

"My darling...it's all right, it's all right..."

She couldn't speak. She was climbing all over him, the hell with a broken leg that had got itself all twisted out of shape again in those comic splints. He seemed surprised at her hysterics, and he said, gently reproving: "You should have known, I don't die quite so easily."

He took her face between his hands—a broken wrist there, too, by the looks of it—and kissed her gently on the mouth, balancing himself on Astrid, trying to sort out one frantic female head from another and not succeeding very well; they were both all over him. He kissed her again, and caught my eye over her shoulder and said gruffly:

"Well, you might at least have the decency to look the other way."

I said: "Not on your life." It's not often you get the chance to see a strong man in a moment of weakness. It was a weakness highly colored by an astonishment that was in itself astonishing; for God's sake, didn't he know how much she loved him?

I said: "So that was you, yelling back there. Pity. I thought for a moment it might have been a *guincho*. I've never seen one, and I was quite looking forward to the experience. Now lie down, if you can tear yourself away from the distaff for a moment, and I'll have a crack at fixing that leg a little more tidily."

Estrilla said quickly: "I'll do it." She wiped a hand at her tears, and laughed, and started crying again and hardly knew which side was up. I was astonished at the sudden change in her. But she pushed me aside, and I sat down with Astrid on the sand and watched her.

Fenrek lay down obediently, and she unwrapped all those pieces of torn shirt, and pulled aside the two crude pieces of wood, and I said:

"You'll never do it alone. He's a weak old man, but there might be a muscle or two left in his thighs. You'd better let me help you."

She said: "No, I can manage."

I looked at Astrid, smiling now so widely that I wondered if she too were going to break out all over in hysterics.

Estrilla put her foot in his crotch, took hold of the ankle with both hands, looked at him in a loving sort of way that can only be described as sickening, and said: "This is going to hurt you very much, would you like some cognac?"

Surprised, he said: "Well, of course I would. Do you have any?"

She shook her head miserably. "No, I don't..." She pulled hard then, and twisted, quite expertly; I heard the broken bone crunch into place. Fenrek gasped and said: "Oh, you...you... bitch" But he took a deep breath and said: "All right, all right, that was fine." He shook his head from side to side, his face very white, and then he shuddered and looked at me and tried to grin. He lay back on the sand and stared up at the sky while Estrilla put those foolish bits of wood back into place again. He said, to no one in particular: "There must be a longer piece of wood lying around here somewhere. A walking stick, a crutch...I found one, but it got away from me in the surf."

I marveled at the strength he must have shown back there, with a broken leg and a busted wrist—the most painful of the breaks—fixing himself up laboriously with torn rag and bits of driftwood. I moved over and took a look at the wrist, a compound fracture with a piece of bone sticking through the flesh, and when Estrilla tried to shove me away again, I said: "That's not going to be quite so easy." But between us we got some rag wrapped around it. Not that that was going to help very much.

And while we were working on it, he said: "Is it too much to hope that Loveless is still in there somewhere?"

"Much too much. Loveless is on his way back from Guincho. He went there to send that telegram, remember? And damn his eyes, he took the Jensen. I only hope he doesn't bash it into a tree."

He surprised me: "The Jensen's still at the top of the Bocea. You can see it from back there."

"Oh? Well, that's a stroke of luck."

It wasn't really. I realized that Loveless was not going to risk driving a car that just might be well-known enough to invite comment. If, as he suspected, the police were out looking for him along the coastal road, one of them might just have decided to pass the time of day with the driver.

I said; "So he's walking there, it'll take him a long time. But then, we always realized that he would have plenty of time, didn't we? Till the dark of the night."

Fenrek said: "Does he have the toxin with him?"

I fished into my pocket and brought out the little box for him to see. Through all that pain, his eyes were shining. "Good. So it's just a question of finding one man." He jerked his head at the shining steel of the container. "How do we destroy that?"

"With heat. What happens when Loveless turns up at Guincho?"

"They don't touch him, in case he was carrying that toxin'

with him. And the big question—is there any more of it?"

I said: "No more."

"Are you sure?"

"Absolutely."

"Good. So now it's up to us."

I said mildly: "It always was."

"The men at Guincho have orders to take no risks, to keep him under surveillance and let us know where he is."

I said: "Some silly bastard is going to take a crack at him, you'll see. He'll make a dive for a gun, and that someone will fire, and he'll be just too late. Because Loveless will have shot him dead before he can even think of pulling the trigger."

Fenrek shook his head. "No. We told them that he might be carrying that botulin on him, in his pockets. If it had been in a simple glass vial, a shot could have busted it open and given us a real lively epidemic. So there'll be no shooting."

"That doesn't go for him."

He said gently, looking at the heights of the sandstone cliff: "The chances are that he is up there now, watching us. What's his weapon?"

"Sawed-off shotgun. A Lames over-under, 12-bore and cut down to a fourteen-inch barrel. Dangerous toy at close quarters, but not much good from up there."

Estrilla was fitting an improvised sling for Fenrek's wrist.

He said: "Get rid of that toxin. Now. I want to know it's gone."

"All right."

While they were helping him to a shelter under the lea of the cliff, close in among the rocks where Estrilla had been, out of the wind and the sun, I clambered up to the little shack, or what was left of it, and ripped off a piece of dry cedar and walked back to the rocks with it, shaving it with my pocketknife into tiny slivers, some not so tiny, and then a few sticks of kindling. I set fire to them with my lighter, in a small hollow of rock, fanned them till they were beginning to blaze, then went back for some heavier pieces, which I wrenched out from the foundations, and lugged them back down there.

In fifteen minutes, the hot embers were glowing nicely, turned by a funneled breeze into a blowtorch. I unwound the wire from the little steel box, and said: "Now everybody keeps well away." I tipped the four glass vials carefully into the middle of the fire, found a long stick and heaped live embers over them, and then got the hell out of there fast. I didn't know whether they'd pop or not, and if they did, I didn't want to be too close.

But they didn't. I took another look in five minutes. The glass had melted already, and I realized that the smart boys who had made these deadly weapons up had taken just that precaution. A fire in the Research Center, otherwise, might have blown loose oddments of toxin all over the landscape. The melted glass had taken on a strange green tinge, and I realized that it had been impregnated with something to absorb enough heat to ensure a rapid melting. Of the powder itself, there was nothing visible at all.

Heat in excess of eight hundred degrees Fahrenheit is about the only thing that will destroy botulinum spores, but to be doubly sure I piled more and more embers up, and threw on more wood; and watching me, Fenrek said (mind reading again!):

"What kind of heat is the minimum?"

I told him: "Eight hundred Fahrenheit, which works out at four hundred and twenty-seven or so in Centigrade,"

Astrid was still worried. She said: "And a driftwood fire is hot enough?"

"Wood burns at twenty-seven hundred and thirty-two degrees, Fahrenheit. Or would you rather have it in Centigrade?"

Estrilla said promptly: "That's exactly fifteen hundred, we're not all stupid, you know."

I was glad to see the enormous change that had come over her. She was bubbling around like a frenzied schoolgirl, fussing over Fenrek and then sitting down, then getting up quickly to fuss some more.

I said: "And the only problem now is where to leave you all while I go and find Loveless. The Alentejano? Are they open for breakfast?"

Fenrek was already struggling to his feet, not without difficulty. Estrilla had found him a long stave, grey-washed by the sea, crooked as a shillelagh, and she was helping him up too, not arguing with his implied authority; the number-two man, just moving out of position as the widowed mistress and getting back into shape again.

Astrid looked at him, worried, and said dubiously: "Well...Estrilla and I can help Cabot, of course, but I really think you ought to...I don't know, to rest up, Uncle? Please?"

He snorted. He said calmly: "No. It's time someone played this game who knows what the score is. I'm taking over now."

Estrilla was delighted; but I thought that was rather unfair of him.

I wanted to carry him up to the top of the cliff where the Jensen was, but he preferred to lean on the two girls, his arm at Estrilla's plump little waist and gloating over it, with Astrid holding uselessly onto the elbow above his broken wrist and the shillelagh under his armpit. He hobbled along happily; and I kept my eyes open for the Major. There was still time for us to come out of all this badly, so I climbed on ahead of them, searching each bush and cluster of boulders very carefully indeed.

I didn't for one moment imagine that he would be there. Fenrek was quite wrong when he suggested that Loveless might even be watching us; it was too much out of character for that sad and reckless man.

Sad and reckless...it was a strange combination, and perhaps the key to his character. Somehow, I was half sure that I knew what Loveless would do now, though I couldn't guess how he would do it; or more importantly, when. I couldn't get out of my mind the memory of that appalling loneliness, a loneliness that perhaps he wasn't fully aware of. Was that the force that had driven him, in the first place, into his profession? How does a man survive when he's at odds with the whole world, even with God himself?

We found the Jensen where I'd left it, and I took the spare key from its hiding place under the dash, and checked the car over carefully first. I didn't suppose anyone had tampered with it, because if Loveless had truly believed that he and I were leaving the country together as soon as the diminishing wind and the darkness of the night allowed us to get the whaler out of its underground pool, then obviously the car would have been just abandoned; and what a terrible thought that was! Or if he'd decided it wouldn't be worth the risk of trusting me, then just as obviously I'd never have use for a car again, I would be lying there dead in a lost lake that had been closed off from public view and was likely to stay that way for eternity.

So I was surprised when I saw the tops of the spark plugs; a thin line had been drawn down them with an ordinary graphite pencil. Nothing serious, just enough to stop the motor from firing. It was a foolish, naïve little trick that wasn't ever going to pay off one way or the other; but somehow, it pleased me. In one respect at least, I'd missed one tiny little value in the man's makeup; I'd never suspected that he had a sense of humor, however fragmentary.

I wiped off the graphite and started the car. We pulled back the passenger's seat to its utmost, to give Fenrek room for his leg, and we put Astrid and Estrilla in the back. I found the flask of cognac still locked in the console at the back of the squab and handed it silently to Fenrek. He shook his head and said: "I need all my wits about me now."

"Since when does one drink deprive you of them? Go on, take a swig, it'll take some of that pain away."

He'd shown no sign of any pain at all, but that leg...and that shattered wrist? They must have been giving him hell. He was about to insist in his refusal, but I said, needling him: "You're not impressing anybody. Drink it, a good long one."

Grumpily, he glared at me. He looked back over his shoulder at Estrilla, saw that she was beaming at him, sighed, and drank.

We drove off, very slowly, across the broken ground, grass-tufted and sweet smelling. And a few minutes later we were on the highway, heading for Guincho. Slowly, very slowly.

I said to Estrilla: "Where's that horrible little bug of yours?"

"That excellent little car of mine is parked on the highway two miles east of the Bocca. Do we need it?"

"No. I just wondered."

I glanced sideways at Fenrek as we went over a pothole in the road. He didn't even wince, The Jensen's a well sprung car, perhaps the only European car that rides as softly as its Detroit counterpart; but the softness of the ride is illusory, the bumps are there even if you don't feel them much, they have to be if the car is going to be safe at the kind of speed Jensens are usually driven at. It felt strange, crawling along now and watching for potholes; not a thing I usually pay much attention to.

We found the first of the police six miles up on the coastal road, just beyond the lighthouse. A barrier had been set up there, a barrier of red-and-white striped wooden bars with a coil of barbed wire beyond it, just lying across the road and ready to do a lot of damage to anyone who thought he could drive his way through all that lumber. An earnest young policeman flagged us down, took one look at Fenrek, at the deep red gash in his forehead and the white, strained look to his face, and said quickly:

"There is an ambulance, *Senhores*, in the lighthouse yard, I will get it..."

He began to move off, but Fenrek said: "No, hold it. You know who I am?"

"*Sim, Senhor Colonelle*, yes indeed."

"Good. What's the disposition now?"

The policeman pointed: "Another barrier, like this one, twelve kilometers east of here on the main road. One on the inland road directly north of us, that's two and a half kilometers, with another one eight kilometers east of that."

"There's a track through the pine trees behind us. Where does that lead?"

"Nowhere, *Senhor Colonello*. A builders track, they are constructing a house there. If there is anyone moving east or west or north of the Bocca, they must use one of the two roads, unless they are all on foot."

"One man now, only one left. The man Loveless. Tell the ambulance men there are two dead bodies on the beach, they'd better be removed."

I said: "One of them was an archer, so if anyone gets interested in his arrows—they're tipped with strychnine, make sure they're handled carefully."

He was puzzled. "An archer, *Senhor?*"

"A toxophilist, a bowman, an *arqueiro*. The heads on his shafts are razor sharp, and all it needs is a scratch, so watch out."

Fenrek said: "The command post, has it been moved?"

"No, sir, still there in the forest."

"Good." He turned to me and said: "This is where it's going to hurt, turn right into the woods."

"If it's not too far you'd be better off walking."

He said patiently: "Why do you always want to argue, Cain? Turn right into the woods here. If this car of yours can take it, so can I."

I pulled the wheel over and crawled at zero miles an hour over the broken pine strewn floor of the forest, squeezing between the trees, looking for smoother surfaces and finding none. In a few minutes we saw the tent they'd put up, a green canvas tent with long black telephone cables snaking off in all directions. A small fire was burning there, with a pot of coffee on it; it looked like a picnic. But Lieutenant Loureiro was there, running out to meet us.

He stared at Fenrek, but before he could speak, Fenrek said: "Later, Lieutenant, we've got work to do. Any report from the men at Guincho?"

"*Nada feito*, nothing doing there yet, *Senhor Colonello*."

"Cascais? Estoril?"

"Nothing, *Senhor Colonello*."

Fenrek looked at me. "He's gone to Lisbon after all. If that damned nonsense about a telegram wasn't just a bit of bull." Fenrek speaks with a markedly Hungarian accent, and the idioms always sound strange. He saw me smile, and said: "He may have been bluffing."

"No. We decided that's what he'd do, and then I heard him tell Histermann he was going into Guincho, At that time, he'd decided one of two things. Either he could trust me, in which case there was no need to hide his intentions; or that I was going to be killed off, in which case it didn't matter much if I knew what he was doing. No, he's gone to Guincho, and even on foot he must have been there by now. What is it they're looking for out there?"

He looked surprised. "Why, for Loveless, of course! Three good men who have an excellent description of him."

I said, turning to Estrilla, who knew this part of the world so very much better than any of us: "In a place the size of Guincho they'll have, what, half a dozen customers a day at the post office?"

"There are three hotels out there, it might be a little more. But not many."

I said to Fenrek: "And with three men watching the place, he's spotted them. One would have been better."

"Not if he chooses to fight."

"You've got a point there" I swung open the car door and got cut. "Let's make some phone calls."

The Lieutenant, very anxiously, helped Fenrek out, put a solicitous arm round his waist, and eased him to a canvas chair in front of the tent. The smell of coffee was ripe and tempting, and I said to Loureiro:

"Now's the time to take you up on that offer of yours again."

It was very pleasant and restful under the tall green trees. A folding table had been set up with a police sergeant handling the radio there, and seven or eight policemen were standing around, waiting for something to happen. One of them wiped the sandy dust off some coffee mugs for us, and Loureiro, beaming, poured while I found one of the telephones and asked for the post office at Guincho. I asked to speak to the Superintendent, and when she came on the line I passed the receiver to Loureiro and said:

"Just make it official, will you?"

He nodded: He said into the phone: "Police business," *Senhora*, Lieutenant Loureiro, Alfama Police, code thirty-seven, Speak here please."

He gave me back the phone, and I said: "In the last two hours, *Senhora*, has a telegram been sent overseas from there?"

She sounded rather crabby, but a code thirty-seven is not to be argued with. She said: "One moment, Excellency." I could hear the papers rustling at the other end. She said in a moment: "One, Excellency, to Larache, in Morocco, that's somewhere near Tangier, I believe."

"Yes, I know where Larache is. Who sent it?"

"One moment, Excellency." I waited a while and she came back and said: "A young man named Miguel Sampaio, Excellency, a page at the Hotel Quinta."

"And he was posting letters, letters from the hotel guests, at the time?"

"*Sim, Excellencia.*"

"Good. Would you read it to me please?"

I heard her clear her throat: "Addressee, Hans Dedijer; Poste Restante, Larache, Morocco. Message reads: *Delayed twenty hours same place one repeat one extra passenger.* Signed, Commander."

"Thank you, *Senhora*. Just tell me what time that was.

"Eight fourteen, Excellency."

"Thank you."

I rang off and repeated the message to Fenrek. I said: "So he was going to take me along after all. That's interesting, isn't it? Interesting—and rather gratifying."

Fenrek said: "Stop preening yourself, Cain, and tell me what that's meant to mean."

I said: "We were almost going into partnership."

Fenrek said expressively: "Huh?"

"One day I'll tell you how I nearly became a mercenary, specializing in mass slaughter by botulin toxin. He must have decided it was safer, on principle, to hand his message and a tip to a pageboy from the hotel."

Fenrek said grimly: "Or, as you say, he saw them watching the place. I'll have their guts for garters."

"No. If he'd seen them, he'd have known he was being carefully trapped. And that extra passenger would have been lying dead in the bottom of the lake, a hundred feet underground and unmourned. The only question is...where is he now?"

"All right, where is he?" Fenrek always suspected that I knew the answer whenever I asked a question.

I said: "He walked up over the dunes into Guincho, and once he knew that was safe he'd presumably take the same way back. So he's probably seen Histermann lying dead there just by the entrance. He may even have seen Van Reck. Or just possibly...No. Where the devil is he, Fenrek? He can't take all that time, not from eight-fourteen to now, to get back to the Bocca. Unless he's decided..."

I broke off when the phone rang. Loureiro reached for it and listened. His face was grave. He put down the phone at last and said: "I'm afraid..." He hesitated, and Fenrek said harshly: "What is it, Loureiro?"

Loureiro said: "It's Loveless, *Senhor Colonello*. That was the post at Cabo Raso. It seems...it seems that one of the men from

Guincho, Patrolman Arisco, walked along the road to the cafe there, to get sandwiches, leaving the two others to watch the post office, you understand? It seems that...he found Loveless sitting in the cafe with a glass of beer."

So that's where he'd gone. Pretty simple, really. Too simple to have occurred to anyone. A man not even on the run, just aware that the police were out looking for him, and with plenty of time on his hands and some thinking to do, some thinking that he'd want to do in the habitual loneliness that was so much a part of his character.

Loureiro said: "He recognized him, of course, from the description, and tried to arrest him."

Fenrek said: "Tried to arrest him? One man?"

"And Loveless shot him. It seems he pulled a kind of shotgun from under his coat, and shot him in the stomach. He ran out, and...and disappeared."

I said: "But presumably Arisco is not dead?"

"*Nao, Senhor*. The cafe proprietor called the police, and they were there in a few minutes. Arisco is badly hurt, but..." I sensed from his tone that he wanted to apologize for his patrolman, but he didn't.

The phone rang again, and as Loureiro went to it, I said: "So now he's on the run with a vengeance."

He had always known, of course, that he was being hunted. But up to now he must have known that the search was centered on Lisbon itself, with its epicenter at the Rua Vicente house. How far around that would we be working? Perhaps within the circle contained by Sacavem, Odivelas, Amadora and Alges, with a subsidiary area around the Bocca itself, where the initial action had been and where he might be presumed to be continuing his activities. But round the peninsula at Cabo Raso and as far to the west as Guincho? Almost certainly not. So, when poor Arisco hopefully tried to arrest him, he must have realized at once that all the events of the past few hours had been nothing more than a careful, well-planned scheme to trap him.

And so? Where would he go now?

I was just deciding that he'd be at his safest heading for Lisbon, to lose himself in the crowds there while he started to plan again from scratch, when Loureiro put down the phone and said:

"A car stolen, *Senhor Colonello*, at Charneca. That's just

outside the barricaded area, about four kilometers outside, up on the mountain."

Estrilla was frowning. "Charneca? That's high up on the *sierra*, why would he want to go there?"

I told her it was nothing but the instinct of the hunted animal. I said: "More important, what kind of car has he got?"

Loureiro said: "An American car, Senhor, a Buick that belongs to Senhor Remedio who owns the flower gardens up there. This year's model, a Riviera, grey, and the license is 428-17. He already had a map spread out on the table. Fenrek hobbled over and stared at it with me. The Lieutenant stabbed at it with his finger and said: "Here, Charneca. But which way he will go...?"

I said: "To Lisbon, without a doubt."

He accepted that. He said at once: "Then this road here, through Cascais, or all the way round, by Sintra."

I said: "Sintra? Not a hope in hell."

Fenrek looked at me. "Why not?"

"Too much narrow road there. Too many places where he can't turn round in a hurry if he has to. Right, Estrilla?"

Estrilla nodded. "If one of the mountain villages there is blocked, he'd have no room to turn, certainly. Some of the streets there are as narrow as they are in the Alfama, just room for a car to squeeze through. Maybe only a small car, even."

And then, just five hundred yards away on the road, we saw the car.

We didn't even hear it, the wind was in the wrong direction, or the rustle of the pines around us deadened it, or perhaps...that's a pretty quiet mill in the Buick anyway.

But we heard the crash. The Riviera went through the red-and-white barricade as though it was made of paper. We saw a policeman leap aside, saw and heard him fire his rifle into the air as a warning to all of us. We saw the great coil of barbed wire wrapping itself round the car and not stopping it in the least. And then, it was gone.

Loureiro was already on the phone, joggling the connection in his impatience and finally yelling: "He's on his way to you in a big American car. Put a truck across the road, quickly, he smashed through our barricade. He'll be there in a few moments."

I said "Keep the line open, Lieutenant. We may as well know when he goes through that one, too."

Twelve kilometers, the man on the barrier had said, "the next barrier kilometers down the road. Seven and a half miles, or say five minutes in a Riviera being pushed. A winding road, but to Loveless that wouldn't matter too much; he would have his foot on the floor and he would keep it there, and the hell with everything and everybody."

I said to Fenrek: "We'll take the Jensen, and this time you stay here."

"This time, I come with you."

"The girls stay behind then."

Estrilla said: "You don't really believe that, do you, Mr. Cain?"

And Astrid said, with a fine disregard for grammar: "Me too."

All I needed was passengers on a hundred-mile-an-hour chase through the streets of Lisbon. Well, you've got to be philosophical about these things. At least, it would help to keep the rear end of the car from taking fight.

We had a few minutes. If he had the sense to turn off instead of trying to get through the second barricade, he could still have made it through be the woods. He wouldn't have gone very far in a Buick without bogging down in soft sand, with no four-wheel drive to help him out of it. But if he stopped to think about it, he'd realize that this was the best thing he could do, get off the road and out of his car so that he'd be closer to what was his own element: the land.

The Lieutenant, phone in hand, was watching as we piled back into the Jensen. I began to say: "We're waiting," when he listened at the earpiece, put down the phone, threw up his hands, and said: "He went through the second barrier too, round the truck. He smashed the barricade."

I yelled: "Tell them to keep it open for us," and touched the starter button.

We knew where he was now, and where he was heading. I gritted my teeth in sympathy for Fenrek as we bounced at forty over the forest's floor, (and not a sound out of him either), and then made a hard left on the smooth highway. I put my foot down and heard the motor start to hum; it never does more than hum.

I drove the first few miles at ninety, till I saw the little bug up on the road ahead of us. I slipped down a gear and shouted to Fenrek: "Brace yourself, were braking hard," and slammed my foot on the Maxarets. She pulled quickly, smoothly, to an incredible halt in fifty feet. I yelled at Estrilla: "Take the side roads."

She was out before I'd finished speaking, and as we leaped forward again I saw that Astrid had fallen out with her and was just getting to her feet and climbing into the bug.

And when we shot by what was left of that second barricade, we were just topping a hundred and thirty miles an hour.

It was exhilarating.

CHAPTER 14

It was, I suppose, a conscious effort to get the girls out of the way, out of the way of the danger that was surely going to wrap itself around us the moment we found that Buick. He had a four minutes start, he was four minutes ahead of us, and that could have been anything up to seven or even eight miles, the way he was likely to drive.

There was no question of the competence of the two cars; mine was immeasurably superior. It's never a question of how fast a car will go—it's more a matter of how well and how long it will sit on the road at maximum speed. In the Jensen I could blow a front tire and still keep a fairly straight line till I stopped; but a Buick?

And the question of driving skill mitigated against me rather than for me. That's a matter of talent and care, and if one man's got less care than the other he can still outrace him, even with a lesser talent; he might break his neck in the process, but he'll get there first.

And now, it was largely a matter of understanding the man we were chasing. If you're on the run in a very fast car, the only way you can make use of your power—and a sad lack of maneuverability—is to bash on regardless, keep going as straight as you can. So he'd take the main highway, the one with the good surface, and bulldoze his way through anything they could get in the time to stop him, rather than attempt the hazards of the winding, narrower back roads, where a sharp bond or a patch of gravel could hurl him headlong into the ditch.

I heard the wail of sirens, and two motorcycle cops were ahead of us, speeding down the highway flat out; they didn't stay ahead of us for long. I passed them easily, wondering where they'd come from and where they thought they were heading. We took the back road through Estoril, well north of the town, hit the highway again beyond Parede, and then began to run into traffic.

It was a question of knowing, or guessing, where he was headed, a question of deciding where a man like Loveless—and I knew him well now—would go to hide himself. To one of the smaller villages, where a stranger would excite immediate comment? Of course not. To Lisbon itself, where he might succeed in getting lost in the crowds? Perhaps. But for how long? I had certain ideas on the subject; for Loveless, it was all a question of ifs and buts now, and I thought I knew every one of them. The mind of a complex man is sometimes more simple than it would appear to be, once you learn which way those twisted passions are heading.

We passed a police car that had crashed at a tight bend, and was sitting there in the ditch with its engine boiling over; the two men standing by it waved us on and pointed ahead. I slammed on the Maxarets again, sacrificing a moment of time for knowledge, and yelled: "How long ago?" I was already moving on again fast when I heard one of them shout back: "Two minutes, Senhor..." The rest of the shout was lost on the wind.

And now, as we drew close to the town, there were police cars and motorcycles all around us, cutting in from the side streets, swinging on two wheels round sharp bends, all heading fast in the same general direction. Fenrek muttered: "For God's sake, we should trade cars, get a police car with a radio in it." It wasn't a bad idea. But better the tool you know than the tool you don't know.

We tore through the heavy traffic of Alges at an alarming speed; and now, we were on the main and busy streets and there was no sense in trying to break our necks any longer. I dropped down to eighty, and a police car pulled alongside us, neck and neck on the wrong side of the road, its sirens blasting, and the officer in the passenger's seat yelled: "Pedroucos, Rua de Pedroucos...He was seen there..." I put my foot down again and cut across his bows, hearing the sudden shriek of his skid behind me as he let me through, and headed up the wide, lovely Avenue of Belem's Tower. I said to Fenrek: "So back there at Praca Manuel, we must have been almost on top of him. That means we've caught up; that means he's out of his element in that car."

"His element?"

"The bush, where else?" He let it go.

The police car we'd almost ditched was tight on my tail now, keeping up with us sensibly. I swing past an alarmed donkey cart and stood on the brakes as a little car shot out of Tristan da Cunha Street ahead of me. It was Estrilla in her bug; she hadn't done badly either to keep up with us.

Fenrek yelled at me: "You've passed Pedroucos."

I said: "I know that. Take a guess at where he's heading."

Fenrek said promptly: "The Alfama, the place he seems to know best. He's probably got a hideout there somewhere."

I said: "No. A bushman on the run is going to head for the bush, and in Lisbon that means only one place."

"Monsanto?"

"Monsanto."

They call it a park, the "Parque Florestal" or forest park. They like to think of it as Lisbon's source of oxygen, and it is perhaps one of the reasons why Lisbon, even densely packed with cars as it is today, has no problem with smog. It's twelve or fifteen square miles of forest, right in the middle of the city, spread out over more of those steep hills, some of them seven hundred feet high, some of them so densely packed with trees and vines that it resembles a jungle. There are sandy roads through them, and half a dozen broad, asphalted highways too; but only a hundred yards from any of those roads, a man can lose himself as surely as he can in the middle of the densest African bush. It's only five miles from north to south, but in those five miles there are hills and valleys, mountains and gorges—and a lonely, primeval silence.

And then, for the second and penultimate time, we saw the Buick; and it was heading straight for us. I'd already swung round on Avenida Restelo, and I saw him less than a hundred yards ahead, coming our way. Restelo is a wide, wide street, and there was little traffic on it, and there was plenty of room to pass. But I knew what he was going to do even before he began to swing the wheel over to ram us.

We were both going more than seventy, maybe eighty miles an hour, and a head on collision at that speed would have been the end of everything for all of us.

I pulled over hard to the left, to full lock, slammed on the brakes again, and missed him by half an inch. There was still barbed wire trailing from under his wheels, locked around the axle no doubt, and it wrapped itself round the edge of my rear bumper, the bumper that had shaved past him, and snapped with the sound of a broken violin string. I heard him hit the police car, a glancing blow that sent the Buick spinning out of control across the road, facing the wrong way, righting itself, side-swiping the wall of a house, and then careening on again. The police car was knocked clear across the road to crash into a lamppost there and wrap itself untidily around it. There were flames coming up from under the hood.

I left the Jensen where it had landed, and yelled to Fenrek: "Stay there!"

It took me ten seconds to get the door of the police car wrenched open and to drag out the officer and his driver. And only just in time. It exploded before I'd got them halfway across the road, dragging both of them by their collars, and the force of the explosion knocked me off my feet and sent me slamming into the adjacent stone wall of a fine old house, highly decorated in the style they call there Manueline, after the gaudy, rococo taste of Portugal's King Emmanuel the First, whose only claim to fame is that he was responsible for the peculiarly flamboyant Gothic style that has become synonymous with Portuguese architecture and decoration, surcharged as it is (those were the great seafaring days of Vasco da Gama and Alfonso de Albuquerque) with marine and nautical designs.

It was a most painful collision. That beautiful wall seemed to lift itself up and hurl itself at me, knocking the wind out of my body and sending bright stars across my vision. I staggered to my feet and looked at the two unconscious policemen, both still breathing and not badly hurt; and then a motorcycle came roaring in and four more cops came running, and I went over to see how the Jensen had fared. Some fragments of metal had damaged the bodywork slightly, and a piece of sharp steel had sliced through the leather of the front seat and opened a new gash in Fenrek's shoulder, but it wasn't very serious; he merely said: "As if I didn't have enough problems already."

I yanked open the door for him. I said: "He practically tore a front wheel off the Buick, he won't get far now."

He hobbled beside me, still on his homemade crutch, round the comer; and there, a front tire burst and the grill smashed in with the radiator steaming, was the Riviera.

Loureiro came running up and stared at the mess, and said: "They tried to stop him at the entrance to Monsanto, to the *Parque Florestal*. But he turned the car round and came racing back. Why would he want to go into the Park?"

The car was a wreck, and the shotgun was gone. And of Loveless, there was no sign at all.

We were in the suburbs here, in the suburb of Belem, which the Portuguese pronounce as though it were spelled Bleng. It grew from the strand called the Restelo, now a main street, which once was an inlet of the river, the narrow harbor the Adventurers used when they sailed off, in the Fourteen Hundreds, to discover new worlds and bring great wealth to their homeland.

The ornate and startling Tower of Belem, surely the most beautiful military fortification in the world, stood watch over the Docks of Success, less than half a mile to the south of us.

Closer still, at the nearest edge of the sea—or rather, the broad river Tagus which they call the Straw Sea—the huge marble caravel of the Discoveries stood like a symbolic stone vessel headed out for strange horizons, with Prince Henry at the prow, pointing the way, and all his sailors and fighting men, cartographers and chroniclers clambering up behind him with the sun on their finely-carved stone faces. Henry the Navigator, they call him, though he never went farther afield than Tangier. But the nobility was remembered there, carved in stone for the world to see, with the sunlight gilding them all beyond the tall masts of the blue and yellow yachts at anchor in the little dock.

To our north, a little over a mile away, the great forest of Monsanto began, with the steeply-winding road leading through the crowded trees up to the Heights of Help, where the old flares once burned that guided the mariners home from their long and hazardous voyages.

You could not forget the sea here; even the lovely old houses, many of them fallen from grace now, with laundry hanging from their iron balustrades, were faced in brightly-colored Faience tiles depicting scenes of the sea, bright in the hot light of the morning.

Fenrek found a police officer and was already giving orders to close the roads into the forest; within minutes, thirty police cars would be covering every entrance on the south, or speeding along the Avenida da Ponte to the north. And in the immediate area, a hundred men, the local police reinforced by the army, would be closing off every road, every alley, every tiny *beco*. A radio truck was already coursing the streets, giving out orders to the patrolling men, and I saw three men carrying a long ladder and running to climb to points of vantage on the rooftops. Two officers were hurrying into the Cathedral; heading for its high towers.

Fenrek said: "As long as we keep him out of the forest, we've got him. Once in there...who knows? With maybe a knife in his pocket he can last for a year, even without the shotgun. I wonder how many shells he has in his pockets?"

I shrugged. "I don't think it matters, really." He looked at me and frowned, remembering the near collision. I said: "You saw the kind of desperation that's on him. The next step's obvious—once he finds he can't break through the cordon."

I'd never seen so many police all together at one place. I'd forgotten, or never realized, that while we were going our own way, setting our own traps, worrying this thing out between the two of us, the whole weighty mass of the law was also there behind us. From the time the first poor fisherman had died, all the resources of the police and the army had been standing by, ready for just this moment. The sheer weight of it, the mass of it, was startling.

I said, brooding about it: "He started this hunt for a new weapon because of the odds against his mercenaries. Now, he's on his own, and look at the odds stacked up against him now."

Wherever you looked, there were men in uniform stringing barbed wire across the roads, climbing up ladders to lookout posts, shepherding people into their houses, clambering over rooftops, standing on balconies and at street corners, their officers giving out orders, quietly and authoritatively, on bullhorns. It seemed as if the whole of the City were mobilized against one man; but that one man was all that was left of a deadly and terrifying menace. I counted twelve official cars in this small street alone.

We heard the squeal of tires, and Estrilla's bug came tearing in, a policeman closing a barricade behind her; even here, she was driving that potent little toy like a racing car. She braked to a skidding stop beside us and said: "I saw him once, driving like a madman." She looked at the steaming Buick, down at the front now with the second tire leaking air, and said: "Do we know where he went?"

I shook my head.

Astrid climbed out and stood there, looking around at the highly-organized chaos, looking at Fenrek's shoulder and worrying how many more wounds would be coming his way before this was over.

Estrilla said: "How big an area?"

I shrugged. "A square mile, two at the most. A hundred men combing it, it's the end."

A doctor, summoned, I learned, by Lieutenant Loureiro, had come to do something about Fenrek's injuries, but he shook his head impatiently and said: "No, when this is all over..."

There was a large-scale map of the area spread out over the hot hood of one of the cars, and Fenrek was staring at it, leaning still on his shillelagh, frowning and unhappy. And then, from the roof across the street, a policeman shouted; he was pointing to the east.

I said to Fenrek: "I'll go see."

A dozen men were already running down Rua do Embaixador, running fast with their rifles unslung, three policemen and a squad of soldiers, a hundred and fifty yards ahead of me. I sprinted and overtook them, and found a long ladder set against the wall of a house, a wall of diamond-pointed bricks that caught the sunlight prettily and cast sharp shadows over the white stone; a woman was leaning over the rail of her balcony on the second floor, a balcony covered with pots of geranium and ageratum, with a long vine of rose-pink *Antigonon Leptopus* trailing handsomely over the wrought iron work, Someone shouted at her: "Get back, Senhora, into the house! There is danger!" She scurried back indoors.

I climbed up the ladder, two rungs at a time, and the man who had shouted was there, a very young corporal in khaki battle dress, camouflaged with patches of maroon and brown and yellow. He said excitedly: "There, Senhor, above the *Chao Salgado*..."

The *Chao Salgado*, the Salted Ground...I remembered the story:

Once, in the Seventeen Hundreds, there was the mansion of the Eighth Duke of Aveiro standing there, and the Duke, an angry and violent man caught up in the protests of the times, had planned an assassination of King Dom Jose, together with four members of a family named Tavora, if my memory is as good as it's supposed to be. They'd all been executed for their pains. The Duke's mansion had been razed to the ground, and the earth had been ceremonially strewn with salt, and cursed. There is a plain and simple marble column standing there to this day to mark the spot, topped by a flaming urn of stone, and decorated with only five stone rings, symbolizing the chains of the conspirators. Now the later-built houses have encroached upon Aveiro's fine old estate, crowding close upon one another, cheek-by-jowl, in Lisbon style; but there is still a little corner the superstitious keep away from, and no one will ever build there.

Even now, two hundred years later, it's as though the specter of the curse still haunts the place. Because of the steep hills, it's hard to find building room within the confines of the City these days, and every inch is taken up; but not here.

There is just a little corner left, an empty corner that has become, as the hesitant houses were built around it, a tiny courtyard. The nearest house to the epicenter of the old curse is only a few feet away from the column, but it gives the impression of turning away from it, of hiding itself; no window overlooks the little monument; the houses seem to hide themselves, turning their backs, ashamed of their proximity. The inscription at the base of the monument, which is no more than twenty feet high, is eroded and scarcely legible; but if you've a curious mind for trivia, and struggle with it, you can still make out the words: *This ground is cursed, and nothing shall live here.*

It's a tiny courtyard, no more than a few feet square, called the Blind Alley of the Salted Ground, with a plain and unpretentious column to tell of the tragic days when the scheming for power was on a much more simple basis. There hasn't been much change in intent, really; the scheming is still going on all over the world, but now the means are more sophisticated, more deadly; and curses don't do much good any more.

We were on a small fat roof, two stories high, abutting onto a fourth floor that was roofed in steeply-pitched red tiles. I found a pipe that would bear my weight, I hoped, and climbed up to take a look. I straddled a ridge and eased my way along. I found a chimney that would take me a few feet higher, and climbed to its top, wrapping my legs around the brickwork. I could see nothing.

I jumped the few feet across the gap onto the next roof, worked my way around to the other side, and stood there looking down into the tiny courtyard. The *Chao Salgado*.

I'd never seen the monument from this high angle before. It looked like a slender spear pointing up at the sky, its top a few feet below me and ten yards or so away.

And then, I saw him.

He was less than five hundred feet away from me, crawling along the lower edge of a steep roof, ready, I thought, to slip at any minute; there was no abutment to break his fall if he should find a couple of loose tiles there. He was reaching for a rope, a long manila rope that was wound once around the chimney stack and dropped down into the street, left there by the workmen cleaning some yellow and blue tile work when they'd been herded away by the police. I saw him haul it up and unhook it from its mooring, and he flung it almost like a lasso, slinging its loop over a cast iron sewer vent on the roof of the house opposite. He missed on the first throw, and on the second as well; but the third try was successful. He put his weight on it and swung out and down, swinging fast like Tarzan on the end of a vine.

He slammed into the opposite wall with an awful force, but he was climbing again immediately, climbing high onto the rooftops once more. He jiggled the rope till the other end was free, and ran fast towards me till he came to the end of the building. I saw him look down into the street and pull back quickly. Following the direction of his look, I saw that five or six policemen were down there, looking up towards him; I didn't know whether they'd seen him or not.

I heard a shout, and Loveless looked round. Three soldiers were crawling along the steep roof-pitch towards him, three houses away, crawling on hands and knees with their rifles across their backs. There was more shouting down on the street below, and I looked down and saw Fenrek there, his white face staring up at me, Estrilla and Astrid were with him, and then they started running into the courtyard of the salted ground itself.

And now, Loveless was getting close. Worming his way along the roof on hands and knees, his rope trailing behind him, his shotgun still in his hand, he was directly opposite me now, less than fifty feet away. Between us, the tiny courtyard was a chasm, the monument poking its morbid spear into the air and looking, from this angle, somehow insignificant. He was groping his way along with a fine disregard for the danger he was in, when a tile fell and crashed to the courtyard below, he paid it no attention at all.

And then, he saw me. He raised his head and our eyes met. I was standing up in full view, because there just wasn't any cover; he would have seen me long before if he hadn't been looking back over his shoulder to where the three soldiers were approaching him. For a moment, he stayed there on his hands and knees, looking me full in the face. And then he stood up and looked to his right; two men there, a house and a half away, were running on a flat roof towards him. To his left there was a wide gap he could never hope to cross, not even with his rope, and a man on the roof there yelled for support anyway. He was still yelling as some men came clambering up on a ladder to join him.

Loveless stood up then, and came to the edge of the roof, his arms held out for balance, walking towards me till we faced each other across the thirty-foot gap that was the Salted Ground. On opposing edges of the buildings, high above the courtyard, we faced each other across the monument, and waited.

He held out his gun in both hands, in front of his body, and broke it open and laughed shortly; it was empty. He said: "Need a good gun, Cain? I've no more use for the bloody thing."

He swung it once round his head and hurled it at me. I ducked, and it smashed into the steep roof behind me, shattering tile with its force, and slid noisily down the slope to crash in the courtyard below. I saw a police officer run and pick it up; it was Loureiro. I saw Fenrek down there put out a preventive hand as someone raised a rifle.

Loveless slung the loop of his rope, then, and it fell on the first throw over the urn on top of the monument. He leaned back and pulled it tight, and said calmly: "I'd liked to have taken you with me, Cain."

An ambiguous remark, if ever I heard one.

And then, quickly, not wasting any time, he slipped the other end of the rope round his throat, knotted it, tugged it tight, and stood there, a man with a gallow's rope round his neck. He stood quite still for a moment, not looking back at the men who were approaching, not even when he must have heard two of them clattering across onto the roof he was standing on. His fists were at his waist, his feet wide apart, his head thrown back. He looked me full in the face for a moment or two, looked around at the crowded, sunlit rooftops, looked at the tightly packed houses teeming with life, looked back at me and shrugged, and half smiled...And then, he jumped.

Just before the sound of Astrid's screaming, I heard the slight, infinitesimal crunch that was his neck breaking. He hung there on the column, his feet no more than a yard from the ground, his head twisted round and his sightless eyes staring up at me.

I turned away and began the slow climb down back across the red and grey tiled rooftops to where the ladder was. And by the time I reached the courtyard, they'd cut the Major down and decently covered his broken, wretched body with a blanket.

We drove up to the Alentejano that night, Fenrek in a couple of casts and still gloating from the roasting he'd given them at the hospital when they expected him to stay there for a few days. He had a pair of shiny aluminum crutches which he was delighted with, like a child with a new toy.

He said: "It's a fine thing to be a cripple, if you've got the leisure and patience for it."

We had thin scallops of pork, tightly rolled and stuffed with squid and sautéed in Madeira, and there were six bottles of *Dao* on the table for the four of us.

It was a wine sort of night, a night when a great deal would be drunk and not much said, the kind of night when the wine would take us, first, through the sharpening of the senses and then through their blunting, with all of us knowing that there was very little that was left to be said now.

No one mentioned the Bocca, nor the Alfama, nor the Salted Ground; we talked, instead, sporadically, of the beaches at Estoril, of the fountains that play in the Garden of Jeronimos, of the horse-drawn carts that lumber their way across the river on the big flat ferry that goes to Cacilhas. We talked of the flower market in the Rossio, of the ancient wrought-iron elevator that takes you down the Baixa to the Upper Quarters, of the splendidly ornate railway station where the trains leave from upstaiss...

Estrilla was happily slicing her Colonel's meat for him, fussing over him like an over-zealous nurse, while Astrid sat close to me and stroked my knee under the tablecloth.

The night was cool and friendly, the scent of honeysuckle strong on the air; and through the trellis work of the patio the sea was blue-white down there in the gleam of the moon. That strange light was hanging over the mountains, the full moon clear as day, casting deep and luminescent shadows among the flowers of the garden. The wind was gentle and fresh, bringing with it the sweet aroma of the pine trees.

Midnight came, and went. We sat back in our chairs, some of us regurgitating gently, and listened to the sad-sweet notes of the *fado*. The dark-haired woman, her fingers tightly clasped, her eyes half closed, her brows drawn down, standing straight and proud, was singing softly:

...the fado is fire and ashes, love and jealousy, grief and sin...And if you want me for your mistress you must tell me, for my lover died last night...If you call me by my name, I will come to you...

The hours slipped by, and soon, there were just the four of us sitting there among the candles under the trees. It was getting cold now, and the wind was swinging round to the southwest. Soon, down there at the Bocca, the waves would be playing tricks again, spewing out their fury to the skies.

But here, and now, there was only peace, and the comfortable quiet of the Lisbon night.

THE END

ABOUT THE AUTHOR

Alan Lyle-Smythe was born in Surrey, England. Prior to World War II, he served with the Palestine Police from 1936 to 1939 and learned the Arabic language. He was awarded an MBE in June 1938. He married Aliza Sverdova in 1939, then studied acting from 1939 to 1941.

In January 1940, Lyle-Smythe was commissioned in the Royal Army Service Corps. Due to his linguistic skills, he transferred to the Intelligence Corps and served in the Western Desert, in which he used the surname "Caillou" (the French word for 'pebble') as an alias.

He was captured in North Africa, imprisoned and threatened with execution in Italy, then escaped to join the British forces at Salerno. He was then posted to serve with the partisans in Yugoslavia. He wrote about his experiences in the book *The World is Six Feet Square* (1954). He was promoted to captain and awarded the Military Cross in 1944.

Following the war, he returned to the Palestine Police from 1946 to 1947, then served as a Police Commissioner in British-occupied Italian Somaliland from 1947 to 1952, where he was recommissioned a captain.

After work as a District Officer in Somalia and professional hunter, Lyle-Smythe travelled to Canada, where he worked as a hunter and then became an actor on Canadian television.

He wrote his first novel, *Rogue's Gambit*, in 1955, first using the name Caillou, one of his aliases from the war. Moving from Vancouver to Hollywood, he made an appearance as a contestant on the January 23 1958 edition of *You Bet Your Life*.

He appeared as an actor and/or worked as a screenwriter in such shows as *Daktari*, *The Man From U.N.C.L.E.* (including the screenwriting for "*The Bow-Wow Affair*" from 1965), *Thriller*, *Daniel Boone*, *Quark*, *Centennial*, and *How the West Was Won*. In 1966-67, he had a recurring role (as Jason Flood) in NBC's "*Tarzan*" TV series starring Ron Ely. Caillou appeared in such television movies as *Sole Survivor* (1970), *The Hound of the Baskervilles* (1972, as Inspector Lestrade), and *Goliath Awaits* (1981). His cinema film credits included roles in *Five Weeks in a Balloon* (1962), *Clarence, the Cross-Eyed Lion* (1965), *The Rare Breed* (1966), *The Devil's Brigade* (1968), *Hellfighters* (1968), *Everything You Always Wanted to Know About Sex* (*But Were Afraid to Ask)* (1972), *Herbie Goes to Monte Carlo* (1977), *Beyond Evil* (1980), *The Sword and the Sorcerer* (1982) and *The Ice Pirates* (1984).

Caillou wrote 52 paperback thrillers under his own name and the nom de plume of Alex Webb, with such heroes as Cabot Cain, Colonel Matthew Tobin, Mike Benasque, Ian Quayle and Josh Dekker, as well as writing many magazine stories.

Several of Caillou's novels were made into films, such as *Rampage* with Robert Mitchum in 1963, based on his big game hunting knowledge; *Assault on Agathon*, for which Caillou did the screenplay as well; and *The Cheetahs*, filmed in 1989.

He was married to Aliza Sverdova from 1939 until his death. Their daughter Nadia Caillou was the screenwriter for the film *Skeleton Coast*.

Alan Caillou died in Sedona, Arizona in 2006.

LOOKING FOR ACTION AND ADVENTURE
AUTHOR ALAN CAILLOU
NOVELS DELIVER!
WWW.CALIBERCOMICS.COM

AVAILABLE IN PAPERBACK OR EBOOK

DON'T MISS ANY OF MICHAEL KASNER'S HARD HITTING MILITARY NOVEL SERIES

BLACK OPS

Formed by an elite cadre of government officials, the Black OPS team goes where the law can't - to seek retribution for acts of terror directed against Americans anywhere in the world.

3 BOOK SERIES

Armed with all the tactical advantages of modern technology, battle hard and ready when the free world is threatened - the Peacekeepers are the baddest grunts on the planet.

4 BOOK SERIES

CHOPPER COPS

America is being torn apart as criminal cartels terrorize our cities, dealing drugs and death wholesale. Local police are outgunned, so the President unleashes the U.S. TACTICAL POLICE FORCE. An elite army of super cops with ammo to burn, they swoop down on the hot spots in sleek high-tech attack choppers to win the dirty war and take back America!

4 BOOK SERIES

FROM CALIBER BOOKS

www.calibercomics.com

DON'T MISS ANY OF NEIL HUNTER'S NOVELS FROM CALIBER BOOKS

Reporter Les Mason is completing an expose on the Long Point Nuclear Plant. But before he can finish he dies an agonizing death. The doctors are baffled—and there are similar cases to follow...Chris Lane, his girlfriend, and organizer of the Long Point Protestors, discovers Mason's notes, and decides to find out for herself what the plant has to hide.

2 BOOK SERIES

In middle of the 21st century America – over-populated decaying cities are ruled by hi-tech gangs pushing every vice and wastelands are controlled by bands of mutants. Ordinary citizens are oppressed and face a hopeless future. But Marshal T.J. Cade is a new breed of law enforcer. Teamed with his cyborg partner, Janek, Cade takes on these criminals and works in the gray areas of the law to get the job done.

3 BOOK SERIES

The village of Shepthorne England wasn't being gripped, but strangled by a winter's blanket of heavy snow and Arctic temperatures. The trouble began innocently enough with a massive pile-up of autos on frozen roads leading to and from the village. Then, from the sky, a military transport plane with its top secret cargo of devastation crashed down towards the center of the village. Hell was just beginning to touch Shepthorne and its unsuspecting citizens...

FROM CALIBER BOOKS

www.calibercomics.com

CALIBER COMICS GOES TO WAR!
HISTORICAL AND MILITARY THEMED GRAPHIC NOVELS

WORLD WAR ONE: MO MAN'S LAND
ISBN: 9781635298123

A look at World War 1 from the French trenches as they faced the Imperial German Army.

CORTEZ AND THE FALL OF THE AZTECS
ISBN: 9781635299779

Cortez battles the Aztecs while in search of Inca gold.

TROY: AN EMPIRE UNDER SIEGE
ISBN: 9781635298635

Homer's famous The Iliad and the Trojan War is given a unique human perspective rather than from the God's.

WITNESS TO WAR
ISBN: 9781635299700

WW2's Battle of the Bulge is seen up close by an embedded female war reporter.

THE LINCOLN BRIGADE
ISBN: 9781635298222

American volunteers head to Spain in the 1930s to fight in their civil war against the fascist regime.

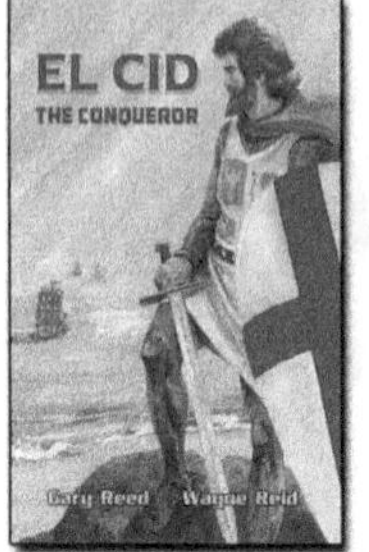

EL CID: THE CONQUEROR
ISBN: 9780982654996

Europe's greatest warrior attempts to unify Spain against invading foreign and domestic armies.

WINTER WAR
ISBN: 9780985749392

At the outbreak of WW2 Finland fights against an invading Soviet army.

ZULUNATION: END OF EMPIRE
ISBN: 9780941613415

The global British Empire and far-reaching influence is threatened by a Zulu uprising in southern Africa.

AIR WARRIORS: WORLD WAR ONE #V1 - V4
Take to the skies of WW1 as various fighter aces tell their harrowing stories.

ISBN: 9781635297973 (V1), 9781635297980 (V2), 9781635297997 (V3), 9781635298000 (V4)

CALIBER COMICS PRESENTS
The Complete
VIETNAM JOURNAL

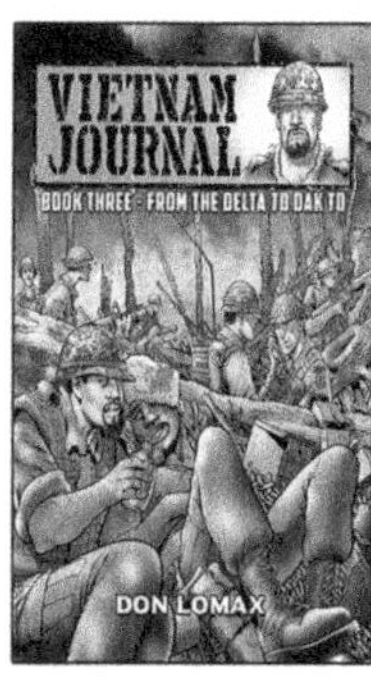

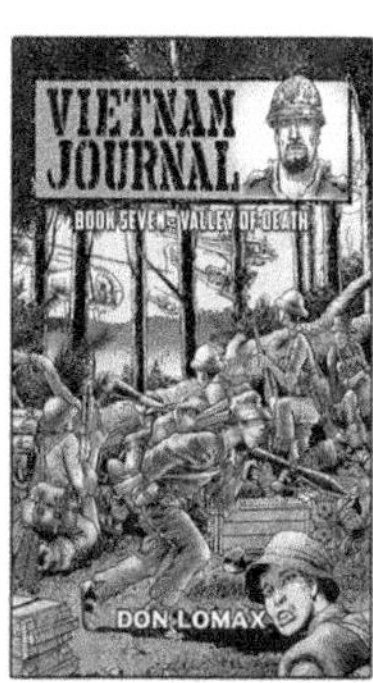

8 Volumes Covering the Entire Initial Run of the
Critically Acclaimed Don Lomax Series

And Now Available

VIETNAM JOURNAL SERIES TWO

"INCURSION", "JOURNEY INTO HELL", "RIPCORD"

All new stories from Scott 'Journal' Neithammer
as he reports durings the later stages of the
Vietnam War.

CALIBER COMICS   WWW.CALIBERCOMICS.COM

CALIBER COMICS GOES TO THE EDGE!
Science Fiction and Horror themed graphic novels

DEADWORLD
ISBN: 9781942351245

RENFIELD
ISBN: 9781942351825

NOSFERATU
ISBN: 9781942351931

**LOVECRAFT:
THE EARLY STORIES**
ISBN: 9781942351634

**THE WAR OF THE WORLDS:
INFESTATION**
ISBN: 9781942351962

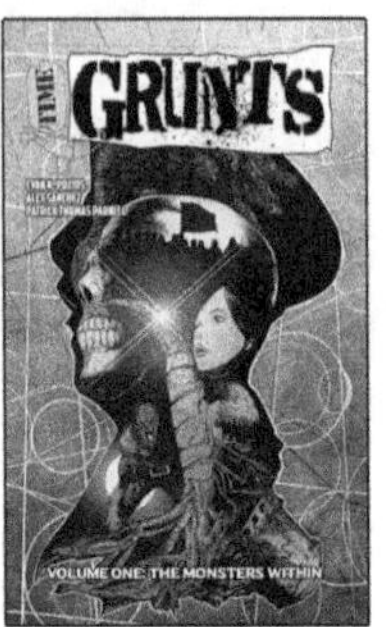

TIME GRUNTS
ISBN: 9781635299472

DRACULA
ISBN: 9780996030649

**DRACULA:
THE SUICIDE CLUB**
ISBN: 9781635299571

**JACK THE RIPPER
ILLUSTRATED**
ISBN: 9781942351917

THE SEARCHERS
ISBN: 9781942351979

A.A.I. WARS
ISBN: 9781635299168

**AUTUMN: TERROR IN THE
LONDON UNDERGROUND**
ISBN: 9781544624020

www.calibercomics.com

ALSO AVAILABLE FROM CALIBER COMICS

QUALITY GRAPHIC NOVELS TO ENTERTAIN

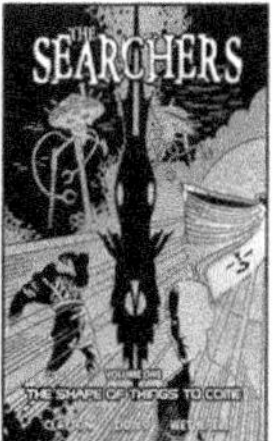

THE SEARCHERS: VOLUME 1
The Shape of Things to Come

Before *League of Extraordinary Gentlemen* there was *The Searchers*. At the dawn of the 20th Century the greatest literary adventurers from the minds of Wells, Doyle, Burroughs, and Haggard were created. All thought to be the work of pure fiction. However, a century later, the real-life descendents of those famous characters are recuited by the legendary Professor Challenger in order to save mankind's future. Series collected for the first time.

"Searchers is the comic book I have on the wall with a sign reading - 'Love books? Never read a comic? Try this one! ....money back guarantee..." - Dark Star Books.

WAR OF THE WORLDS: INFESTATION

Based on the H.G. Wells classic! The "Martian Invasion" has begun again and now mankind must fight for its very humanity. It happened slowly at first but by the third year, it seemed that the war was almost over… the war was almost lost.

"Writer Randy Zimmerman has a fine grasp of drama, and spins the various strands of the story into a coherent whole… imaginative and very gritty."
- war-of-the-worlds.co.uk

HELSING: LEGACY BORN

From writer Gary Reed (Deadworld) and artists John Lowe (Captain America), Bruce McCorkindale (Godzilla). She was born into a legacy she wanted no part of and pushed into a battle recessed deep in the shadows of the night. Samantha Helsing is torn between two worlds…two allegiances…two families. The legacy of the Van Helsing family and their crusade against the "night creatures" comes to modern day with the most unlikely of all warriors.

"Congratulations on this masterpiece…"
- Paul Dale Roberts, Compuserve Reviews

DEADWORLD

Before there was The Walking Dead there was Deadworld. Here is an introduction of the long running classic horror series, Deadworld, to a new audience! Considered by many to be the godfather of the original zombie comic with over 100 issues and graphic novels in print and over 1,000,000 copies sold, Deadworld ripped into the undead with intelligent zombies on a mission and a group of poor teens riding in a school bus desperately try to stay one step ahead of the sadistic, Harley-riding King Zombie. Death, mayhem, and a touch of supernatural evil made Deadworld a classic and now here's your chance to get into the story!

DAYS OF WRATH

Award winning comic writer & artist Wayne Vansant brings his gripping World War II saga of war in the Pacific to Guadalcanal and the Battle of Bloody Ridge. This is the powerful story of the long, vicious battle for Guadalcanal that occurred in 1942-43. When the U.S. Navy orders its outnumbered and out-gunned ships to run from the Japanese fleet, they abandon American troops on a bloody, battered island in the South Pacific.

"Heavy on authenticity, compellingly written and beautifully drawn."
- Comics Buyers Guide

SHERLOCK HOLMES:
THE CASE OF THE MISSING MARTIAN

Sherlock is called out of retirement to London in 1908 to solve a most baffling mystery: The British Museum is missing a specimen of a Martian from the failed invasion of 1899. Did it walk away on its own or did someone steal it?

Holmes ponders the facts and remembers his part in the war effort alongside Professor Challenger during the War of the Worlds invasion that was chronicled in H.G. Wells' classic novel.

Meanwhile, Doctor Watson has problems of his own when his wife steals a scalpel from his surgical tool kit and returns to her old stomping grounds of Whitechapel, the London

CALIBER PRESENTS

The original Caliber Presents anthology title was one of Caliber's inaugural releases and featured predominantly new creators, many of which went onto successful careers in the comics' industry. In this new version, Caliber Presents has expanded to graphic novel size and while still featuring new creators it also includes many established professional creators with new visions. Creators featured in this first issue include nominees and winners of some of the industry's major awards including the Eisner, Harvey, Xeric, Ghastly, Shel Dorf, Comic Monsters, and more.

LEGENDLORE

From Caliber Comics now comes the entire Realm and Legendlore saga as a set of volumes that collects the long running critically acclaimed series. In the vein of The Lord of The Rings and The Hobbit with elements of Game of Thrones and Dungeon and Dragons.

Four normal modern day teenagers are plunged into a world they thought only existed in novels and film. They are whisked away to a magical land where dragons roam the skies, orcs and hobgoblins terrorize travelers, where unicorns prance through the forest, and kingdoms wage war for dominance. It is a world where man is just one race, joining other races such as elves, trolls, dwarves, changelings, and the dreaded night creatures who steal the night.

TIME GRUNTS

What if Hitler's last great Super Weapon was – Time itself! A WWII/time travel adventure that can best be described as *Band of Brothers* meets *Time Bandits*.

October, 1944. Nazi fortunes appear bleaker by the day. But in the bowels of the Wenceslas Mines, a terrible threat has emerged . . . The Nazis have discovered the ability to conquer time itself with the help of a new ominous device!

Now a rag tag group of American GIs must stop this threat to the past, present, and future . . . While dealing with their own past, prejudices, and fears in the process.

www.calibercomics.com